FAMILY
PATTERNS

FAMILY PATTERNS

KRISTIN ECKHARDT

Guideposts
New York, New York

www.guideposts.com
(800) 932-2145
Guideposts Books & Inspirational Media

Cover design by Wendy Bass
Cover illustration by Joyce Patti
Interior design by Lorie Pagnozzi
Typeset by Aptara

Printed and bound in the United States of America
10 9 8 7 6 5 4 3 2 1

DEDICATION

I am so grateful to my editor, Beth Adams, for believing in this series and bringing it to life. Thank you, Beth, for your gentle guidance, wisdom and support. I'd also like to thank author Carolyn Greene, a good friend, fantastic plotter, and a blessing in my life. I couldn't have done this without her.

PATCHWORK MYSTERIES

FAMILY
PATTERNS

PROLOGUE

Maple Hill, Massachusetts • December 1920

Molly Drayton rose silently from her warm bed, the frigid night air biting into her bare feet as she crept across the wooden floor. She hadn't taken the time to slip a robe over her long flannel nightgown, afraid she might awaken her young husband. She couldn't let Noah discover her.

Not if she wanted to survive the night.

Shivering, Molly stepped into the front parlor before lighting a candle. The flickering flame cut through the darkness and illuminated the small quilt crumpled on the settee. She picked it up and wrapped it tightly around her shoulders as the frightful howl of the wind drew her to the front window.

She parted the heavy drapes just far enough to see through the frosted windowpane. A light snow had begun to fall, swirling around the bare tree branches and dusting the front walk with a fine white powder. There were footprints in the snow. Molly let the drapes drop from her hand, hastened toward the long staircase, and began her quiet ascent. She was careful to avoid the squeaky spots on the steps. Her six-year-old son, William, slept on the second floor of the house. William had fallen asleep on the settee shortly after supper and hadn't stirred when Noah carried him up to bed.

When she reached the top of the stairs, Molly paused by William's bedroom to make sure his door was tightly closed, then she walked to the room at the end of the hall. She turned the glass doorknob, wincing at the loud creak of the door. Molly sucked in a deep breath, listening closely for any movement from her husband in the bedroom below.

All was quiet in the house. She hurried over to the mahogany desk and opened the top drawer, lifting the candle higher. She pulled out a sheet of notepaper and a pencil, her hand shaking as she began to write.

That's when she heard it. The sound of a footstep on the stairs. Then another. A heavy, deliberate step.

She blew out the candle. The darkness only amplified the sound of the approaching footsteps. He was at the top of the stairs now and moving toward her. She backed into the far corner of the room, clutching the quilt tightly around her shoulders, praying for a miracle.

CHAPTER ONE

Maple Hill, Massachusetts • Present Day

S arah Hart had been twelve years old the last time she'd set foot in the rambling Victorian house on Bristol Street. Familiar scents of cedar and cinnamon seemed to still linger in the air, bringing back memories of her grandfather, whose blue eyes would twinkle with delight whenever she and her brother came tumbling through the front door.

"Hey, Mom," Jason said as he entered the front parlor. "You're right on time."

"Hope you don't mind that I let myself in," she said, leaning up to kiss his clean-shaven cheek. At thirty-six, Jason was a handsome man, with a square jaw and short, dark hair. "The door was standing wide open."

"That's Maggie's doing." He smiled. "She already loves living in a place where you can leave your doors open in the middle of the day."

Jason and Maggie had recently purchased the old family home and moved here from Los Angeles. Sarah was still pinching herself. She couldn't believe they were really living so close after all this time.

"Just be sure and lock the house up at night," she said, setting her purse on the marble top parlor table. She probably worried too much, but something still unsettled her about this house, even after all these years.

"We'll be fine, Mom."

Sarah looked around the parlor, which was filled with many of Maggie's treasured antiques. A pale blue camelback sofa sat in the corner next to an upright piano with elaborate scrollwork on the front and beautiful inlaid wood trim. A mahogany phonograph stood in the opposite corner near an antique brass floor lamp. "Your grandpa didn't believe it when I told him you bought this place."

"He remembers it?" Jason asked.

"At times." Sarah said. Her father, William Drayton, lived at Bradford Manor Nursing Home in Maple Hill. "His memory comes and goes. You'll visit him soon, right? I know he'd love to see you."

"I will," Jason said. "I've just got a lot on my plate right now."

Jason was going to practice family law in Maple Hill. He'd bought out the practice of a retiring lawyer and was now in the process of sorting through outdated files and putting the office back into shape.

Footsteps sounded in the hall and a moment later Jason's wife Maggie appeared in the arched doorway. She was a year older than Jason, but in her denim shorts and lime green shirt, it didn't show. Her shoulder-length auburn hair was swept back into a messy ponytail and there was a spot of white paint on her chin.

"Hi, Sarah." Maggie walked over to give her a hug. "Isn't it a gorgeous day? I've been painting the back porch."

"I can tell." Sarah pointed to her chin. "Looks like you missed a spot."

"Oh, dear." Maggie's eyes flashed in amusement as she reached up to rub her chin. "I seem to get more paint on me than on the porch rails." She looked up at her husband. "Maybe I should go upstairs and freshen up before we leave."

"No time, Magpie," he said. "It's at least a thirty-minute drive and we don't want to be late to the contractors."

"All right." Maggie smoothed back her hair as best she could and turned to Sarah. "I'm not sure what time we'll get back. We'll try not to be gone too long, but as you can see"— she pointed at the strips of water-stained wallpaper on the ceiling—"there's a lot to go over."

Jason and Maggie were in the process of restoring the old Victorian to its original condition. The previous owner had modernized the house, removing much of its charm in the process; he'd lowered the ceilings, installed cheap shag carpet over the beautiful hardwood floors, and removed the gingerbread trim from the exterior of the house.

Sarah knew that Jason and Maggie had a huge task in front of them, but they seemed excited about bringing Grandpa Noah's house back to life and were working hard to restore it faithfully. She'd lent them all of Grandpa Noah's old photographs of the house, taken both inside and out, so they could see the place in its original condition.

"I can stay until six," Sarah told them. "Then I've got to interview a new boarder. She called just this morning and sounded desperate to find a place."

"We should be home well before then," Maggie slipped her purse over her shoulder. "Thank you for doing this. I hope it's not too much bother."

"Of course not." Didn't Maggie realize how much she relished the time with her granddaughters? For so many years she had hardly seen them at all, and now she intended to savor every moment.

"The girls are upstairs," Jason said. "They're a little homesick today, so I'm afraid they might not be very good company."

Sarah assured him that they'd manage. "Good luck with the contractor."

"Thanks." Maggie sighed as she looked up at the ceiling. "We're going to need it."

As soon as the door closed behind them, Sarah went in search of her twelve-year-old twin granddaughters and found Audrey upstairs, lying sprawled on top of her bed, her long, sandy blonde hair spread out around her. The charcoal pencil in her hand moved slowly over the sketch pad in front of her.

"Hello there."

Audrey didn't look up from her drawing. "Hi Grandma."

Sarah approached the bed. "What are you drawing?"

"Me and my best friend."

Sarah looked down at the small photograph next to the sketch pad. A ginger-haired girl with a wide smile had her arm wrapped around Audrey's shoulder. "You're doing a wonderful job."

"No, I'm not." Audrey scribbled over the page, then closed the sketchbook. "I can't even draw here. I can't do anything here. It's so boring."

"Maybe we can make cookies this afternoon."

Audrey rolled onto her back and stared up at the cracked, white plaster ceiling. "Whatever."

"Where's your sister?" Sarah asked. She would ignore Audrey's attitude for now.

"I'm right here, Grandma," said a muffled voice behind her.

Sarah turned around, but she didn't see anyone. "Amy?"

"Yes," a voice answered, but from close to the corner of the room now.

Audrey sat up on the bed. "Hey, where are you?"

Sarah was wondering the same thing. She looked around, hoping to catch a glimpse of Amy's freckled face.

"Here I am." Amy replied. Her voice was now coming from a spot near the bed.

Audrey hopped off the bed with a delighted squeal. "You're freaking me out! Are you in the wall or something?"

The sound of Amy's giggles filled the room. "Hold on, I'll be there in a minute."

A few moments later, Amy appeared in the doorway, her cheeks flushed. She looked identical to her sister, but her blond hair hung in two long braids down her back. "Hey, Grandma."

"Hello, dear." Sarah reached out to pull a cobweb from Amy's T-shirt. "So tell us the secret to your vanishing act."

Amy grinned. "I'm not sure I want to tell. It could come in handy if I want to do a little spying."

"Oh, come on," Audrey peered past Amy. "This is like the only interesting thing that's happened since we moved here. You can't keep it to yourself."

"Okay." A mischievous twinkle gleamed in her blue eyes. "I found a secret passageway."

Sarah gasped. As a child, she'd explored all the hidden nooks and crannies in her grandfather's house, but she'd never found anything like that. "Where is it?"

"In the weirdest place." Amy moved out the door. "Come on, I'll show you."

The twins raced out of the room and Sarah followed a step behind. It couldn't really be...could it? A secret passageway?

Jason and Maggie had already been hard at work in Amy's room. The wallpaper had been scraped off and they'd removed the orange shag carpet, although small pieces of the foam padding were still stuck to the hardwood floor.

"It's in here." Amy led them to the walk-in closet, where strips of carpet tack still lined the floor. "I was hanging up some of my clothes"—she gestured toward the half-full boxes on the floor—"when I noticed one of the floorboards was loose."

Amy knelt down to demonstrate, removing the loose floorboard to reveal a small metal wheel underneath. When she turned the wheel, a creaking noise sounded beside them.

Sarah turned to see a narrow panel in the closet wall slide open to expose a dark passageway behind it.

"Cool," Audrey said, stepping inside the passageway.

"Wait a minute, girls," Sarah said, reaching for Audrey's arm. "You never know what could be in here. It could be dangerous."

But the girls didn't stop, and, if Sarah was honest, she was as curious as they were about what lay hidden behind the wall. Hesitantly, she took a step into the passageway behind them.

Amy led the way with a flashlight, the beam stretching just far enough ahead to light their way. "There are lots of cobwebs. Probably lots of spiders, too."

Audrey stopped in her tracks. "Gross. Let me hold that thing so I can see them before I run into them."

Amy handed the flashlight to her sister, and they moved slowly along the corridor. Dust tickled Sarah's nose, and she inhaled a faint, musty odor. The passageway was still and dark, almost smothered in darkness except for the narrow beam of the flashlight, which revealed glimpses of bare wood walls and a thick layer of dust on the wood floor.

"I hope the batteries don't go out," Audrey whispered as they shuffled along. "How far does this thing go, anyway?"

Sarah wondered the same thing. She'd lost her sense of distance in the darkness. The passageway seemed narrower now, and she reached out one hand to feel her way along the rough-hewn wall.

"I don't know," Amy replied. "I was exploring it when I heard you and Grandma talking in the bedroom. I couldn't resist trying to scare you."

Sarah glanced behind her into the endless blackness.

"You know, girls," she whispered, "I bet nobody has been inside this passageway for over fifty years. I used to play in this house all the time when I was a little girl and I didn't even know about it."

"Maybe we should go back." Audrey halted in her tracks. "What if we get lost in here?"

"Don't be such a baby." Amy turned and plucked the flashlight out of her hand. "There's nothing here that can hurt us, right, Grandma?"

"That's right," Sarah said. She tried to sound confident, but a part of her wondered if Audrey was right. An odd chill filled the small passageway.

"Why is it cold in here?" Audrey asked, wrapping her arms around herself. "It shouldn't be so cold, should it?"

Sarah moved closer to her. "We're probably near an air conditioner vent that's blowing cold air into this part of the passageway."

"Or, it's a ghost," Amy whispered, holding the flashlight under her chin in a way that made her sweet face look distorted. "I'M COMING TO GET YOU, AUDREY MARIE HART," she howled.

"Stop it," Audrey said, grabbing the flashlight. "That's not funny!"

The flashlight beam dropped to the floor, illuminating something by the wall. Sarah crept closer to the spot. "Hey, shine the light over here again."

Audrey aimed the flashlight at her as Sarah cautiously reached out to pick up what looked like an old blanket. "What is it, Grandma?"

Sarah's heart began to pound as she looked down at the bundle in her arms. It was a child-sized quilt made of vintage fabrics. She moved the quilt closer to the light, startled to see three letters stitched into one of the corner fabric pieces.

It couldn't be... She'd heard about her father's baby blanket that had disappeared, a small quilt he had lost when he was only six years old on the same night that Sarah's grandmother, Molly, had vanished, but ... "It's an old quilt."

"That's weird." Amy said. "I wonder what it's doing in here."

Sarah was wondering the same thing. She smoothed her fingers over the vintage fabrics as she admired the workmanship. It had been up here for a very long time. Dampness had stained some of the fabrics, and there were a few small holes here and there.

As she looked more closely at the quilt, she noticed something odd sticking out from a small opening in the seam between two square patches. She eased one finger into the loose opening, then carefully slid out a brittle, yellowed piece of paper.

Audrey leaned over her shoulder, shining the light on the slip of paper. "What's that?"

"Something I've never dreamed existed," Sarah breathed, as she read the faded, handwritten scrawl. "It's a clue. The only clue to the disappearance of Molly Drayton."

arah ran down the stairs to find some brighter light so she could get a better look at the quilt and the note. She hurried into the dining room, one of the few rooms in the house not under construction. She didn't want to take the chance of smearing any wet paint or varnish on the quilt.

"What's going on, Grandma?" Audrey asked as both girls followed her into the room. "Who's Molly Drayton?"

"My grandmother." Sarah spread the quilt out on the antique mahogany dining table, then moved one of the spindle-back chairs out of her way.

"So Molly Drayton is our great-great-grandmother?" Audrey asked.

"That's right," Sarah said. "She was married to your great-great-grandpa Noah when she disappeared one night and no one ever saw her again."

"How long ago was that?" Amy asked.

"Ninety years. December 12, 1920, to be exact. She was only twenty-four years old." Sarah's fingers trembled as she smoothed out the wrinkles and bumps in the quilt top. "Open those curtains for me, Audrey. We need more light in here."

Audrey walked over to the window and parted the long, forest green drapes that had been left by the previous owner. They were among the few items in the house Maggie hadn't junked yet. Sunlight streamed though the beveled glass window, illuminating a palette of deep blues and yellows among the small, square fabric pieces. The half-inch binding around the edge was a rich, blue silk taffeta. The quilt was small and square, approximately four feet wide and four feet long. She couldn't believe they'd found this treasure in the old forgotten passageway.

Amy peered over Sarah's shoulder. "Why is it so small?"

"It was made for a child," Sarah replied. "The pattern is a classic design called Sunshine and Shadow."

Audrey joined them at the table "That's a weird name for a quilt."

"Look at the pattern." Sarah pointed to the center squares of dark blue cotton. "See how different fabrics are used to form diagonal rows that radiate outward from the center? It's called Sunshine and Shadow because it uses varying shades of both light and dark fabrics to create the diamond patterns."

Audrey flipped one corner of the quilt over and slid her hand along the light blue fabric. "This side is so soft."

"It's flannel," Sarah said. "The fabrics on the quilt top are velvets, silks, brocades, cottons, and taffetas. And look at this stitching." Sarah pointed to the tiny, hand-quilted stitches. "Each square is quilted with outline stitches, and these stiches on the binding are called crosshatch stitches."

"What about the note you found?" Amy said. She was apparently not interested in the quilting lesson. "What does it say?"

Sarah pulled the slip of paper from her pocket and laid it on the table next to the quilt. "212 Elm Street. It looks like something else was written below the address, but it's been scribbled out."

"Whose address is it?" Amy asked.

"And why was it hidden in the quilt?" Audrey slid into a chair, her eyebrows knit in confusion. "And why was the quilt in the secret passageway?"

"I don't know." Sarah couldn't stop touching the quilt. "Your great-grandfather had a quilt just like this that disappeared at the same time Grandma Molly disappeared. I can't believe it, but I think we've found it."

Amy rocked back in her chair, balancing it on two legs. "How can you be sure it's the same one?"

"Be careful, Amy," Sarah warned her, then moved to the opposite end of the table. "Do you see the letters embroidered here in this corner block?"

Audrey leaned across the table. "W.J.H."

"Those are my dad's initials," Sarah explained. "William James Harrison. Grandma Molly made the quilt for him when he was a baby and he slept with it all the time."

Amy walked over for a closer look. "This sure doesn't look like a baby blanket to me."

"They didn't have cartoon or Disney-style fabrics back then, and pastels didn't become popular until the mid-1920s. Most of the time, a child's quilt was made in a traditional quilt pattern, only small enough to fit in a crib. But it's easy to tell this one was made for a young boy."

"How?" Audrey asked.

"Most of the squares are cut from blue fabrics, for one thing. And see how Grandma Molly embroidered different animal shapes on the yellow squares?"

"I didn't even notice that before," Amy said, leaning in for a closer look.

Sarah began pointing them out, thrilled to see none of them had suffered much damage. "On this side of the quilt are a rabbit, a fox, and a frog. Over there are a lamb, a duck, and a butterfly."

Audrey kept staring at the initials on the monogrammed block. "Wait a minute. I thought their last name was Drayton, not Harrison."

Sarah sat down at the table to explain their family history. "Grandma Molly gave birth to my dad when she was married to her first husband, Charles Harrison. They lived in Boston and he was killed in battle during World War I."

Amy blinked. "So Grandpa Noah wasn't his father?"

"Not his biological father," Sarah said, "but his father just the same. Grandpa Noah adopted William when he and Grandma Molly were married."

Sarah's mind drifted back to a conversation she'd had with Grandpa Noah when she was a teenager. He'd told her about the first time he'd seen Molly walking down a Boston street.

I fell in love at first sight, literally, he'd said, chuckling. *I took one look at her and tripped over a hitching post, scraping my hands and elbows. She tended to me and was so sweet I decided to hitch myself to her forever.*

He'd done just that, too, marrying Grandma Molly after a whirlwind courtship and bringing her and her five-year-old son home with him to Maple Hill. Sarah could remember the love she'd heard in his voice whenever he'd talked about his wife. After she disappeared, he'd showered that same love on his stepson, protecting Sarah's father from the scandal as much as possible.

"Earth to Grandma," Audrey said, waving a hand in front of Sarah's face. "Tell us the rest of the story. How old was Grandpa William when his mom disappeared?"

Sarah took a deep breath, surprised at how vivid those memories were after all these years. The quilt had brought them all back, the good and the bad.

"He was six." She placed one palm on the quilt. "He told me once that this quilt was his security blanket. It had traveled with him from Boston to Maple Hill after Grandma Molly married Grandpa Noah."

"So it's special to him?" Audrey asked.

"Very special," Sarah replied. "The last time he saw the quilt was also the last time he saw his mother. She laid him down on the parlor sofa one evening and covered him with the quilt. When he awoke the next day in his bed, both his mother and the quilt were gone."

"I can't believe they never found her," Audrey said.

Amy's eyes widened. "Maybe she was up in the passageway too. Maybe she died there!"

"Don't be silly," Audrey said before Sarah could say a word. "There weren't any bones up there."

Not any they'd noticed, anyway. "It wouldn't hurt to take another look," Sarah said. "I was so excited to examine the quilt I rushed out of there before we came to the end of the passageway."

Audrey shuddered. "I'm not going back in there."

"Suit yourself," Amy said, heading toward the doorway. "I'll go with you, Grandma."

Sarah followed Amy back upstairs "Do you have any other flashlights?"

Amy shook her head. "That was the only one I could find."

As they passed an empty bedroom, Sarah saw a small, portable work light sitting on the floor. "That's just what we need." She walked inside and picked it. "Do you have an extension cord?"

"There's one in my room," Amy said. "One of my outlets doesn't work, so Dad used an extension cord to hook up my CD player."

"Perfect."

When they reached Amy's bedroom, Sarah attached the long, orange extension cord to the portable lamp, then switched it on as she and Amy headed back into the secret passageway.

"Wow," Amy said as the portable work light illuminated their path, "it looks totally different in here now."

She was right. The bright light lit the passageway from floor to ceiling. Sarah could see wormholes in the bare stud walls, along with some protruding nails.

"Watch out for the nails," Sarah said, grateful none of them had encountered a nail on their first walkthrough. She kept her gaze on the floor as they walked, looking for anything unusual.

"I see some bones," Amy said, pointing to a spot on the floor next to her. "But I think they're from a mouse."

Sarah directed the work light at the tiny rodent skeleton.

"I think you're right."

"Wait until Audrey hears we found a mouse skeleton up here," Amy said with a grin. "She'll really freak out."

Sarah just hoped they didn't encounter any other kind of skeleton. As gruesome as it sounded, she had to admit there was a possibility Grandma Molly had died in this passageway.

As they walked, Sarah carefully scanned the walls for any other doors that might lead into another room. The ceiling rafters were a good ten feet above her, making it impossible for anyone to reach them without a ladder.

"I think I see the end of the passageway," Amy said as she edged in front of Sarah.

The light landed on a brick wall blocking their way.

"It's the chimney." Sarah slowly aimed the light around the edge of the bricks. The mortar had crumbled in a few places, but it was still solid.

Amy reached out a hand and pressed against several of the bricks. "I guess there's no other way out of here."

"No," Sarah said. Grandma Molly had left the passageway, either by force or of her own volition, leaving the quilt behind.

When they returned to the dining room, Audrey was lying on the green velvet fainting couch in the corner. She didn't look up from her cell phone as her thumbs moved furiously over the keypad. "Find anything?"

"Just some mouse bones," Amy told her. "Who are you texting?"

"Mom. I'm telling her about the secret passageway."

Amy scowled. "I wanted to tell Mom and Dad. I'm the one who found it."

"Too late now," Audrey said.

Amy turned to Sarah. "Even if we didn't find anything else in the passageway, she still could have been murdered in this house, right?"

"That's what the police first suspected," Sarah said. "And Grandpa Noah was their prime suspect.

"No way." Audrey stood up, looking warily around the dining room. "She wasn't murdered here."

"It's possible." Amy's eyes gleamed with ghoulish curiosity. "What do you think happened to her, Grandma?"

"I don't know." Sarah remembered the raw pain she'd hear in her father's voice whenever he talked about his mother. "All I know is that my dad has missed her every single day since she disappeared."

Amy leaned against the antique sideboard, her cheeks flushed.

"Poor Grandpa William." Audrey tucked the cell phone in her pocket as she walked toward the table. "He was such a little guy when it happened. He must have been so scared."

"Grandpa Noah took good care of him," Sarah assured them. "My dad told me they used to go fishing together all the time just to get away from town and all the nasty things people were saying. The worst part was they tried to take Dad away from Grandpa Noah when they gave up on finding Grandma Molly."

"That's awful!" Audrey exclaimed. "It would be bad enough to lose your mom, but then your dad too? What were they thinking?"

They were thinking Noah Drayton killed his wife. Sarah didn't say the words aloud, but it was clear from the expressions on the twins' faces that they'd figured out that part themselves.

"It was primarily one family who believed Grandpa Noah was guilty," Sarah explained. "Arthur Turnquist, who had lost the town selectman election to Grandpa Noah, was determined to convince everyone in Maple Hill that Noah Drayton had murdered his wife. He didn't get him thrown in jail, but Grandpa Noah did have to resign from office because of the scandal."

Amy cleared her throat. "Are you sure Grandpa Noah didn't do something to her?"

"Positive," Sarah said without hesitation. "If you'd known him, you wouldn't have any doubts either. Dad never did, and he knew Grandpa better than anyone."

The girls nodded but didn't look entirely convinced. Sarah wished she could persuade the girls, but how could she prove his innocence? Unless—

A beeping sound from Audrey's pocket broke Sarah's reverie. She looked up to see the girl pull the cell phone out and begin texting again.

"Now who are you texting?" Amy asked.

"Dad. He wants to know more about the passageway."

"Let me tell him," Amy said as she headed toward the doorway. "I'll get my phone."

"I'll just tell him about the note," Audrey said, following her out of the dining room.

"No, let me."

Their voices faded, leaving Sarah alone in the room. She got up from her chair and walked slowly around the table to view the quilt from every angle. Then she turned it over, noting that the faded backing had been constructed from four strips of blue flannel sewn together lengthwise.

There was nothing fancy about this quilt. It was made of recycled fabrics on both the top and the bottom, but it was priceless to her. She leaned over the table for a more detailed inspection of the squares. Most were in good shape, but a few had been severely damaged by time and moisture and insects. Many of the quilting stitches were broken and loose, too. She studied the wide variety of vintage fabrics on the quilt top, impressed with the way Grandma Molly had put them together to form the Sunshine and Shadow pattern.

The chime of the grandfather clock finally made her look up from the quilt. Her back creaked as she straightened. She'd been bent over the quilt for too long.

She picked up the slip of paper with the address on it. *212 Elm Street.* Was that where Grandma Molly had gone the night she disappeared? Sarah had always enjoyed reading mysteries, but she'd never tried to solve one herself. Certainly not a ninety-year-old mystery that had gone cold long ago. She reached out and smoothed one finger over the block monogrammed with her father's initials, imagining her grandmother placing those stitches with loving care. "What happened to you, Grandma Molly?"

"Did you say something, Grandma?" Amy asked, as she and Audrey walked back into the dining room carrying a large bowl of popcorn.

"I was just talking to myself." She moved toward them. "Looks like you decided to make a snack."

"Searching for clues made me hungry," Amy said.

"Why don't we eat on the front porch?" Sarah said. "It's a beautiful day and I don't want to risk getting butter stains on the quilt."

Amy shrugged. "It's already got a lot of stains on it."

"Those can be fixed." The Drayton name had a stain on it, too, thanks to decades of accusations and innuendo aimed at Grandpa Noah. Now that she'd found the quilt and the note, could that be fixed too?

As they walked toward the front door, Audrey said, "There's something I still don't understand. Why did the quilt disappear at the same time as Grandma Molly?"

"I don't know." Sarah remembered the stories she'd heard as a child. "Some people said she took it with her to remember her son. Others said she was buried in it. At least we now know that last part isn't true."

"I don't think the first part could ever have been true either." Audrey opened the front door. "She wouldn't have taken Grandpa William's blanket when she knew how much it meant to him."

Sarah agreed. So why had the quilt been in the secret passageway? And what had happened to her grandmother? A strange fluttering in her stomach made her aware that she had to find the answers. For her grandparents. For her father. For herself. The mystery of Molly's disappearance had haunted them all for far too long. It was time to find out the truth.

CHAPTER THREE

Sarah arrived home only a few minutes before six o'clock. Jason and Maggie had been amazed by the discovery of the secret passageway and had insisted Sarah take the quilt home with her. She set in on the table in her sewing room, then headed toward the back porch to retrieve the jar of sun tea she'd left brewing there. The glass jar warmed her hands as she carried it into the kitchen.

When the doorbell chimed, Sarah glanced over at the stove clock. Right on time.

She set the sun tea on the counter, then headed for the front door, where she found a young woman standing on the wrap-around porch. Mousy brown hair framed a heart-shaped face and a pair of sunglasses shielded her eyes. "Are you Mrs. Hart?"

"Yes, but please call me Sarah."

"I'm Katie. Katie Campbell."

"Nice to meet you, Katie." Sarah opened the door wider. "Please come in."

Perspiration stains dotted Katie's long-sleeved white blouse, which, along with her black slacks, looked much too warm for the July heat, but Sarah was more concerned by the slender girl's pale face.

When Katie removed her sunglasses, Sarah's concern grew. The dark circles under her brown eyes only added to the girl's haggard appearance. She looked as if she hadn't slept or eaten in days.

"Please have a seat," Sarah said, "while I pour us some iced tea."

Katie sank onto the sofa as Sarah turned and walked down the hall into the kitchen. She planned to give the girl more than tea. Within a few minutes, she'd put together a plate of ham and cheese sandwiches cut into quarters and a basket of potato chips. She carried the food and drinks out on a tray and set it on the coffee table.

"It's close to dinner time," Sarah said, handing a glass of tea to Katie, "so I hope you don't mind joining me in a bite to eat."

Katie looked at the tray. "That's very nice of you. I am a little hungry."

Sarah picked a sandwich, gratified to see Katie follow her example. "Why don't we eat first? Then we can talk about the room."

Katie nodded as she took a bite of the sandwich. She'd barely chewed it when she took another bite. Sarah pushed the basket of potato chips toward her. "I'm so glad you're here to help me finish these. I'm afraid they'll grow stale if we don't eat them tonight."

Katie took a chip from the basket and took a dainty bite, obviously trying to slow her eating. Sarah grabbed a chip and popped it in her mouth.

"I forgot the napkins," Sarah said, rising to her feet. "I'll be back in a minute."

Sarah returned to the kitchen and gathered napkins slowly enough to give Katie some privacy while she ate. The poor girl was obviously famished and seemed barely able to restrain herself from gobbling down the food. She'd seen it before. Too many young people lived hand to mouth these days, and boarders often showed up at her door with an empty stomach.

She tidied up the kitchen for a few minutes before returning to the living room. In that short amount of time, Katie had eaten half the sandwiches and made a serious dent in the basket of chips. Sarah was gratified to see a hint of color returning to her cheeks.

"So what brings you to Maple Hill?" Sarah asked her, reaching for one of the remaining sandwiches.

"Actually, it's not a what, but a who," Katie replied with a shy smile. "Nathaniel Bradford." Nathaniel Bradford was a Revolutionary War hero from Maple Hill. There was a life-size statue of him in Patriot Park. He'd also been dead for at least two hundred years.

"I'm not sure I understand."

"I'm a graduate student at Northwestern in Chicago and I'm writing my thesis on Nathaniel Bradford. I decided the best way to really understand the man was to come to the town where he lived and get to know the area."

She was a starving college student. Now it all made sense. "That sounds interesting. You should check out the Maple Hill Historical Society. I'm sure Irene Stuart, the director there, will be happy to assist you in your research. The library is full of books about Nathaniel Bradford too."

"Perfect." Katie reached for her glass. "I like the town already. All the shops downtown and the maple trees lining the sidewalks and the village green. It's so quaint."

"I agree." Sarah finished her sandwich, then brushed the bread crumbs from her fingers. "I've lived here all my life."

"I can see why." Katie set her glass on the coffee table. "How long have you rented rooms?"

"About four years. After my husband died, I needed a project to keep me busy so I remodeled the house, including the second floor. Once that was done, I figured it was a waste to let those two bedrooms sit empty."

Katie nodded. "Do you have anyone else living here now?"

"A woman named Rita. She makes a lot of day trips, something about birding in the Berkshires, so she's not around much."

"So you have a room for me?"

"I do," Sarah said. "Why don't I give you a tour of the house and explain how it works around here, then you can decide if you'd like to stay."

"That sounds good."

Sarah rose to her feet, then led Katie to the hallway. "That's the dining room," she said, pointing to the arched doorway opposite the living room, "and the kitchen is this way."

She walked past the staircase and into the kitchen. She'd remodeled it, too, since Gerry died, and loved her new classic New England style with its wide plank floor, cranberry red walls, and contrasting cream-colored cabinetry. A round, pine table and two chairs filled the small nook near the window.

"This is so cozy." Katie turned in a slow circle. "I love it."

"You're welcome to use anything in the kitchen," Sarah told her. "All I ask is that you clean up after yourself. Each boarder gets his or her own refrigerator shelf and freezer shelf for food. I've found it's less confusing for everyone that way."

"Makes sense."

Sarah pointed to a door opposite the table. "That's the laundry room, along with a bathroom. The door on the left leads to my sewing room. I restore vintage quilts, so I spend a lot of time in there."

"Is that a hobby or a job?"

Sarah smiled, thinking of her weakness for buying beautiful fabrics. "A little bit of both."

When they reached the top of the stairs, Katie's pale face brightened when she saw the small sitting room. "Wow, this is nice."

The second level had been converted from four bedrooms to three. Sarah had used the extra space to expand the master bedroom and to create an open sitting area at the top of the stairs. Along with a love seat and two overstuffed chairs, there was a small television set in the sitting area, and a bookcase with a bunch of novels. Her personal library grew every year and she loved rereading her favorite mystery authors like Agatha Christie and Rex Stout. Which reminded her—she had her own mystery to solve. She itched to get into her sewing room and start cataloguing the vintage fabrics in the quilt. But she kept going with the tour, telling herself she could wait a few more minutes before she tackled the ninety-year-old mystery.

"You're welcome to use the living room whenever you like," Sarah said, "but I thought it would be nice to create another space for my boarders to relax in."

Katie smoothed one hand over the flying geese quilt draped over the back of the love seat. "This looks like a great place to study."

Sarah walked straight ahead and opened the door to her bedroom. "This is my room."

The door was open far enough to reveal the antique mahogany sleigh bed and matching dresser she'd found at an estate auction years ago. She'd fallen in love with it and Gerry had surprised her by bidding on it. He'd always been a kind, generous man. Someday she'd give the set to her daughter Jenna, who lived in Texas with her husband and two sons.

"Everything is so nice," Katie said. "It's like something out of a magazine."

Sarah laughed. "I'm not sure I would go that far, but thank you for the compliment. I've lived here since I was first married, so I've had a lot of years to get it just right."

She turned around and motioned to the two closed doors on either side of the stairwell. "Those are the guest rooms. Rita's room is on the right and the one on the left would be your room."

Katie followed her to the room, looking dead on her feet in spite of the light supper she'd just eaten. She stood in the doorway, her gaze taking in the soft yellow walls, the tall oak dresser, and the green and pink nine-patch quilt on the twin-size bed.

"Well?" Sarah asked.

"It's perfect." Katie walked over to the window and peeked through the blue gingham drapes. "And it looks out over the street in front of the house."

"That's right, but you don't have to worry about traffic noise. This is a very quiet neighborhood." Sarah pointed to a door near the closet. "That leads to your bathroom. Each bedroom has its own bath, so you don't have to share."

"Cool."

"There's some storage space in the cellar," Sarah added, "so you're welcome to store items down there if need be."

"I don't have much with me," Katie said. "Just my suitcase."

"How long are you planning to stay in Maple Hill?"

Katie paused for a moment. "I'm not sure. As long as it takes, I guess."

Sarah found her reply a little curious, yet something about Katie appealed to her. She was like a stray kitten needing a home. "So do you want the room?"

Katie bit her lower lip. "Can I ask how much you're asking for rent?"

"My usual rate is one hundred fifty dollars a week in the summer."

"Oh." Katie's face fell and Sarah's heart went out to her.

"But this room's been empty for a while ..." Sarah tried to determine a fair rate that Katie would be able to afford. Jason would chide her for not being a better businesswoman, but there was more to life than business. Sometimes God called you to act, and Sarah felt that he was calling her now. This girl needed her help. And Sarah had always had a compassionate heart. Her parents would groan whenever they saw her walk through the door with a wounded bird or an abandoned puppy in her arms. When she'd been old enough to realize the way some people in the community treated Grandpa Noah because of Grandma's unexplained disappearance, she'd been heartsick.

She'd always believed in helping others, finding guidance in one of her favorite Bible verses: "Give, and it will be given to you. A good measure, pressed down, shaken together and running over, will be poured into your lap. For with the measure you use, it will be measured to you."

"So I'm willing to reduce the rate," Sarah continued, "to one hundred dollars a week."

Katie beamed. "I'll take it!"

Sarah breathed a sigh of relief. "Good. I have a rental form for you to fill out and sign. It's a week-to-week tenancy, with payment due every Thursday. I'll need seven days notice when you decide to move out."

Katie hesitated. "What about a security deposit?"

"That won't be necessary," Sarah told her. Katie probably didn't even have enough spare money to feed herself, much less pay a security deposit. Jason wouldn't approve of that either, but what her son didn't know wouldn't hurt him. "Just promise me you won't throw any wild parties."

"Believe me, Sarah, you'll hardly know I'm here."

CHAPTER FOUR

fter settling Katie in her bedroom and giving her the rental form, Sarah headed for her sewing room. The quilt lay on the table where she'd left it and Sarah walked over to look at it once more. The fact that she'd found it after all these years still hadn't quite sunk in. She couldn't wait to tell her father about it, hoping he'd be lucid enough to understand. His memories often got mixed up, but he'd never forgotten losing his mother. Some pain went so deep that it could never be erased.

The tattered note sat on top of her desk. She picked it up, wishing she knew what it meant. Had 212 Elm Street been Grandma Molly's destination the night of her disappearance? Sarah moved to the window and held the paper close to the glass, hoping the fading light would illuminate the words that had been scribbled out below the address. She could make out a few pencil strokes, but the words were still indecipherable.

She sat down at her computer and pulled up an online phone directory. Then she typed in *212 Elm Street, Maple Hill, Massachusetts*, and clicked the search button. A moment later, she had a name.

"D. Hatch," she said aloud, writing it down on the memo pad in front of her. She didn't know anyone by that name and, although there was a telephone number listed, she didn't want to explain the situation over the phone, especially when she hadn't figured out what to say.

She placed the crinkled note carefully in her desk drawer, then grabbed a pen and a spiral notebook from her desk before returning to the quilt.

She usually started a new notebook for each new quilting project, recording her progress and making detailed notes along the way. It not only helped her keep track of her work, but writing things down longhand seemed to spur her creativity. Whenever she had a problem with a quilt, writing it out always seemed to help her find a solution.

Her first problem with this quilt was what to do with the binding. The blue silk taffeta edging the quilt was starting to fray in several places and she feared manipulating the fabric in any way would destroy it. Once she settled into the chair, Sarah pulled the notebook toward her and wrote: *Bias binding—blue silk taffeta—fraying in several places. No stains or moth holes. Need to research ways to stabilize this fabric. Perhaps a special fabric adhesive for taffeta???*

Sarah decided to leave the binding on the quilt for now. She could always remove it later and, in the meantime, look for ways to save it.

Reaching across the table, Sarah picked up her wide acrylic ruler and flipped on the gooseneck lamp that provided enough illumination for her to see even the tiniest stitch. She clipped her special magnifying lenses on top of her glasses, preparing to list each of the individual fabric pieces on the quilt top.

The border of the quilt contained a row of white two-inch equilateral triangles, cut from cotton fabric. The rest of the quilt top was made of two-inch squares of blue and yellow fabrics, arranged so that diamonds radiated out from the center. She started at the bottom corner of the quilt, moving left to right.

1. Triangle – white cotton. Brown stain.
2. Triangle – white cotton. No damage.
3. Triangle – white cotton. No damage.
4. Triangle – white cotton. Brown stain.

Sarah continued along the border until she'd documented all twenty-four white triangles and their setting triangles. Then she moved up to the first row in the body of the quilt.

49. Square – light blue satin. Letters W. J. H. embroidered with matching blue silk thread.
50. Square – medium blue satin. Loose stitching at seams.

51. Square – dark blue satin. No damage.

52. Square – deep yellow satin. Fraying at seams.

Sarah catalogued many of the quilts she restored, finding it helped her organize the process and provided her with an opportunity to closely study each individual fabric piece before she began working on it. After completing a quilt restoration, she used the list to check off each piece and make sure she hadn't missed anything.

To keep track of her progress, she placed a T-pin in each fabric piece as she recorded it. That was the best way to keep from accidentally listing a piece twice. She stopped after documenting the first six rows of blue and yellow squares, her fingers starting to cramp. She set down her pen, then massaged her right hand. She'd documented 144 squares, which meant there were still 432 to go, plus the fabric pieces in the three other borders. But that would have to wait until later. The sun sat low on the horizon, casting long shadows in the room. Sarah got up from her chair, turned on the overhead light, and walked over to close the curtains. A yawn escaped her. She was looking forward to climbing into bed, but first she wanted to complete one more step in her preparation work.

She retrieved her digital camera from the desk drawer and took pictures of both the front and the back of the quilt. She'd add these to her notebook, providing color images to go along with her written record of the fabric pieces.

Then she got another idea.

Sarah headed for the living room, where she switched on a lamp by the bookcase. Family photographs filled the shelves, including a black-and-white photo of Grandpa Noah and Grandma Molly on their wedding day. She wore a flapper-style dress adorned with ribbons and lace, and carried a small bouquet of flowers. Grandpa Noah stood beside her in a dark suit and tie. They both looked very solemn as they faced the camera.

Although the photograph had been around since Sarah was a little girl, she suddenly saw the grandmother she'd never met in a new light. Despite all the stories she'd heard, Grandma Molly had never quite seemed real.

Now that she had the quilt Grandma Molly had sewn for her baby boy, Sarah felt a special connection to her. Grandma Molly's hands had sewn every stitch with love and Sarah could feel that love every time she touched the quilt. In some small way, it made her grandmother come alive for her.

Sarah held the camera in front of her, centering the LCD screen until the wedding photo came into focus. She snapped the picture and looked at the result on the LCD screen. It was a perfect replica of the photograph.

She would place it in the quilt notebook as a special reminder of what was at stake. Grandpa Noah's life had been ripped apart when his wife disappeared, but he'd never lost his love for her. Sarah would need that kind of dedication while putting the pieces of this puzzle together.

There were so many questions that needed answers, but she wouldn't let them overwhelm her. She knew from working with quilts that the most complicated patterns could be broken down into simple, manageable pieces. That's how she needed to approach solving this mystery—one piece at a time.

CHAPTER FIVE

The next morning, Sarah sat at the kitchen table and sipped a cup of coffee. She hadn't heard a peep from Katie and hoped that meant the girl was getting some much-needed sleep. Katie had filled out the rental form and given Sarah a twenty-dollar bill before going to bed the night before, promising more money in the coming days.

Sarah studied the rental form now, noting Katie's small, neat handwriting. The form was a standard room rental agreement Jason had insisted on drawing up for her when she'd expressed an interest in taking in boarders; it included the length of the agreement, which Sarah had decided to make week-to-week, because she wasn't dependent on the rental income. It also spelled out a few household rules, such as no overnight guests of the opposite sex, no smoking, and no alcohol in the house.

The agreement outlined the use of the common areas and appliances, and stated that the tenant would need to obtain

Sarah's permission in order to bring a pet into the house. She loved animals, but one boarder had owned a ferret which she'd let run loose in her bedroom, and it had destroyed a set of bedroom curtains.

Sarah also had each boarder list someone to notify in case of an emergency. She was surprised to see that Katie had listed a professor at Northwestern University. Most people wanted you to contact a family member in an emergency, but Katie hadn't revealed anything about her family during their interview last night.

"Good morning!" Rita French walked into the kitchen, although bounced might be a better way to describe her stride. She and Sarah were about the same age, but the petite woman was so energetic that some days Sarah got tired just watching her.

"Good morning," Sarah replied, admiring the turquoise jogging suit Rita wore.

"It looks like I have a new neighbor upstairs." Rita opened the refrigerator door and retrieved a small bottle of orange juice from her shelf. "I heard someone moving around in the other room last night."

Sarah had been asleep before Rita arrived home, so she hadn't had a chance to introduce the two boarders to each other. "Yes, you do. Her name is Katie and she's here doing graduate research for a history degree."

"That sounds like fun." Rita caught her reflection in the window glass and combed her fingers through the fringe of caramel brown above her eyes. "I wish I had studied history in college instead of accounting." She laughed. "Do you think sixty is too old to go back to school?"

"Not at all."

Rita shook her head. "I'm not sure I could sit in a classroom all day with students young enough to be my grandchildren. Besides, I'm having too much fun tooling around the country looking for birds." She opened the freezer and grabbed a plastic-wrapped bran muffin. "I'm off to the Museum of Science in Boston today."

"Will you be back tonight?"

"No." Rita tucked the orange juice bottle in the pocket of her lightweight jacket. "I plan to spend at least a couple of days there."

"Well, have a good trip," Sarah said as Rita headed out of the kitchen.

"Thanks, I will."

Sarah took a sip of her coffee. It had cooled during her conversation with Rita, so she got up to add some more from the pot. Just then a knock sounded at the back door and Sarah's best friend Martha Maplethorpe appeared in the doorway that separated the kitchen from the back porch.

"Good morning," Martha greeted Sarah, a cloth bag slung over one arm. "I brought back your copies of *Country Cottage Magazine*." She dug into her bag, then pulled out three magazines and set them on the table. "I found some great recipes and a couple of interesting crochet patterns."

Martha was like a sister to Sarah. They'd been friends for decades and Martha had helped Sarah through Gerry's death. Martha was a round jolly woman with graying brown hair and hazel eyes. Her four children and nine grandchildren all lived in or near Maple Hill. Sarah had always envied her for having grandkids so close by. Now that Jason and his family had moved to Maple Hill, Sarah could share in that joy.

"You didn't have to make a special trip to bring them back."

"I know, but I needed some excuse to get out of the house for a while." Martha settled herself onto a kitchen chair. "Ernie's been driving me crazy."

Her husband could be as dour as Martha was cheerful, but she didn't usually let his moods bother her.

"What's he done now?" Sarah asked as she poured her friend a cup of coffee.

"He's barely said two words to me in the last few days." Martha reached into her bag and pulled out a ball of thread and a crochet hook. "All he does is stomp around the house or stare out the window. He hasn't gone out to his shop much either."

Ernie liked to tinker with old cars, fixing them for his grandchildren to drive. Whenever Sarah had trouble with her Grand Prix, she always took her car to Ernie first, who could usually fix the problem without charging her an arm and a leg.

"I probably did something to make him mad." Martha chuckled as she looped the white cotton thread around one finger, then began to crochet. "I'm sure he'll get over it in a day or two."

Sarah set the coffee cup in front of Martha. "What are you working on now?"

"A lace tablecloth. Ernie spilled grape juice on my old one and I can't get the stain out."

"That might explain his bad mood. Maybe he feels bad."

Martha smiled. "Then he's got a funny way of showing it." She reached for her coffee cup. "So what's new with you?"

"I got another boarder last night." Sarah told her about Katie and her research project.

"Maybe I should have Kyle talk to her. I told him to write a story about Nathaniel Bradford for the *Monitor*, but he just rolled his eyes at me." She laughed. "I guess I don't have a good nose for news." Kyle was Martha's oldest grandson and he was working as a summer intern at the newspaper office.

Sarah watched the crochet hook fly in Martha's hands, always fascinated by how fast she could make such tiny, intricate stitches. "Is Kyle enjoying his stint at the newspaper?"

"He seems to be." Martha pulled more thread from the ball. "He wants to be a sports reporter, so he's been itching to cover some of the local ball games."

"Amy plans to play softball next summer. She didn't want to join in the middle of the season."

"It's hard to come into a new town," Martha commiserated. "We'll have to introduce the twins to my granddaughters when they come back from summer camp. That will help break the ice with other kids around town."

"That's a wonderful idea." Sarah smiled. "The twins are pretty bored. I think they're homesick."

"That's only natural at their age. Moving from Los Angeles to Maple Hill has got to be a bit of a culture shock."

"True." Sarah took another sip of her coffee. "Although we did have fun yesterday. Amy found a secret passageway in Grandpa Noah's house."

Martha jerked her head up. "Really?"

Sarah recounted what had happened the day before and then added, "And guess what we found? Dad's quilt."

Martha's mouth gaped. "No!" Martha had heard Sarah talk about Molly Drayton's mysterious disappearance and the quilt that disappeared with her countless times.

"I'm sure it's my dad's quilt. It has his initials on it and is just like he described it."

Martha sat back in her chair. "That is amazing. Imagine it being there all these years."

"I haven't told you the most mysterious part," Sarah said. "I found a piece of paper stuck inside the quilt, with the words '212 Elm Street' scribbled on it."

"212 Elm Street?" Martha echoed. "Our Elm Street?"

"I hope so. I'm going there today to see what I can find out."

"Do you know who lives there?"

"D. Hatch. I looked up the address on the computer last night in the Maple Hill online directory. Does the name sound familiar?"

"Not at all." Martha let out an envious sigh. "Oh, I wish I could go with you. I invited Pastor John over for lunch today and just wanted to stop by here for a quick visit." She glanced at her watch. "In fact, I probably should get home and put my roast in the oven."

"Don't worry," Sarah said as Martha packed up her crocheting. "I'll tell you if I find anything. And that's a big if after all these years."

"Don't be so sure. You found the quilt, didn't you?"

"With the help of the twins."

"Maybe that secret passageway is connected to Molly's disappearance. It *must* be if that's where you found the quilt."

A thrill shot though Sarah at the possibility of answering the questions that had been plaguing the Drayton family for decades. But she was getting ahead of herself.

Martha bid her goodbye, then left through the back door. Sarah cleaned up the coffee cups, then wondered if she should wait until Katie awoke to go on her fact-finding mission. She glanced at the clock, noting that it was just past ten o'clock. Maybe if she left now, she'd be back before Katie got out of bed.

If not, she was sure the girl could fend for herself for the next hour or so.

She scribbled a quick note to let Katie know that she'd be back soon, then left her a key to the house before grabbing her purse and heading out the door. Her silver Pontiac stood in the driveway, decorated with dusty paw prints from the neighbor's cat.

Sarah settled into the car, then pulled out of the driveway. She drove toward Elm Street, wondering what she should say to the owners of the house. If she was lucky, they'd know some of the house's history and might be able to tell her the significance of the note in the quilt. If not ... Sarah shook her head, figuring she'd cross that bridge when she got to it. Her car rolled along the wide street, the windows open so she could enjoy the warm breeze. She drove past Patriot Park, where children played on the playground under the maple trees and the bronze statue of Nathaniel Bradford gleamed in the summer sun, then headed toward the village green.

A farmer's market was set up in the center of the green with long tables of fresh produce sitting under a blue and white striped canopy. Sarah made a mental note to stop there later and pick up some sweet corn for supper. It was a beautiful day in Maple Hill.

CHAPTER SIX

When she reached Elm, Sarah slowed the car to a crawl so she could read the address numbers on the houses.

"200 ... 204 ... 208," she murmured. "212!"

The two-story brick house was crumbling around the edges, and several shingles were missing from the steep roofline. Only the towering chimney and the stained glass adorning the windows hinted at the majestic home it must have been a century before.

Sarah caught a glimpse of the rotting cellar doors at the back of the house. They were padlocked with a thick chain, although they looked fragile enough to be easily broken through. Tall weeds flourished in the yard, leaving little room for the sparse blades of grass struggling to find sunlight between the spindly fir trees dotting the front yard.

Sarah parked her car against the curb, then got out and walked to the front gate. It emitted a bone-chilling squeal when she opened it, the wrought iron bar leaving a residue of rust on her fingers. She wiped them off as she approached the front door. The covered porch floor creaked as she stepped onto it, no doubt announcing her arrival to the residents of the house.

She knocked on the door and waited for someone to answer. A minute later, she knocked again, louder this time in case the owner was hard of hearing.

At long last the front door slowly opened a crack, but Sarah couldn't see anyone on the other side.

"Hello?" Sarah called out, feeling a little uneasy. "Is someone there?"

"Who is it?" a woman's voice asked.

"My name is Sarah Hart. I was hoping I could talk to you about the history of your house."

"Why?" asked the voice.

"Well," Sarah said, not certain where to start, "it's a long story, but I promise not to take up too much of your time. I'd just like to ask you a few questions."

After several moments, the door opened wider. "Okay, you can come in."

Sarah took a deep breath, then stepped over the threshold and into a drab living room. The beige furniture blended with the beige walls and the worn beige carpet on the floor, the monotony broken only by a small pea green rug at the base of a recliner. The only sign of life, other than the woman standing in front of her, was a philodendron plant on the fireplace mantel, the green, leafy tendrils drifting toward the blackened grate.

Given the blandness of the living room décor, Sarah was stunned to see the decorative plaster ceiling above her. Long ago, someone had painted swirl patterns and other fine detail with gold leaf. There were muted reds and blues as well, adding to the intricate pattern.

"Now who did you say you were again?" the woman asked her, reminding Sarah of the reason she was there.

"Sarah Hart. Thank you for letting me intrude on you this way."

"I don't get many visitors."

Sarah judged her age to be about fifty. Silver threaded her dark hair, which was pulled back into a messy ponytail. Her black polo shirt was matted with white hairs, the source of which became apparent when a white Persian cat appeared in the open doorway between the living room and the kitchen. The cat's neatly combed fur hung almost to the floor.

"That's a beautiful cat."

"Her name is Bianca." The woman reached down to scoop her up, cradling her in her arms.

"Are you Ms. Hatch?"

"Yes. Doris Hatch."

"It's nice to meet you, Doris. And you too, Bianca." Sarah reached out to pet the cat, but it ducked away from her hand.

"Bianca is shy of strangers," Doris said, taking a step back from Sarah.

"I don't believe I've seen you around town," Sarah said. "Have you lived in Maple Hill long?"

"Six years."

Sarah had hoped to break the ice with some small talk, but Doris wasn't making it easy for her. There was something strange about the woman, but Sarah couldn't quite put her finger on it. If she didn't know better, she'd think Doris knew exactly why she was here and was playing games with her, but that surely wasn't possible, was it? "So what brought you here?"

"Someone had to take care of my aunt."

"I see."

Doris stared.

"Is your aunt here?" Sarah asked, hoping the woman might be more chatty than her recalcitrant niece.

"She died."

"Oh, I'm sorry for your loss." Maybe grief explained her odd behavior. "Was it recent?"

"No," Doris said. "Aunt Cleo passed away three years ago."

The name gave her pause. "Cleo?" It wasn't a common name. "Cleo Turnquist?"

"That's right. Did you know her?"

Cleo Turnquist had been Arthur Turnquist's daughter, and she had been as forthright in her belief in Grandpa Noah's guilt as her father had. Sarah had crossed the street to avoid her on more than one occasion.

"We met a few times," Sarah replied at last. Any hope that she'd receive help from Doris Hatch was quickly fading. No doubt Cleo Turnquist had told her niece all about

Maple Hill's "most notorious murderer," as she'd once called Grandpa Noah within earshot of Sarah. The memory still made her angry and more determined than ever to prove her grandfather's innocence.

An oven timer buzzed, startling the cat. Bianca jumped out of Doris's arms and onto the floor. "I'll be right back," Doris said, disappearing into the kitchen.

Left alone in the living room, Sarah looked around. Had her grandmother sought sanctuary here the night she disappeared? Had it belonged to a Turnquist back in 1920? That possibility implied all sorts of complications that Sarah didn't want to entertain until she knew it to be true.

She turned her attention to a display of framed photographs on the wall opposite the window. They were all scenic photos of exotic places, each one filled with bright, vibrant colors. Just like the ceiling, they looked out of place amid the sea of beige.

A few minutes later, Doris walked back into the living room carrying a plate holding pea-sized pieces of pastry. "Look, Bianca," Doris said, "your catnip biscuits are done. I cooled them off for you too." As she set the plate on the green rug, Bianca padded over and gave the doughy lumps a delicate sniff before turning her back on them.

After an awkward moment, Sarah decided to get to the point of her visit. "This might seem odd, but I was hoping you could tell me something about the people who lived here in 1920."

Doris frowned. "That was ninety years ago. How old do you think I am?"

"Certainly not that old," Sarah hastened to clarify, "you're younger than I am. I just meant that your aunt might have mentioned previous owners. Could the house have belonged to the Turnquist family for the last ninety years?"

"Aunt Cleo bought it after her mother died, and that was only twenty years ago."

"Do you know who owned the house before that?"

"No idea. I don't think I can help you."

Sarah wasn't ready to leave. The piece of paper with this address scribbled on it was the only clue she had so far. This house had been important to Grandma Molly for some reason and she was determined to find out why.

"I must say, this is a beautiful ceiling," Sarah arched her neck to study it once more. "Unusual, too. I've never seen one like it before."

"That's because it's the only one in Maple Hill."

"Really?" Sarah looked at her. "How do you know?"

Doris blinked at the question. "I just do."

"But how?" Sarah asked gently. "You've only lived here for six years."

Doris hesitated for several moments as the cat wove around her ankles. "You know, I may have something that could help you after all."

arah followed Doris down into the dark, dank cellar. "I don't come down here very often," Doris said when they reached the bottom of the stairs. "I mainly just use it to store Aunt Cleo's stuff."

The cool air made Sarah shiver a little. The cellar was unfinished, with concrete block walls and a cracked concrete floor. There were boxes stacked haphazardly around them, along with some broken-down furniture and a metal filing cabinet.

"I think it's in here," Doris said as she walked over to the filing cabinet. "I went through all my aunt's papers after she died and I remember something…" She sorted through the file folders. "Here it is."

Doris handed Sarah a folder. "It's some kind of certificate dedicating this house as an historic landmark because of the ceiling upstairs."

"Really?"

Doris nodded. "It was painted by a guy named Luther Endicott. He must be famous or something now since they made it a landmark."

The name didn't sound familiar. Sarah looked down at the certificate. "The ceiling was painted in September 1920."

"Do you think this will help?"

"It's a start," Sarah replied. If this house was the only one in Maple Hill painted by Luther Endicott, then she might be able to find the name of the owner by researching the painter. "Thank you for showing this to me."

A plaintive meow sounded at the top of the cellar stairs. Sarah looked up to see the cat sitting on the upper landing. "I think Bianca misses you."

"She refuses to come down into the cellar." Doris turned to look at her. "I wonder if that means something. They say cats have a sixth sense."

Sarah didn't know about a sixth sense, but she didn't blame Bianca for staying upstairs. A touch of mildew hung in the air and cobwebs arched across the ceiling beams. The room definitely had an eerie feeling to it.

"You can take that certificate with you," Doris said as she headed toward the stairs.

"Thanks. I promise to return it soon." Sarah slipped the certificate back into its envelope, then placed it in her bag.

Doris took the stairs slowly, using both hands on the stair rail to pull herself up as Bianca sat at the top watching her.

Sarah saw the stiffness in her legs and hips as she mounted the stairs, something she hadn't noticed before. She wondered if Doris suffered from arthritis or, perhaps, an old injury. That could explain why the yard was such a mess.

When they finally reached the top of the stairs, Sarah closed the cellar door behind her, feeling a little guilty for her earlier doubts about Doris. The woman might suffer from some social awkwardness, but she'd been kind enough to help a total stranger. "Thanks again, Doris. Maybe I can take you out for lunch sometime. That's the least I can do for all your help."

"I don't like to go out much."

"Is there anything I can do for you?"

"No," Doris replied, her hand stroking Bianca's head. "I'm fine. I haven't met many people in Maple Hill, so it is nice to make a new friend."

"Here," Sarah said, reaching into her purse and pulling out one of her business cards. "I use these for my quilt restoration business, but it has my home phone number on it. Please feel free to call if you ever need anything."

Doris hesitated a moment, then took the card from her. "Thank you."

Sarah bid her goodbye, then walked down the porch steps. The yard really just needed a good sprucing up. Maybe she could convince Audrey and Amy to mow the grass and pull weeds. It would get them out of the house and give them something to do. She wasn't sure how to approach Doris about it, but she would give it some thought.

The sky darkened as Sarah set the landmark certificate on the seat beside her. She pulled away from the curb and headed for the village green, rethinking her plan to stop for sweet corn and wishing she'd brought an umbrella. As she drove past the storefronts and restaurants surrounding the green, the mouthwatering aroma of barbecue filled the air. In her opinion, Maple Hill offered the best of both worlds, the quaintness of an historic village and all the modern conveniences of the twenty-first century.

One of those modern conveniences was the new computerized records system at the county courthouse. She'd read about the new system in the newspaper and decided now was the perfect time to try it out. At the end of the green, instead of continuing on her way home, she turned left and headed toward the courthouse. She found an empty parking space right in front of the building.

The four-story courthouse sat atop a hill, overlooking the tree-lined streets of downtown Maple Hill. The rusticated stone building had stood on that spot since the mid-1800s and still retained the intricate, hand-carved wood moldings and embossed tin ceiling tiles that gave the building much of its charm.

Sarah mounted the steps leading to the front entrance, then headed for the Register of Deeds office. The young clerk, Tim Barclay, according to the nameplate on his desk, looked up as Sarah walked through the door.

He brushed back the wavy red hair that hung past his white shirt collar. "May I help you?"

"I hope so," Sarah said, glimpsing a solitaire game on his computer screen. "I need to find out who owned the property at 212 Elm Street in 1920. I understand all the town records are digital now."

"They sure are." He remained seated in his chair as he pointed to a computer station in the corner near the door. "That computer is available to the public during courthouse hours and has all the public documents on it. The log-in information is taped to the desk."

"Thank you."

"That's what I'm here for," he said, turning back to his game.

Sarah walked over to the computer and sat down. She took a moment to read the log-in instructions, then accessed the file containing all the property records. There were links for each decade, so she clicked on the 1920–1929 link.

A moment later the file opened, but instead of a long list of property deeds, there was one simple sentence: *Records destroyed in a storage room fire.*

Frustrated, Sarah returned to the original Web page and clicked on the link for 1910–1919, only to find the exact same message: *Records destroyed in a storage room fire.*

Sarah looked over at Tim. "Excuse me?"

"Yeah?" he said, his gaze fixed on his computer screen.

"Do you know anything about a storage room fire that destroyed property records in the early twentieth century?"

"I sure don't."

"Wouldn't new deeds have been issued?" Sarah asked.

"Beats me," he replied. "All I know is that every record we have is on the computer. If it's not there, we don't have it."

She turned back to the computer screen, not ready to give up. Sarah clicked the 1930–1939 link, then groaned when she saw the same message. *Records destroyed in a storage room fire.**

Then she noticed the asterisk. She scrolled down on the page until she came to another link that read: *Duplicate property deeds from 1910 to 1939.*

She clicked on the link and a long list of deeds appeared on the screen. She moved the cursor to the search box in the corner, then typed in *212 Elm.*

The photocopy of a deed popped up on the screen. Sarah quickly scanned it, looking for the information she wanted. *On this eleventh day of October, 1936, First National Bank conveys property deed at 212 Elm, Maple Hill, Massachusetts, to Elmer Dowling.*

She knew there had been a lot of foreclosures during the Great Depression, which explained why the bank had title to the house in 1936, but there must have been no other copies made during that time period. Further searching only revealed a notification that the records were incomplete for this time period.

Leaning back in her chair, Sarah mentally sorted through the information she had so far. Then she searched for property deeds for 212 Elm after 1936, but the only one she found was a transfer of property from Elmer Dowling to Cleo Turnquist in 1990.

Now Sarah knew that no one else had owned the house between 1936 and 1990. But who had the bank foreclosed on? And had that person owned the house in 1920?

Fortunately, she knew just whom to ask.

When Sarah pulled into her driveway she was thrilled to see her neighbor sitting on his front porch. Elmer Dowling, Jr., had moved next door to her five years before when he'd married his third wife, Imogene Smythe Dowling. At eighty-four, Imogene was ten years his senior, but the age difference didn't seem to bother Elmer or Imogene. He spent most of his time fishing in the lakes and streams of the Berkshire Mountains while Imogene filled her days watching soap operas on television.

Elmer's tackle box was open beside him as Sarah mounted the steps of his Tudor-style home. "Hey, neighbor," Elmer greeted her as he carefully examined a green fishing lure. He was a tall, wiry man with snow white hair and bright blue eyes.

"Hi, Elmer. Going fishing today?"

"Sure am." He set the lure back in the tackle box, giving her his full attention. "I wanted to wait until the rain passed, so I'm getting a late start."

"I'd like to ask you a quick question if you have time."

"Shoot," he said, leaning back in his porch rocker.

"I'm researching the house at 212 Elm Street and discovered that your dad purchased it back in 1936."

"He sure did," Elmer replied. "We moved in right after I was born."

"Do you happen to know who owned it before he bought it?"

"The bank. They were selling it cheap or my dad never would have bought it."

"I mean, who owned it before the bank?"

Elmer thought for a moment, then shook his head. "I don't recall. My dad got it for pennies on the dollar. Kept bragging about that bargain until the day he died." He squinted up at her. "Why are you looking for the owner after all these years? I'm sure he's dead and buried by now."

"I'm just doing some family research," Sarah said. "I thought the Draytons might have some connection to that house."

Elmer closed his tackle box and snapped it shut. "Well, I do my best thinking with a fishing pole in my hand. If I remember anything about the house, I'll let you know."

"Thanks," she said, moving toward the steps. "I appreciate it."

When she crossed the front yard to her house, she was surprised to see Katie out on the front porch watering the hanging flower baskets. It was something Sarah usually did most mornings after breakfast, but she'd been in such a hurry to check out the house on Elm Street that she'd completely forgotten.

"I just love it here," Katie said as Sarah approached her. "It's so quiet and peaceful. I can't remember the last time I slept so well."

Sarah could see she looked more rested than she had last night. The circles under her eyes had faded and she had color in her cheeks. "Thank you for watering my flowers."

"It's my pleasure." Katie set the watering can on the porch floor. "I love gardening, but it's been a long time since I've gotten to do any."

"I suppose your graduate work keeps you pretty busy." Katie looked away for a moment. "Yes."

Sarah moved toward the front door. "Have you eaten yet?"

"You don't have to feed me again," Katie replied. "That's not part of our rental arrangement."

"Nonsense. I know you haven't had time to go to the grocery store yet and I certainly won't miss a bowl of soup or a cup of oatmeal."

Katie hesitated. "Oatmeal does sound good."

"I have some raisins you can put in it, too," Sarah said as she walked into the house. "I'll show you where the pots and pans are so you can make yourself at home."

When they reached the kitchen, Sarah walked over to the pantry and pulled out the box of oatmeal, then retrieved a pan from the cupboard. When she handed them to Katie, she noticed the younger woman's eyes watering. "Are you all right?"

Katie blinked back her tears. "It's just that you're so ... nice. I feel like ..."

Sarah waited, but Katie didn't finish her sentence. Instead, she blinked back her tears and started measuring out the oatmeal.

Sarah leaned back. Tears seemed a bit much. Why was Katie so surprised that someone could be nice to her? What could have happened in her past to elicit such a reaction? Questions tingled on the tip of Sarah's tongue, but she resisted the temptation to ask them. Once she and Katie knew each other better, the girl might confide in her. Sarah didn't want to meddle in her tenant's personal life.

"I'll probably be out researching Nathaniel Bradford most of the day," Katie said, stirring the oatmeal in the pan, "but I'll make time to go to the grocery store this afternoon. Is there anything I can pick up for you?"

"I can't think of anything," Sarah replied. "I'm heading out again myself to do some research at the historical society. If you want to come with me, I can introduce you to the director."

Katie smiled. "That sounds perfect. Just give me time to eat and clean up. It won't take long."

"Just let me know when you're ready," Sarah said before walking into her sewing room.

The notebook still lay open on her desk, so she sat down and added the latest information about the house on Elm Street to it. There wasn't much, but she knew from her quilting experience that what looked like a useless, stray thread could unravel an entire quilt. She couldn't afford to overlook anything.

Sarah turned to the quilt on the table, wondering if she'd overlooked something there too. She'd fingered all the squares after she'd first found the quilt, searching for other concealed notes. Now she did it again, just in case she'd missed something hidden in the batting.

To be completely thorough, Sarah planned to search the quilt one more time, but that would have to wait for another day. First, she needed to gather all the information she could find about an artist named Luther Endicott.

CHAPTER EIGHT

The Maple Hill Historical Society sat nestled among a stand of red maple trees just south of the town square. Sarah turned into a parking space in front of the white clapboard building while Katie took the spot next to her. They both climbed out of their cars and met on the sidewalk.

"Cool building," Katie said.

"And even better on the inside." Sarah slipped her car keys into her purse. "I can spend hours here and never get bored."

"Sounds like my kind of place." Katie followed her to the door, then noticed the placard on one of the porch columns and read the words aloud. "Maple Hill. Incorporated 1786."

"We'll be celebrating our bicenquinquagenary soon."

Katie gaped at her. "What's that?"

Sarah laughed at her expression. "Our 225-year anniversary. Irene told me about it the last time I was here. I have to admit that's a word I haven't heard before. I even made her spell it out for me."

"It's a new word for me, too."

When Sarah walked inside the building she was greeted by the familiar scents of aged cedar and parchment. Irene kept the building clean and well-dusted, but you couldn't hide the smell of the past. The pine plank floor squeaked as they walked toward the counter. There was no sign of Irene, so Sarah rang the bell on the countertop.

A moment later, Irene Stuart appeared through the arched doorway, her brown hair swept into a neat French twist. Her heels clicked on the wooden floor as she headed toward them.

"Hello, there, Sarah," Irene said. "It's nice to see you again." Her gaze moved to Katie. "And I see you've brought someone with you today."

"Irene Stuart, this is Katie Campbell. She's taking a room at my house and has come to Maple Hill to research Nathaniel Bradford for her graduate thesis."

Irene's brown eyes lit up. "I love Nathaniel. He's such a cutie. I just had coffee with him yesterday."

Katie blanched as Sarah bit back a smile. Irene was perfectly sane, but she did have a tendency to talk about historical figures and events in the present tense, which could be disconcerting for people who didn't know her.

"You had coffee in the park?" Sarah said, trying to clarify Irene's meaning for Katie.

"That's right. I sat right on the base of Nathaniel's statue. I love this place, but it's nice to get outside once in a while." She turned to Katie. "You chose a wonderful subject, Ms. Campbell. Nathaniel is our hometown hero."

"Please call me Katie."

Irene smiled. "I suppose we should be on a first-name basis since you'll no doubt be spending a lot of time here. Just let me know what you need and I'll be happy to help you."

"Thank you," Katie replied. "I'm still settling in, so I probably won't be too bothersome for a while."

"It won't be any bother at all," Irene assured her. "Nathaniel and I go way back. We have quite an extensive collection of items and documents concerning him."

"Why don't we let Katie look around and get her bearings?" Sarah suggested.

"That's a wonderful idea," Irene agreed, rounding the counter to give her a visual tour. "Those display cabinets can be opened if you wish to take a closer look at an item." She pointed at four long display cabinets along one wall. "There are periodicals and other documents in the filing cabinets. They're arranged alphabetically by subject. You'll see that Nathaniel takes up practically an entire file drawer by himself."

"I may start with some books," Katie said, her gaze moving over the rows of bookcases. "Can they be checked out?"

"Most of them," Irene replied. "I prefer to keep all the reference books here, of course. There's a computer work station in the corner if you want to access the online catalog or the Internet." She craned her neck toward one of the bookshelves. "You'll find the volumes pertaining to Nathaniel Bradford and the Revolutionary War over there."

"Thank you," Katie said as she headed for the bookcases.

Once she was out of earshot, Irene turned to Sarah. "She seems like a nice young woman. Where is she from?"

"Chicago. She's a student at Northwestern."

Irene's brows rose in approval. "Good school. I wonder what got her interested in Nathaniel."

"That's a good question," Sarah said.

"A man with both brain and brawn," Irene said, then launched into a lengthy monologue about his fame, for saving the farms from being burned to the ground by the Brits and other heroic deeds, as if Sarah were unaware of these things. As Irene spoke, Sarah realized she hadn't asked Katie many questions about her project, and Katie hadn't offered much information. Sarah loved history, although it often took some effort to find the truth behind the fiction.

"Sarah?"

She blinked, aware that she'd been daydreaming. "I'm sorry, Irene. What did you say?"

"Nothing important. It looks like you've got something on your mind."

"More like someone. My grandmother, Molly Drayton."

Irene's eyes widened. "Really?"

Sarah didn't have to recount Molly's story for Irene. As the historical society director, she knew all of Maple Hill's famous and infamous citizens, but she was too young—only forty—to fully understand how the scandal had affected the

Drayton family. "Have you discovered something new about her disappearance?"

"Maybe. I'm trying to find out who owned the house at 212 Elm Street in 1920. There are no property records because of a storage room fire, so all I have is the name Luther Endicott."

"The name sounds familiar, but I can't quite place it." Then her eyes widened. "Is he one of your suspects?"

"No," Sarah said with a smile. "He painted the living room ceiling of the house at 212 Elm in September of 1920. That's all I know about him so far, although the house was declared a historical landmark due to his work."

"Oh, you mean Cleo Turnquist's old house? I remember her coming in here to talk to me about that a number of years ago." Irene rolled her eyes. "Or should I say, talk at me."

That described Cleo to a T. She'd always enjoyed acting superior to other people, a trait she'd inherited from her father.

"Any idea where I could start looking?" Sarah asked her. She was new to the sleuthing business.

"I'd start with the microfilm machine," Irene said, pointing it out to her. "We have back issues of the *Maple Hill Monitor* dating back to the 1870s. There's no subject guide, so you'll have to search by the approximate day, month, and year you're looking for."

An elderly couple walked through the door and approached the counter.

"Thanks," Sarah said, heading toward the microfilm machine. "I'll see what I can find."

"Good luck," Irene said before turning to help the newest arrivals.

Sarah sat down at the microfilm machine and turned it on. She spent several minutes fiddling with the machine, figuring out how it worked. At last, she began to search for newspaper articles from September 1920.

There were several stories about how veterans were adjusting to returning home from the Great War, including casualty lists of soldiers from Maple Hill and the surrounding area. She shook her head at the large number of names, regretting the loss of so many young men.

She scrolled through the pages, resisting the urge to read every article, and searched for news about Luther Endicott. She soon moved on to October, then November. There were several local stories about different people in the community, but none about the painter.

One article did catch her eye. It was a feature story about the newly elected town selectman, Noah Drayton, and included a grainy photograph of her grandfather.

She stared at the picture of the solemn young man in the same dark suit he'd worn at his wedding. The article stated that he'd recently married Mrs. Molly Hollis Harrison, a widow from Boston.

Sarah blinked, realizing she'd never heard her grandmother's maiden name before. Molly Hollis Harrison Drayton. Four names, but still so hard to find.

Her gaze went back to her grandfather. He looked just as dignified in this photograph as he had in his wedding picture, completely unaware of the scandal that would soon shatter his world.

So many memories came rushing back to her. Grandpa Noah had been such a loving, caring man. As a little girl, she'd spent countless hours on his knee as he'd read books to her, his voice taking on the inflections of the various characters in the stories. He'd always had a smile, had always been willing to listen whenever she'd had a problem, no matter how small.

Her grandfather hadn't deserved the scorn and shame that had rained down on him after Molly's disappearance. As she scrolled to another page on the machine, a vivid memory came rushing back to her.

When Sarah was ten years old, her grandfather had taken her to get an ice cream soda at the drugstore and Cleo Turnquist had confronted him at the door. Even after fifty-two years, Sarah could still remember every word of their conversation.

"Where's your wife, Mr. Drayton?" Cleo had demanded, placing her stocky body squarely in front of him. "What did you do to her?"

"Please let us pass," Grandpa Noah said quietly.

"I know what you did." She turned her gaze to Sarah, "and someday this little girl will know it, too. Judgment Day is coming, Mr. Drayton. You can count on it."

The expression on Cleo Turnquist's face had scared Sarah even more than the harsh words that had come out of her mouth. It was filled with hate. After the woman left, Sarah asked her grandfather what she'd meant.

Instead of brushing off her question, Grandpa Noah kneeled down so his face was even with hers. "She thinks I did something bad and that makes her angry."

"Did you do something bad, Grandpa?"

He hesitated for a moment, then shook his head. "No, Sarah. Not the bad thing she thinks I did."

"Then she's the bad one," Sarah proclaimed.

"Sometimes people get angry when they don't understand something. It doesn't help us to get mad at them, too. We should pray for them instead."

"Can I pray that I never see her again?"

At that, Grandpa had just smiled. "Well, it might be better for us to pray that she finds peace in her heart."

The front door opened, breaking Sarah's reverie. She looked up to see a young man walk inside. As he moved to the counter, Sarah looked around for Katie but couldn't see her. No doubt she was buried deep in the book stacks. If she was anything like Sarah, she could be lost there for hours.

She turned her attention back to the microfilm machine. She continued to scan the papers, growing desperate as she searched for any information about Luther Endicott but finding nothing. When she finally reached the holiday edition, she saw that Molly Drayton was the front-page story.

YOUNG WIFE DISAPPEARS AMID
RUMORS OF MARITAL DISCORD

Mrs. Noah Drayton mysteriously vanished three days ago from her home on Bristol Street in Maple Hill and hasn't been seen since. According to her husband, town alderman Noah Drayton, Mrs. Drayton was at home on Monday night, but gone from the home when he awoke on Tuesday morning.

Mr. Drayton has offered a reward for any information concerning his missing wife, but has yet to answer rumors that they were heard arguing on the day prior to her disappearance. A handyman in the Drayton's employ, Mr. Horace Lynch, reportedly told neighbors about the volatile relationship between Mr. and Mrs. Drayton. Mr. Drayton was seen with a black eye on the morning of his wife's disappearance, which he blamed on a mishap while playing ball with his stepson. Others point to it as the sign of a violent struggle between him and his wife.

It has been suggested that Mrs. Drayton would never leave voluntarily so close to Christmas. Friends and neighbors say she was a loving mother to six-year-old William Drayton.

While authorities cannot confirm that Mr. Drayton used foul means to rid himself of his wife, there are growing suspicions among those in the community....

Sarah couldn't read any more. She scrolled to the next page. The reporter's snide innuendos made her feel sick. With reporting like this, it was no wonder so many people in Maple Hill believed Grandpa Noah had murdered his wife.

But there had been facts mixed in with the fiction. Sarah hadn't known about the black eye before, and even she might have found the timing suspicious if she hadn't believed in her grandfather's innocence.

She quickly scrolled through the remaining newspaper articles for the year, almost ready to give up on finding any information on Luther Endicott when his name flashed in front of her, then disappeared again. She sat up in her chair and scrolled back a page.

"How's it going?" Irene asked as she strolled over to the microfilm machine.

"I think I found something." Sarah pointed to the headline on the screen. "Endicott Goes to Washington." Then she began reading the article aloud.

"Renowned local artist Luther Endicott will take his talents to Boston to paint a mural in the one of the corridors of the Massachusetts State House. Endicott is a longtime resident of Maple Hill. Although Endicott usually confines his talents to painting murals and portraits, he recently completed an artistic ceiling project at the home of Mr. Clayton Wiggins at 212 Elm Street. Mr. Wiggins is offering tours on Sunday afternoon for anyone who would like to see Endicott's unique handiwork."

"Clayton Wiggins," Irene echoed. "Is that who you're looking for?"

Sarah jotted the name down in her notepad. "That's the one."

Irene's eyes sparkled with excitement. "So what's next?"

"Lunch." Sarah glanced at her watch. "No wonder I'm starving, it's almost two o'clock!" She looked around the room. "Where's Katie?"

"She left about twenty minutes ago." Irene looked surprised. "Didn't she say anything to you?"

"No." Sarah couldn't hide her concern as she turned off the microfilm machine. "She didn't say a word."

CHAPTER NINE

When Sarah walked out of the historical society, Katie's car was gone. A warm breeze ruffled her hair as she pulled her cell phone out of her purse and dialed the cell phone number Katie had listed on the rental form.

"We're sorry," said an automated voice, "but this number is no longer in service."

Sarah dialed her home phone.

Katie picked up on the third ring. "Sarah Hart's residence."

"There you are. I was worried when you disappeared from the historical society."

"Oh, I'm sorry," Katie said breathlessly. "I started getting a migraine and didn't want to disturb you, so I just left."

Sarah walked toward her car. "Are you all right?"

"I will be. I just need to rest for a while. Sleep is really the only cure when one of these headaches kicks in."

"Would you like me to come home?" Sarah asked, fishing her car keys out of her purse.

"Oh, no," Katie said. "I'll be fine. I just need a nap."

"All right," Sarah said, sensing there was more going on with this girl. She didn't sound like someone suffering a debilitating migraine. "I'll see you later."

"Bye."

Her stomach rumbled as Sarah placed her cell phone back in her purse, so she headed across the street to the Spotted Dog Bookstore and Café, one of her favorite places in Maple Hill. The striped awning over the door featured a painting of a giant Dalmatian.

Inside, there was a cozy bookstore on one side of the shop, where jazz played on the speakers and people sank into overstuffed armchairs to browse the latest releases.

Soft chatter emanated from the café opposite the bookstore, where a dozen tables were scattered over black-and-white checkered tile. A row of bright red bar stools lined the counter and Sarah was delighted to see her son sitting on one of them.

"This is a nice surprise," Sarah said as she approached him.

Jason put down his menu. "Hi, Mom. Care to join me for lunch?"

"I'd love to."

He lifted himself off the bar stool and followed her to a table that bordered the checkered tile of the café and the wooden floor of the bookstore. "Do you come here often?"

"Probably more than I should," she said with a smile. "Martha and I like to meet here for coffee quite often. Their spiced chai latte with whipped cream is one of my favorites."

Jason pulled out a chair for her. "I hear they have great clam chowder."

"The best." Sarah sat down, then watched her son take a seat opposite her. "It's wonderful to be able to run into you like this. I hope it happens a lot."

He laughed. "Are you sure you won't get tired of me?"

"Never," she vowed, watching him open his menu.

A few moments later, Liam Connolly, the proprietor of the Spotted Dog, approached the table and greeted her with his deep Irish brogue. "Hello, there, Sarah."

"Hello, Liam," Sarah said, brushing her graying blonde hair off her collar. "This is my son, Jason Hart. He and his family recently moved here from California. Jason, this is Liam Connolly. He's the owner."

Jason rose from his chair and shook Liam's hand. "Nice to meet you."

"Same here," Liam said as Jason returned to his seat. "Your mother is one of my favorite customers."

Jason looked between the two of them. "Is that right?"

Sarah chuckled. "I told you I come here too much."

"Nonsense." Liam's smile deepened the laugh lines around his green eyes. "I don't see enough of you."

To Sarah's mortification, she felt a blush steal up her cheeks. It was a ridiculous reaction. Liam surely acted this way with all his customers. She struggled to find a neutral subject. "Where's Murphy?"

"He's over there," Liam said, pointing to the bookstore portion of the shop, "under the chair."

Sarah leaned across the table to catch a glimpse of the scruffy white corgi with a black spot on his back. "Looks like he's sleeping."

Jason looked baffled as he leaned forward for a better view. "Who's Murphy?"

"My dog," Liam replied. "He's all tuckered out from the walk we took earlier."

Jason grinned. "So is he the Spotted Dog?"

"I guess you could say that," Liam confirmed, "although Murphy makes me do all the work around here." He pulled an order pad from his pocket. "Are you ready to order or would you like some more time?"

"We're ready," Sarah replied, and they placed their order.

After Liam left, Jason leaned back in his chair and sighed. "This is nice. So different from L.A. Most of the time I ordered food in for lunch or, in some cases, skipped it all together if I was too busy to eat. I have to admit, I've been enjoying going home for lunch with my family."

"So what made you come here today?"

"Maggie took the girls to Pittsfield to do some shopping. We needed to find some way to get them out of the house."

"Are the girls still homesick?"

He sighed again. "Worse than ever. According to them, they hate Maple Hill. They'll never be happy here. Never make any friends. It's doom and gloom all the time."

"It's a big change for them, especially at their age. At least they've got each other."

"True. They can commiserate together. They're also on the computer all the time talking with their friends back in California."

"That's the nice thing about technology," Sarah said. "You don't have to lose touch with friends even if you move far away."

Liam silently deposited tea in front of Jason and a chai in front of Sarah, and left.

Jason shrugged. "I don't know if it's a blessing or a curse. I think they might be more motivated to find new friends here and try to fit in if they weren't so connected to their California friends."

"I have an idea that might help."

Jason picked up his tea. "I'm all ears."

"Well, when Martha came over this morning, we were discussing how homesick the twins are. She suggested introducing them to her granddaughters. The girls are about Amy and Audrey's age, so they should have a lot in common."

"That's a good idea. Starting to meet kids here should really help." He leaned back in his chair. "So what's new with you? Have you looked into that Elm Street address?"

Sarah filled him in on her progress so far. "I'm not sure my leads will go anywhere, but I'm not about to give up.

The sooner I can learn more about Grandma Molly and why she wrote that note, the sooner I can solve this mystery."

Liam walked over to their table carrying a tray. "Here's your soup and ham sandwich," he said to Jason, setting the cup and basket in front of him before turning to Sarah. "And your tuna salad and sweet potato fries."

"It all looks delicious, Liam," Sarah told him. He'd given her an extra portion of fries. "Thank you."

"Just let me know if you need anything else." Liam wiped his hands on his apron. "We've got fresh peach pie for dessert."

Jason groaned as he walked away. "Peach pie! And I've already put on a few extra pounds since we moved here."

"You were too skinny before," Sarah said as she picked up her fork. "Now you're just right. Besides, the pie here is delicious."

"Okay, if you twist my arm like that."

She watched him eat, wondering if the twins were the only ones who were homesick. She'd been so thrilled Jason had moved his family here she'd never wondered if he had any second thoughts.

"Jason." Sarah knew she had to tread lightly. "Are you and Maggie happy here?"

He looked up from his soup. "What? Where did that come from?"

"I was just wondering."

He pondered her question for a moment, then shrugged. "It's an adjustment, but we knew it would be. I'm spending more time with Maggie and the girls than I ever have before. It helped to get rid of the two-hour commute to downtown L.A. every day. The hours I kept at my office there were insane." He set down his spoon. "But that's not the main reason we moved here..."

His voice trailed off and he looked thoughtful. Sarah took a sip of her tea, waiting for him to finish.

"I didn't tell you before, but I had some health problems back in Los Angeles."

Sarah's food turned to dust in her mouth. "What happened?"

"It's nothing serious," he assured her. "I was having some chest pains and ended up in the emergency room a few times."

"A few times?" Sarah put down her fork. "Jason, why didn't you tell me?"

"I'm okay." He waved off her concern. "I took a bunch of tests, but all they found was some high blood pressure. The doctor said my chest pains and other symptoms were caused by stress."

Chest pains? "Is he sure? Did you get a second opinion?"

"He's sure, although he advised me to reduce the stress in my life or it could develop into something more serious. That's when Maggie and I started talking about moving to Maple Hill. Just driving through this town is like taking an antianxiety pill."

She couldn't bring herself to laugh at his joke. Jason had always pushed himself to the highest level. He'd earned a college scholarship and graduated in the top of his class at law school. Now it seemed his drive to succeed was starting to hurt him.

"Relax, Mom," Jason said, watching her expression. "I'm taking my blood pressure medication and exercising and doing all the other things the doctor prescribed." He reached for another fry. "These are really good. I'll have to order some next time."

"Help yourself," she said, pushing her basket closer to him. "I don't seem to have much of an appetite."

He looked up at her. "Why is that?"

"Too much excitement, I guess. I found the quilt and a new boarder moved in..."

"What's her story?" Jason asked.

Sarah nodded. "Her name is Katie. She's a graduate student working on a thesis about Nathaniel Bradford."

He took a sip of his tea, then wiped his mouth with a napkin. "Something tells me you didn't check out her references before she moved in."

"I'll get to it soon," she promised, not telling him about the girl's disconnected cell phone. Maybe Katie had just been unable to pay her bill. "She listed a college advisor and a former employer, so I doubt they'll have anything bad to say about her."

"That's not the point." Jason scrubbed one hand over his jaw. "You shouldn't let anyone sign a lease and move in before you check their references. We've talked about this before, Mom."

She could be stubborn too. "This girl isn't dangerous. In fact she looked awful when she showed up at my door. I got some food into her as fast as I could."

He laughed. "You've always liked taking in strays."

"Maybe Katie will let me read her thesis when she's done with it. Maybe I'll find out something about Nathaniel Bradford that I don't already know."

"That's usually how it works with historical figures—we only see one side of them." Jason looked at her for a long moment. "I suppose the same could be true about Great-Grandpa Noah."

"What do you mean?"

He leaned forward, setting his forearms on the table. "I mean you're really digging deep into the family's past. What if you find some answers you don't like?"

"I already have." She told him about the newspaper article reporting Molly's disappearance. "It was awful, like reading a tabloid instead of a legitimate news report. Full of speculation about their marital discord and ..."

"Was there marital discord?"

She shrugged. "I don't know. I'm sure they had a few bumps in the road, just like most newlyweds. But I do know my grandfather and he was never a violent man."

"Not when you knew him," Jason said gently, "but people change. You told me that Grandpa Noah's faith got him through those difficult times. Maybe it changed him into the gentle man you knew."

Sarah didn't like what she was hearing. "My grandfather did not murder his wife."

"Maybe he didn't," Jason said, "but he might have driven her away. It's not normal for a wife to just up and disappear in the middle of the night. If you only investigate Grandma Molly, you'll be missing half the picture."

As much as Sarah hated to admit it, she knew he was right. So many of the townspeople had been ready to believe her grandfather was capable of murder. Maybe they had reasons other than the inflammatory newspaper articles.

As difficult as it might be, she had to keep an open mind.

"Now how about a slice of that peach pie?" Jason asked, rubbing his hands together.

CHAPTER TEN

The following day, Sarah picked up the twins and took them with her to Bradford Manor.

"Does Grandpa William know we're coming?" Audrey asked from the passenger seat. There had been a slight tussle over who would get to sit in the front seat with Sarah, but she'd finally settled it by letting Audrey sit in the front on the way there and Amy sit in the front on the way back.

"No," Sarah replied, "he wouldn't remember it even if I had told him. He's ninety-six and sometimes he doesn't make a lot of sense. You'll just need to be patient with him."

"Why are we going if he doesn't know who we are?" Amy asked.

Sarah glanced at her through the rearview mirror. "Because we know who he is. I think he'll be happy to see you."

"At least it's something to do," Audrey said. "Can I turn on your radio, Grandma?"

"Sure, but not too loud."

While Audrey fiddled with the radio, Sarah glanced in the rearview mirror at Amy. "You okay?"

"Yeah." Amy replied, her gaze fixed on the window.

Sarah knew a trip to the nursing home wouldn't be too exciting for the girls, but she wanted them to get to know their great-grandfather. She just hoped her dad was having a good day.

Audrey finally settled on a radio station, then wiggled her body to the fast beat of the music as she sang along. Sarah didn't recognize the tune or the lyrics, but she was glad Audrey was enjoying herself.

She drove along Creek Side Road, then turned onto the private gravel drive that led to the parking lot. The nursing home was a red brick colonial-style building with four white columns bracketing the front entrance. Situated on a knoll overlooking the town of Maple Hill, the building was surrounded by lush lawns, and the back patio provided a splendid view of the Berkshire Mountains.

Sarah and the girls climbed out of the car and headed for the building. One of the residents sat outside on a bench, her face lighting up as Sarah approached.

"Hello, Olive." Sarah greeted her, then turned to the twins. "This is Mrs. Cavanaugh. She was your father's Sunday School teacher when he was a little boy."

Olive's eyes widened. "These two cuties are Jason's girls?"

"That's right," Sarah said, standing between the two girls. "This is Audrey and the one with the ponytail is Amy."

"My, they've grown." Olive said. "It seems like just yesterday you brought their baby pictures to church to show everybody. You sure were a proud grandma."

Sarah laughed. "I still am. Jason and his family have just moved to Maple Hill, so you'll probably see these two quite a bit around here."

"I sure hope so." Olive looked at the girls. "How old are you two now?"

"Twelve," Audrey answered for both of them.

Olive leaned forward, tapping one ear. "I couldn't hear you, dear."

"Twelve," Audrey shouted loud enough to make Sarah wince, but Olive didn't seem to mind.

"Well, that's a nice age." Olive adjusted the shawl around her shoulders. "I'm sure William will be happy to spend time with you two."

Sarah gave her a wave as they walked inside "It was nice to see you again, Olive."

"You, too, Sarah. Goodbye, girls."

The front entrance opened into a large sitting room with furniture on both sides of the doorway. Soft colors and gentle lighting gave the room a tranquil, cozy atmosphere. A console piano stood against one wall and just across from it was a tall aviary filled with small, colorful birds.

Several residents sat in the room, many of them dozing in their wheelchairs. Amy stuck to her grandmother like glue as they walked through the room. Sarah led them toward the nurses' station in the center of the building, then turned left down a long hallway.

"What's that weird smell?" Sarah heard Amy whisper to her sister.

"It's old people," Audrey whispered back. "Just pretend you don't notice."

When they reached her father's room, Sarah tapped gently on the door, then pushed it open. "Dad?"

He sat in a wheelchair next to his window, a copy of the *Maple Hill Monitor* spread out on his lap. He looked up when he heard Sarah's voice, then a smile crinkled his face. "There's my little girl!"

She smiled, glad that he recognized her today. It didn't matter if she were six or sixty-two, her father would always see her as his little girl. He'd moved to Bradford Manor eight years ago, shortly after her mother, Ruth, had passed away from cancer. Sarah had offered to let him move in with her and Gerry, but he'd refused, saying he didn't want to be a burden.

Over the years, he'd grown more frail. Sarah came to visit her father often, feeling blessed to still have him in her life and cherishing every moment of the time they got to spend together.

"Look who I brought with me," she said, turning around to introduce him to his great-granddaughters. Audrey stood right behind her, but Amy was still in the doorway.

"Come in, Amy," Sarah prodded. "Grandpa William won't bite."

"I can't," he proclaimed. "I don't have my teeth in."

That made Audrey snort with laughter, but Amy remained stone-faced as she took a few halting steps into the room.

Sarah sat down on the chair beside her father, knowing she couldn't force him on Amy. "These are Jason's girls."

"Jason who?"

"My son, Jason, who just moved back to Maple Hill. These are your great-granddaughters. They're twins."

His brow crinkled as he looked them over. "Is that right?" That was his stock phrase whenever he was surprised or confused by something and didn't know what else to say.

"This is Audrey," she said, reaching out one hand to pull the girl closer to her. "She likes to sing and dance and draw."

"I used to take tap lessons," Audrey volunteered.

"So did I," he said.

Sarah smiled as she shook her head. "When did you take tap, Dad?"

"Back in the army. They made me play a trumpet."

"So you played taps on the trumpet?" Sarah said.

He nodded. "Yes, but I don't play the trumpet anymore."

Out of the corner of her eye, Sarah could see Amy edge a little closer in the room. "That's probably a good thing, Dad, or they might kick you out of here."

Audrey plopped on the end of the bed, then looked around the small room, taking in the light green walls and the long shelf below the window. "Do they let you have any decorations in here?"

"Oh, sure," he told her. "Fred down the hall has a silver star and Mason Lowe has a purple heart."

Sarah could see that he was still stuck in World War II mode. He'd served in the war before coming back home and working as Maple Hill's postmaster for thirty years.

He looked over at Amy. "Do you have any decorations, girl?"

Amy moved next to Sarah. "I don't know what he means," she said, her voice barely a whisper.

"Do you have any medals or awards," Sarah explained.

"Oh." Amy thought a moment, then turned to her great-grandfather. "I have a softball medal."

"Softball, eh?" he said. "Have you ever hit any home runs?"

"One or two," Amy replied. "I mostly like to pitch."

The discussion about softball made Sarah remember something she'd read in the newspaper article. "Dad," she leaned closer to him. "Do you remember ever playing ball with Grandpa when you were a little boy?"

He turned to her, one hand reaching out to gently pat her arm. "My dad bought me peanuts at a ball game once. We didn't play though."

Sarah let it go. Even if his memory were clear, he'd been only six years old and suffering the trauma of losing his mother. If his father had had a black eye, he probably wouldn't even have noticed.

Her dad rolled his wheelchair over to the small desk in the corner. "I have some peanuts in here." He picked up a box and held it out toward Audrey. "Do you want some?"

"Sure," Audrey said, taking it from him. She took off the lid, then stared down at the contents. A blush crept up her face as she looked over at Sarah and whispered, "These are chocolates."

"That's okay," Sarah told her, taking the box from her. "Dad, these are chocolates. Did Pastor John bring them for you?" She knew the pastor was a frequent visitor at Bradford Manor and often brought small treats for the residents.

"Who?" her dad asked.

"Pastor John, from Bridge Street Church."

He shook his head. "No, it was just me and Dad."

Sarah handed him a dark chocolate and let each of the girls take one before she replaced the box on his desk. Then she returned to her chair, reaching over to smooth her father's sparse white hair over the top of his head. "How have you been feeling, Dad?"

"Pretty good," he answered. "Played checkers with Hoy Clifton yesterday. Beat him three times in a row."

"Hoy died twenty years ago, Dad," Sarah said gently.

"Is that right?" He licked the chocolate off his thumb. "Seems like he was just here."

Sarah looked over at the girls. "Do you want another chocolate?"

"No, thanks," Audrey said. "We're good."

Amy edged back toward the door. "Is it okay if I go look at the birds in the front room?"

"Sure," Sarah replied, seeing her discomfort. Amy might be the risk taker in the family, but she'd always been shy around people she didn't know well. No doubt it would take a few more visits until she felt comfortable with her great-grandfather.

"Do you want to go with me?" Amy asked her sister.

"I guess," Audrey said, rising off the bed.

A loud, beeping alarm sounded and both girls jumped.

"What's that?" Audrey asked her grandmother.

"Nothing serious, you just tripped the alarm." Sarah reached over to shut it off.

Audrey froze, as if fearing she might set off another alarm if she moved. "But why did it go off?"

"It's a bed alarm," Sarah explained. "A lot of nursing homes have them in case one of the residents gets out of bed without assistance. It could be dangerous for them if they fall."

"My legs ain't what they used to be," Dad said, patting one knee, "but they've held up pretty good over the years, so I'm not complaining."

"Why don't you stop by the nurses' station," Sarah told the girls, "and let them know that great-grandpa is fine and they don't need to come down here."

"Okay," Audrey said, as both girls moved toward the door. "Bye, Grandpa William."

He looked up at her. "Bye."

Sarah watched the girls leave.

Dad smiled at her. "Kind of a scary place, isn't it?"

Despite his spotty memory, her father was still sharper than she gave him credit for. He missed little of what happened around him.

"I guess it is," Sarah replied. "Don't take it personally, Dad. I think they're still overwhelmed by the move from California."

"I don't mind. I'm just glad they came here for a visit."

Sarah noticed the plant on his window sill looked a little droopy so she walked over to his sink and filled up a plastic cup with water. Then she walked over to the window and poured the water on the plant.

"I never did have a green thumb," Dad said.

Sarah placed the cup back on the sink, then sat back down on the chair near her father. She'd been struggling to think of a good way to start this conversation, but it was more difficult than she'd imagined.

"Dad, I have something to tell you."

"What's that?"

She took a deep breath. "I found your quilt, the one that disappeared..."

Tears gleamed in his blue eyes. "Where?"

"In the house. Jason's living there now and one of the girls found a passageway behind the walls."

"Is that right?"

She didn't say anything for a long moment, allowing the news to sink in. He'd been so young when his mother disappeared and she could only imagine the trauma he'd suffered. And Noah Drayton had never remarried after Molly vanished. How could he when it was possible she was still alive?

"Mama used to sing me to sleep at night," Dad said softly. "She always smelled like lavender."

Tears stung her eyes at the emotion in his voice. She reached out to hold his hand.

He gave her hand a squeeze, then breathed a deep sigh. "I'm glad you found the quilt. I'd like to see it sometime."

"I'll bring it," she promised. "I need to fix it up a little first, though. It's not in the best shape."

"My mom made it for me," he said. "She was angry at Dad for tying up the bad man."

Sarah blinked. "What bad man?"

He picked up the newspaper in front of him and tapped his finger on a front-page photograph of a convicted felon. "This one. He's very bad."

"Yes," she murmured, wondering if her father was mixing up his memories again. He'd been reading the newspaper before they'd arrived, and he might have combined the story of the felon with his mom's disappearance. There was no way to know.

"Anything else in the newspaper today?" Sarah asked gently.

He opened it up. "Not too much. Bridge Street Church is having a bake sale. I'll have to tell Ruth to make some brownies."

"Mom passed away a few years ago."

He looked up from the paper. "Is that right?"

Sarah leaned over and kissed his forehead. "I'll make the brownies, Dad, and I'll bring you a nice batch of goodies from the bake sale."

He reached up to cradle her cheek with one hand. "You're a good girl, Sarah Drayton."

"Maybe I can get the twins to help me do some baking," she mused. "They might enjoy looking for recipes on the Internet."

"My mom used to make the best cookies in the world."

"What kind were they?"

"I don't know, but I've never had any like them since she went away."

Sarah rose from the chair, aware that the twins were probably anxious to get home. She leaned over to give him a hug. "Bye, Dad. I'll stop by again soon."

"Okay, Sarah. Don't forget to do your homework."

Sarah might not be in school anymore, but she had plenty of homework to do if she wanted to solve her mystery.

As she walked down the long hallway, she tried to make sense of her father's latest revelation.

She was angry at Dad for tying up the bad man.

Sarah had no way of knowing if that was true or simply another tangled up memory. But Grandpa Noah could have gotten that black eye in a struggle to tie someone up.

CHAPTER ELEVEN

After Sarah dropped off the twins at their home, she drove downtown to her favorite store in Maple Hill. The Wild Goose Chase was a fabrics and craft store run by her friend, Vanessa Sawyer. Although Vanessa was about half Sarah's age, their love of fabrics and quilting had formed a bond between them.

The bell above the door tinkled as Sarah walked into the store. She was surprised to find it empty in the middle of the day, but relished the opportunity to spend some one-on-one time with Vanessa. The mother of two young children, Vanessa was estranged from her husband and had her hands full running both a home and a store by herself.

"Vanessa?" Sarah called out as she looked around the store. She didn't see her friend, but found a romance novel sitting on the counter, which meant that Vanessa was near.

"I'm in the storeroom," Vanessa shouted back to her. "I'll be out in a minute."

There was barely room to squeeze between the bolts of fabric as Sarah made her way to the back of the store. Vanessa kept a couple of chairs there, as well as a tea kettle for her customers.

Vanessa emerged from the back storeroom. She was a petite, African-American woman. "I thought I recognized that voice. It's so nice to see you, Sarah. It's been a while."

Sarah laughed. "I was just in last week."

"I know, but you usually come even more often than that. You're one of my best customers."

"I guess fabric is an addiction for me, I just can't seem to get enough of it."

Vanessa's big eyes flashed with amusement. "I feel the same way. That's why I opened this store and stuffed it with fabric from the floor to the rafters."

Her description wasn't far off. Vanessa carried one of the largest supplies and varieties of fabrics in Berkshire County. She had other crafting supplies too, including yarn, jewelry beads, embroidery kits, and painting supplies. She'd recently begun carrying raw wool for spinning, and Martha had been tempted to buy a spinning wheel to make and dye her own yarns.

"What are you working on now?" Vanessa asked.

"Actually, I've decided to take on a very special project."

"Wait a minute." Vanessa held up both hands. "Let's sit down and pour a cup of tea. I've been on my feet all day and something tells me I'm going to want to hear every detail."

Sarah laughed. "I think you know me too well."

Once they were settled in their chairs, each holding a cup of tea, Sarah told her the whole story.

Vanessa looked awestruck by the time Sarah had finished. "I can't believe you found that quilt after all these years. And a secret passageway? I thought those only existed in books."

"Me too—it was quite an adventure."

Vanessa tucked her legs under her. "And now you're going around town searching for clues. How exciting!"

"More like frustrating. One clue leads to the next, but I'm starting to feel like I'm going around in circles. All I have so far is a secret passageway, a ninety-year-old quilt, an address, and a shaky account of my Grandpa Noah tying up a bad man."

"That just makes it all the more intriguing." Vanessa rubbed her slender hands together. "Who knows what you'll find next?"

Sarah took a sip of tea, hoping Vanessa was right. She certainly wasn't ready to give up. In her mind, solving this mystery was very much like putting together a quilt; it took patience, logic, and determination to see the project through to the end.

Vanessa brushed a stray curl out of her eyes. "Please let me know if there's anything I can do to help."

"Oh, I will," Sarah promised. "The first thing I need to do is pick up some supplies for repairing the quilt."

"How bad is it?"

"Really, not too bad," Sarah replied, "considering how many years it's been in that secret passageway. There's moth damage on several of the fabric pieces. Some I can fix, but others will have to be replaced. The binding is in bad shape and there are loose threads to sew up."

Vanessa grinned. "That's your specialty."

"I really want to do a good job on this one, Vanessa." Her throat caught and she had to pause a moment to collect herself. "When I told Dad about finding the quilt, he started reminiscing about his mother and how she used to sing to him."

"Your poor father," Vanessa said. "Did it upset him to have the subject brought up again after all this time?"

Sarah shook her head. "I don't think so. It seemed to bring back some good memories for him, like the singing and the cookies she used to bake for him."

"I'm starting to understand why this project is so special to you."

Sarah nodded. "I'm giving the quilt to my father after I've finished restoring it. It will warm his body on chilly days and warm his heart just knowing it was made by his mother."

Tears shone in Vanessa's eyes and she placed a hand on her chest. "That is so sweet. I'm sure he'll love it."

"I think he will. I just hope I can find out what happened to the woman who made it."

"You will," Vanessa proclaimed. "I have every faith."

Sarah set down her empty tea cup. "Then I'd better get to work."

Vanessa rose from her chair. "What do you need to get started?"

"Thread and some binding material. I think I'll pick up some light blue flannel, too, if you have any. That's what she used for the backing."

"Have you cleaned the quilt yet?"

"Not yet. That's the next step in the process."

"I hope you're recording this restoration."

"I am. It's a family heirloom and I want all of my grandchildren to know the history behind it."

Vanessa took a step toward her. "It would also make a wonderful presentation. I've been meaning to ask you to give a workshop about vintage quilt restoration for my customers. The notebook would be a wonderful way to show them how it all works, especially with the quilt's backstory."

"I don't know…" Sarah imagined presenting the quilt's story without a resolution to the mystery. She couldn't face a roomful of people speculating that Grandpa Noah had murdered his wife. She couldn't let that happen. Nothing was going to stop her from solving this mystery.

"Just think about it," Vanessa said.

"Okay, I'll think about it," Sarah promised. "Now I'd better get those supplies and head home. I can't wait to get started restoring my dad's quilt."

When Sarah arrived home, the wind practically blew her into the house and she couldn't have been happier about it.

She retrieved the quilt from the sewing room and carried it to the backyard, where she attached it to the clothesline with wooden clothespins. She'd finished documenting the individual fabric pieces on the quilt top late last night, and now she wanted to freshen it up.

Wind was one of the best tools for cleaning a vintage quilt. It not only aired the quilt out, but it removed much of the dust that had settled into the fabric pieces over the years.

Sarah made certain the quilt was well fastened on the line before she walked back to the house. Katie's car was parked on the street, but there had been no sign of her downstairs. That meant she was still holed up in her room. Sarah hoped she was getting a lot of work done on her thesis.

When she entered the kitchen, she started putting together the ingredients for the organic buttermilk soap she intended to use to wet wash certain stains on the quilt. The last thing she wanted to do was damage the fabrics in any way, so she was being very careful every step of the way.

As she stood at the kitchen counter, she looked out the window, gratified to see the wind whipping the quilt about. "God's washing machine," Sarah mused as she pulled a large mixing bowl from the cupboard. Then she retrieved a quart of low fat buttermilk from the refrigerator.

She poured the entire carton of buttermilk into the bowl, then added a gallon of water and a tablespoon of lemon juice. She stirred the milky concoction together, then pushed the bowl aside to let it set.

The ingredients were all organic, which meant she shouldn't get any of the nasty surprises that sometimes occurred when one used chemical-laced soaps. Still, she'd keep the wet wash away from the more delicate fabrics on the quilt, like the velvets, silks, and satins. She didn't want to run the risk of ruining any of the fabric pieces.

As she reached for a dish towel to wipe her hands, she heard the buzzer sound on the dryer in the laundry room.

Katie must be doing her laundry, she thought, aware that Rita hadn't been home all day. She tossed the dish towel aside, then walked over to the stairs, wondering if she should let Katie know the dryer was done. She hated to think of all those clothes wrinkling as they cooled off.

She climbed the stairs, still torn between letting Katie know about the dryer and leaving her to her studies. But when she reached Katie's door, she heard a strange sound emanating from inside.

It was a sob. A deep, wrenching sob.

Sarah froze, wondering what to do. Katie was obviously upset about something, but she was in the privacy of her room. The last thing Sarah wanted was for Katie to think that her landlady liked to listen at the door. But she couldn't walk away either. Not when it was so obvious that the girl was in distress.

She tapped lightly on the door. "Katie?"

There was no response. Sarah waited, wondering how long she should stand there.

At last, Katie's strained voice sounded through the door. "Yes?"

"I just wanted to let you know that your laundry is done. The buzzer just went off."

"Okay," Katie squeaked. "Thanks."

Sarah stood there a moment longer, then turned and walked back down the stairs. There was nothing more she could do, no matter how unsettling it was to hear Katie weeping like that.

Leave it alone, Sarah admonished herself as she headed back to the kitchen. She was here if Katie wanted to talk. Until then, she needed to give the girl some space. Please, Lord, let her be all right.

She walked out the back door to retrieve the quilt. She removed the clothespins, dropping them back into the cloth bag that hung on the line. Then she carefully folded the quilt and carried it back inside the house, where she laid it out once more on the table in the sewing room.

That short stint on the clothesline, with the combination of wind and summer sun, had removed much of the dust and done wonders for brightening the fabrics, giving new life to the quilt.

Sarah retrieved her bowl of buttermilk soap from the kitchen counter and carried it into her sewing room. She dipped a small sponge into the liquid soap, then carefully dabbed at a small stain on a green cotton fabric piece until it looked clean. Then she stepped back, waiting for the piece to dry completely so she could make certain no damage had been done.

While she waited, she turned to her computer and typed in the name Clayton Wiggins, the man for whom Luther Endicott had painted the ceiling of the house at 212 Elm Street in 1920.

To her surprise, several links came up with the name Clayton Wiggins highlighted on them. Most were on social networking sites, and none appeared to be the Clayton Wiggins she wanted to find. Most were young teenagers from different parts of the country who just happened to share the same name.

So much for the World Wide Web, she thought to herself as she closed the Web site. The Wiggins name wasn't a local one as far as she knew, but that didn't mean there weren't descendants of Clayton Wiggins living in the area. She picked up the Maple Hill telephone directory and thumbed through it.

No Wiggins.

As she thought about what to do next, Sarah heard footsteps on the stairs. She rose from her chair and walked into the kitchen. A moment later, Katie appeared holding an empty laundry basket under one arm. Her eyes were rimmed with red, further evidence that it had been sobs Sarah had heard upstairs. Despite her earlier intention not to pry, she couldn't let Katie disappear into her room again without knowing if something was seriously wrong.

"Are you all right?" Sarah asked.

"Me?" Katie said, her voice cracking a little. She cleared her throat, then flashed a smile. "Oh, I'm fine. My allergies are acting up a little. There must be something in the air here."

Sarah nodded, but she didn't believe a word the girl said. "How's your work going?"

"My work?" Katie blinked. "Oh, right. It's fine. I've been doing a lot of reading. It's pretty intense."

"I'd love to take a peek sometime. Nathaniel Bradford is such a fascinating character."

Katie started moving toward the laundry room. "Well, I'm really not comfortable with people reading my work in progress. It's pretty rough. I hope you don't mind."

"Not at all," Sarah replied. "I feel the same way about my quilts. They look like a chaotic mess when I'm in the middle of putting them together."

"Exactly." Katie cleared her throat. "Well, I'd better go fold my laundry."

"Okay." Sarah watched her disappear behind the laundry room door, feeling oddly dissatisfied with their conversation. Why was Katie being so secretive? She sensed there was something the girl was hiding from her. Something important.

Sarah sighed as she returned to the sewing room. The fabric piece had dried and showed no damage from the wet wash. Sarah picked up the sponge, dipped it into the buttermilk soap, and dabbed at another stained square.

As she worked, Sarah wondered how to get Katie to open up to her. If the girl was having problems, she wanted to help. In the meantime, Sarah realized there *was* something she could do for Katie.

After setting down the sponge, Sarah folded her hands together and bowed her head. *Dear Lord,* she prayed softly. *I'm so worried about Katie. Please watch over her and protect her. Let her know that she's not alone. Keep her close to you, Lord, and heal her pain. Amen.*

CHAPTER TWELVE

Sarah stood on her front porch the next morning and lifted the watering can above her head to reach the hanging pot of petunias. When water dripped from the coconut fiber liner, she knew it was time to move on to the next basket.

The front door opened and Rita bounded outside. "Good morning. I can't believe I slept so late."

"You've been so busy, you probably needed the sleep." Sarah had slept later than usual too, having stayed up late to finish wet washing the brown stains out of the quilt top and backing. It was a painstaking process, and she'd found satisfaction in watching the blemished fabric pieces return to their original state. If only it were as easy to fix the other problems in her life.

Rita smiled. "I've been having a great time. Who knew birding could be so much fun?"

Sarah emptied her watering can into the last basket. "I'll have to try it some time."

"You should. It's great exercise, too, with all the walking we do. I'm gearing up for a four-week birding tour in Canada next month."

"That sounds like quite an adventure."

"I'm looking forward to it, but I hate leaving here." Rita pulled an envelope from her pocket. "Here's my rent money for the next two weeks. I guess this is my official notice."

Sarah took the envelope. She'd miss Rita's energetic spirit. "Well, you've been a great boarder. You're welcome back anytime."

"Thank you," Rita said. "I'll miss this place. Maple Hill has a way of growing on a person."

"That it does."

"I've especially enjoyed your library. That librarian is so knowledgeable." She grinned. "Handsome, too. He'd be perfect for my niece."

Spencer Hewitt had referred Rita to Sarah's house when she'd asked him about local rooms to rent. A bachelor, he'd found himself the victim of matchmakers on more than one occasion.

Sarah glanced at her watch, surprised to see it was already after nine o'clock. "Oh, my goodness," she gasped. "I'm going to be late." She and Martha had made plans to meet for coffee this morning at the Spotted Dog Cafe. They were supposed to meet at nine, but now Sarah wouldn't get there until at least nine fifteen.

"I'm sorry, I didn't mean to keep you."

"It's not your fault." Sarah set her watering can on the porch. "I just lost track of time."

"Well, you have a nice day," Rita said, heading for her car.

"You too." She hurried into the house and heard the sound of water running above her. That meant Katie was awake and in the shower. Sarah had already showered, but she still needed to apply some make-up and run a comb through her hair.

She'd just reached the top of the stairs when the telephone rang. She moved quickly toward the bookcase to pick up the extension. "Hello?"

"Hi, Sarah, this is Martha."

"Oh, Martha, I just noticed the time. Are you already there?"

"I'm still at home," Martha said. "I'm glad I caught you. I just tried your cell phone, but there was no answer."

"I'm sorry," Sarah said. "I was outside."

"I'm afraid I can't make it for coffee after all," Martha said. "Ernie's not feeling well and I don't want to leave him home alone."

"Oh, dear." Sarah settled onto the love seat. "Is it some kind of bug?"

"I guess so. He's been feeling off for a couple of days now."

"Well, tell him I hope he feels better soon."

"I'm sure he will," Martha said. "In fact, let's go ahead and plan that picnic for our granddaughters for the day after tomorrow. The girls are coming home from camp today, so they'll have time to settle in."

"That sounds wonderful," Sarah said. "I'll have to make sure the twins are free, but I'm almost certain they will be."

"Then it's a date."

A man's voice rumbled in the background, then Martha said, "Sorry, Sarah, I have to go. Ernie needs something."

"Okay. Talk to you soon."

She hung up the phone, relieved that Ernie seemed to be talking to his wife again, even if the reason was a touch of the flu. As she set the cordless receiver back on the base, she wondered what to do next. The house was due for a good dusting, but that didn't sound like much fun, especially since she'd been planning to spend the morning with Martha. Her thoughts moved to the quilt in her sewing room downstairs.

Dusting or quilting? Not a hard choice at all.

An hour later, Sarah stood in her sewing room measuring a length of white flannel and thinking about what steps she should take next in her sleuthing. She needed information about Clayton Wiggins and wasn't exactly sure where to look next.

She pictured the house at 212 Elm. It might be a crumbling mess now, but back in 1920 it would have been one of the nicest homes in Maple Hill, which meant Wiggins had to have been a man of some wealth. Perhaps he'd been a business owner or a professional of some sort. She might be able to find information about him in the local Chamber of Commerce records. It wasn't much to go on, but at least it gave her a place to start.

Picking up her rotary cutter and her acrylic ruler, Sarah sliced through the flannel, the razor-sharp blade rolling along the green plastic cutting mat underneath the fabric. She folded the newly cut strip and placed it on the table. She planned to dye the flannel blue and then use it to replace the moth-eaten flannel on the back of the quilt.

She walked over to her closet, opened the door, and was greeted by row after row of fabric remnants, all crowded onto the closet shelves. She'd picked up most of them from the bargain bin at the Wild Goose Chase, although she always kept her eyes open for good fabric bargains whenever she traveled. With any luck, she could find the replacement fabrics here.

She was just pulling out several remnants in various shades of blue when the doorbell rang. Sarah dropped the remnants on the table, then headed for the door.

"Hello, there." Maggie stood on the front porch in a red knit top and denim capri pants. "I promise not to make a habit of dropping in unannounced, but this couldn't wait."

If it wasn't for the sheepish smile on Maggie's face, Sarah might have thought something was wrong with Jason or the girls. "What is it?"

Maggie hesitated. "I'd really like to show you rather than tell you. Are you busy right now?"

Sarah shook her head. "Not really. I was just working on Dad's quilt."

"Can I tempt you into doing something else? It won't take long."

"Depends what it is," she quipped. Maggie's unexpected appearance this morning intrigued her, especially since her daughter-in-law hadn't had much time for Sarah since they'd moved to Maple Hill. Maggie was always buzzing here or there, involved in some new project for the house. "I've already talked myself out of dusting today," Sarah continued, "so I'm not in the mood for cleaning."

"It's not housework, I promise."

"Then what is it?"

Maggie sucked in a deep breath. "Come with me and I'll show you."

Ten minutes later, Maggie steered her red Chevy Tahoe toward the village green. "We're getting closer."

Sarah had been trying to guess their destination ever since she'd climbed into Maggie's car. "Martha stood me up for our coffee date this morning, so if we're headed for Liam's, I'm all for it."

"No hints until we get there."

"There" turned out to be a parking spot near the Galleria, a shop filled with beautiful paintings, framed scenic photographs, and sculptures made out of various pieces of colored glass, metal, and wood. "Are we picking out some art pieces for your home?"

"No," Maggie said as she turned off the ignition. "Just the opposite in fact."

Sarah followed Maggie out of the car, still perplexed by her behavior. She met her daughter-in-law on the sidewalk in front of an abandoned storefront.

"Well?" Maggie asked.

"Well, what?"

Maggie motioned to the empty store in front of them. "What do you think of this place?"

Sarah went over and peered through the large plate glass window. "It looks dusty."

Maggie chuckled and pulled a key out of her pocket. "Let's go inside."

Sarah followed her inside the shop, starting to feel uneasy. The shop was nice enough, very rustic, with wide plank floors and brick walls. It was also very empty. She turned to Maggie. "Did you buy this place or something?"

"No," Maggie said, "but I did just sign a one-year lease. I've decided to open an antique store!"

Sarah blinked. She knew Maggie loved antiques, but she hadn't realized Maggie wanted to go into the business. "Well, this is a surprise."

Maggie nodded. "For me, too. I'd been toying with the idea for a long time, and it's something I thought I might finally try when we moved here. And then I found this place, and I knew this was it. So I signed the lease yesterday afternoon."

"Is Jason as excited as you are?"

Maggie winced. "Well, I haven't exactly told him yet."

Sarah looked at her, stunned. "You haven't told him?"

"You know how he is," Maggie said with a dismissive wave. "He'd insist on going over all the legal forms with a fine-tooth comb. The owner told me there were several other interested parties, so I didn't want to risk losing it."

Sarah swallowed. She and Gerry had never made big decisions unilaterally. They'd always talked things over, making sure they were both on board before going forward. "Oh, Maggie, I'm not sure that was a good idea."

"That's why I brought you here," she explained. "I knew once you saw what a great place this is, you could help me convince Jason that it was the right thing to do."

Her stomach sank. She didn't want to be put in the middle between her son and daughter-in-law.

Maggie walked across the room, obviously determined to bring Sarah around to her way of thinking. "I'm going to keep the floor and the brick walls as they are. The ceiling adds the perfect ambience."

Sarah tilted her head back to view the embossed, silver tin ceiling twenty feet above. "It is beautiful."

"The place just needs a little cleaning up," Maggie said, "and a few shelves for me to get started. I've already applied for a sales tax permit and plan to hold my grand opening next week."

"So soon?" Sarah said.

"Well, I don't want to miss out on all these summer tourists, so the sooner I can open, the better."

"Don't you have to find some antiques first?"

Maggie waved away that concern. "Oh, I brought enough antiques with me from California to fill a storage unit. I didn't even realize how much I had until we moved here.

I could never resist an estate sale," Maggie said. "Jason groused about dragging all those antiques with us to Maple Hill, but now I have some inventory for the store, enough to start with, anyway. And the money we'll save on the monthly storage unit fees will help defray the cost of the building lease."

Now it sounded like she was trying to convince herself more than Sarah. Or rehearsing the speech she planned to give her husband.

"I'm going to name my store Magpie's Antiques," Maggie continued. "Isn't that perfect?"

Magpie was Jason's nickname for his wife because she liked to collect things—something told Sarah Jason wouldn't be thrilled about this latest addition to his wife's collection. "It is a cute name," she conceded. "I just hope you haven't taken on more than you can handle."

Maggie frowned. "I thought you'd love the idea. I've always dreamed of opening my own antique store and this seemed like the time to do it. It's hard moving away from family and friends and starting all over again."

"I'm sorry, Maggie." Sarah reached up to rub her temple, feeling caught in the middle, a place she definitely didn't want to be. "I do support you. I'll be happy to help at your grand opening and do anything else you need."

"Like talk to Jason?"

Sarah shook her head. "I don't feel comfortable getting involved with that. That conversation should be between the two of you."

Maggie grew quiet. "Okay. That's fine."

Sarah could tell it wasn't fine, but she wasn't willing to overstep her bounds by interfering in her son's marriage. "Am I still invited to your grand opening?"

Maggie's expression softened. "Of course."

They didn't speak much on the drive home. Sarah didn't take it personally, aware that Maggie was apprehensive about telling Jason she'd committed to a one-year lease without his knowledge. That was probably another stress he didn't need in his life, but his marriage was his business, no matter how much she might want to help smooth the waters.

As the Tahoe pulled up to the house, Sarah turned to Maggie. "Can I take the girls on a picnic Thursday afternoon? Martha and I want to introduce our granddaughters to each other."

"I'm sure they'd like that," Maggie said. "It's been lonely for them here, too."

That one little word—"too"—helped Sarah understand a little better why Maggie had embarked on a new project. Running her own store would give Maggie a chance to meet a lot of people and engage in the community. Sarah just wished she'd included Jason in the decision.

"There's someone else I'd like them to meet," Sarah continued. "Her name is Doris Hatch and she lives at the address I found in the quilt."

Maggie arched a brow. "Really? Does she know anything about it?"

"No, she just moved to town a few years ago. But she has health problems and could use some help around her yard. Do you suppose the girls would be interested in lending her a hand?"

"It won't hurt them to help out someone in need." A tiny smile tipped up the corners of her mouth. "And it will give me time to get the shop ready for next week."

When Sarah climbed out of the car, she stood on the sidewalk a moment watching the red Tahoe disappear down the street. "Be with Maggie and Jason, Lord," she whispered. "I think they're going to need you."

CHAPTER THIRTEEN

Sarah awoke the next morning to the sound of the vacuum cleaner.

"What in the world?" she murmured, lifting her head off the pillow to check the clock on her nightstand. The digital numbers read eight o'clock. Had she let the house go so long without cleaning that one of her boarders had been forced to do it herself?

Rising out of bed, she slipped her feet into her blue slippers and pulled on her robe before heading downstairs. Katie guided the upright vacuum cleaner over the red Oriental rug covering the wide plank floor, her brown ponytail swinging back and forth.

The girl stood with her back toward Sarah, oblivious of her presence, while she picked up the vacuum cord and swung it over the coffee table. A feather duster lay on top of the coffee table, along with a bottle of glass cleaner.

"Katie?" Sarah called out in a voice loud enough to be heard over the vacuum.

Katie turned around, then flipped off the vacuum and pulled a pair of ear buds from her ears. The cord from the ear buds led to an MP3 player sticking halfway out the back pocket of her jeans.

From the way the woodwork and windows shined, Sarah assumed Katie had been at this for a while. All the surfaces gleamed, free of the dust Sarah had avoided taking care of yesterday.

"I hope you don't mind," Katie said. "I snooped around a bit until I found the vacuum cleaner and duster and stuff."

"I don't mind." Sarah stepped into the living room. "I know I let it go too long, but don't ever feel like you have to clean. That certainly isn't part of our rental agreement."

Katie bit her lip. "Actually, I was hoping we might be able to strike some kind of bargain."

"What do you mean?"

Katie's gaze dropped to the floor. "Next week's rent was due yesterday and I...don't quite have it yet. I was hoping you'd let me do some work around the house until I have the money."

Sarah watched a hot blush creep up the girl's neck and cheeks as she waited for Sarah's answer. "I think that sounds like a good plan. But if we're going to use the barter system, then let's play fair. You won't owe me any money for next week's rent."

Relief flashed across her face. "Really?"

"It seems like more than a fair exchange to me. You probably think I'm a horrible housekeeper."

Katie's eyes widened in horror. "Not at all! Oh, I hope you don't think that's why I did this. Your house is beautiful. I'm lucky to be here."

Sarah reached out to pat her arm. "I'm the lucky one. I've been so busy with my work lately, I've neglected the house, so thank you for doing this."

Katie looked sheepish. "I figured it was the least I could do after..." Her voice trailed off and she cleared her throat. "Anyway, I'm going to tackle the kitchen next, then the sitting room upstairs." She cocked her head. "Do you want me to clean your sewing room, too?"

"No, thank you." Sarah didn't usually let people in her sewing room when she was in the middle of a quilt restoration project, afraid they might accidentally misplace a vital fabric piece or one of her tools. "I can handle that room by myself."

"Okay." Katie placed the ear buds back in her ears. "I think I'll get back to work now.

"Just don't let cleaning interfere with your thesis work."

"That won't be a problem," Katie replied, then flipped on the vacuum before Sarah could say anything else.

Sarah watched her for a moment, then turned around and headed back upstairs. Now that Katie had freed up some extra time for her, she didn't intend to waste a moment. As soon as she showered and dressed, she intended to head to the library for a date with Clayton Wiggins.

Soon Sarah was walking through the walnut door of the Maple Hill Library, a lofty building located near the village green.

"Hi, Spencer." Sarah approached the handsome young librarian behind the circulation desk. He was in his midthirties with short, dark hair, penetrating blue eyes and a slightly receded hairline. "How have you been?"

"Very busy." He shifted the pile of books in front of him to another spot. "Summer is always crazy around here. Tourists like to take advantage of the free Internet service and access to magazines and newspapers, plus all the kids are out of school. It keeps me hopping, but I love it."

That was apparent in every inch of the library. The former librarian had been a spinster who had held the position for almost forty years. She'd ruled with an iron fist, successfully intimidating the library board and anyone else who took issue with her way of running things. She didn't like change, which meant she'd been resistant to anything more technologically advanced than pen and paper.

When Spencer had taken over five years ago, he'd found an electric typewriter to be the most modern piece of technology in the building. In less than a month, he'd reworked the budget to make funds available to buy three computers, and he'd asked the library's patrons to donate DVDs and CDs. He'd also arranged the tall bookcases in a way that created small nooks where readers could sit undisturbed.

"How's that boarder I sent your way?" Spencer asked.

"Rita is wonderful. You're welcome to send me boarders any time."

He chuckled. "That's what I'm here for, to provide information to people who need it."

Sarah leaned her forearms on the counter. "Then I hope you can help me. Where would I find archived records from the Maple Hill Chamber of Commerce?"

"Well, that's not a request I get every day. I've got them stored in binders in the back room. Any particular date you're looking for?"

She thought for a moment. "How about 1919 through 1921?" That should cover enough time to reveal if Clayton Wiggins was an active member of the community and if he had any connection to Grandma Molly or Grandpa Noah.

"Okay, I'll be right back," Spencer said before disappearing behind a door.

Sarah still hoped to find some descendants of Wiggins who could help her figure out why Grandma Molly had written his address on the note. Perhaps he'd been married to a friend of hers or ...? She shook her head, tired of speculating. She wanted some solid answers.

A few minutes later, Spencer reemerged with two large blue binders in his hands. He set them on the counter in front of Sarah. "This top volume covers 1917 through 1919 and the bottom volume is 1920 through 1922."

"Thank you." Sarah carried the binders over to one of the long oak tables and sat down. When she opened the first binder, full of a thick sheaf of paper, she realized the wisdom of eating a big breakfast this morning.

She was going to be here for a while.

CHAPTER FOURTEEN

On Saturday afternoon, Sarah and the twins arrived at Patriot Park.

"There's the statue of Nathaniel Bradford," Sarah told them, motioning toward the bronze sculpture in the center of the park. Bradford was seated on a horse, his right arm extended in front of him, pointing the way to freedom.

"I've never heard of him before." Audrey got out of the car, pulling her short-sleeved top, adorned with a rhinestone butterfly, over the waistband of her skinny pink jeans.

"Well, he's pretty famous around here." Sarah handed her a sack filled with paper plates, napkins, plasticware, and cups. "I'm sure you'll learn about him in school. He was a high-ranking general in the Revolutionary War and one of George Washington's key advisors."

"I can't wait," Amy said wryly, grabbing her basketball as she climbed out of the back seat.

Sarah handed her the picnic basket, then picked up the pie carrier she'd filled with cupcakes. After locking her car, she led the girls to the picnic area on the other side of the park.

There was a playground nearby with swings, slides, and a tether ball. Farther out were winding trails that led to the thickly forested hills.

"Are they here yet?" Audrey leaned against a picnic table, adjusting one of her butterfly earrings.

Sarah set the pie carrier on the table. "I don't see them yet."

Amy placed the basket beside it. "Maybe they're not coming."

"They're coming," Sarah assured them. "I talked to Martha this morning and she said that all three girls are very excited to meet you."

"Okay," Audrey said. "I just don't want this to be lame, like we're desperate for friends or something."

"We are desperate." Amy tossed the basketball back and forth between her hands. She wore an orange T-shirt and a pair of denim shorts. "We haven't met anybody in Maple Hill yet."

"Just give it some time." Sarah pulled the tableware out of the sack. "Before you know it, you'll have more new friends than you can count."

Audrey slumped down onto the bench and placed her chin in her hands. "I miss my old friends in California. I'll probably never see them again."

Amy rolled her eyes. "You see them all the time. You're always video chatting with them."

"It's not the same," Audrey said. "We're thousands of miles away from California. It's like we moved to a different planet."

Sarah suppressed a smile, realizing it had been a while since she'd listened to the drama preteen girls could create. Her own daughter, Jenna, had been the same when she was young.

"I haven't seen any cute boys around here, either," Audrey said.

Sarah set a jug of juice on the table along with a stack of paper napkins. She was glad it wasn't windy today. The air was hot, but not unbearable. A fly buzzed near her cheek and she brushed it away.

"We can ask the Maplethorpe girls where to find cute boys," Sarah suggested.

Audrey's blue eyes widened in horror. "Oh, Grandma, you have to promise not to say *anything* about boys. I'd die if you did!"

"We don't want them to think we're both boy crazy," Amy said. "Because *I'm* not."

"That's just because no boy's ever noticed you."

"Then no boy has noticed you, either. We're twins, so you just insulted yourself."

"That's enough, girls," Sarah said as she saw Martha's green minivan pull into the parking lot. "It looks like they're here."

Audrey and Amy suddenly got very quiet as Martha and her three granddaughters approached them. Sarah noticed Audrey fiddling with her hair while Amy began dribbling the basketball, her gaze fixed on a spot on the ground.

"We meet at last," Martha announced, her face wreathed in a smile as she made the introductions. "Amy and Audrey Hart, these are my three granddaughters: Lexie, Trina, and Prudence."

"It's Pru," Prudence hastily informed them. She had long, dark hair and wore a pair of silver wire-rimmed glasses. "Nobody calls me Prudence except Grandma."

Martha circled her arm around Pru's shoulders and gave her a squeeze. "That's because Prudence was my mother's name and she never let people call her anything else."

Pru heaved a weary sigh. "I know. You've told me that a thousand times. I like Pru."

"So do I," Martha said, a teasing glint in her eye. "I just like Prudence better."

Trina looked back and forth between Amy and Audrey, her red ponytail bobbing behind her. "Wow, you two really are identical twins. Which one is which?"

"I'm Audrey," Audrey said, stepping forward with a smile.

Trina smiled back. "I love your jeans."

"Thanks."

The conversation dwindled and soon the only sound was the basketball hitting the ground.

"Do you play basketball, Amy?" Martha asked at last.

Amy shrugged, not meeting her gaze. "Just for fun. I like softball better."

Lexie tossed her blonde hair behind her back. "Well, if you two were dressed the same, I don't think I'd be able to tell you apart."

"That's what everybody says at first," Audrey replied, "but all our friends back home can tell us apart. We can't even trick them anymore, although we do like to trick new teachers."

Lexie flashed a grin, revealing a pair of silver braces with hot pink bands on them. "That's wicked awesome! You'll have to do that at Hawthorne Middle School. All the teachers there are really lame."

Martha heaved her bulging picnic basket onto the table. "Who's hungry?"

"Me," the girls all chorused.

They sat down at the table as Martha and Sarah set out the food they'd brought along. Sarah had fried up a couple of chickens while Martha had made cold cut sandwiches and a big tub of potato salad. Martha poured juice for all of them while Sarah removed the cupcakes from the pie carrier and placed them on the table. They were topped with pink frosting and sprinkled with colorful jimmies.

"Those look great," Lexie exclaimed. "What kind are they?"

"Half are chocolate," Sarah replied, "and half are vanilla, because I have two picky granddaughters."

Audrey laughed. "At least we both like frosting."

Sarah and Martha sat down to eat, each of them taking a little bit of everything.

"Oh, I almost forgot," Sarah said, reaching for her basket. "I brought a jar of my pickled beets."

Audrey wrinkled her nose. "Pickled beets sounds gross."

"Don't say that until you've tried one," Martha told her. "They're actually quite good."

Pru shook her head. "They're gross." Then she winced. "I'm sorry, Mrs. Hart. No offense."

"None taken," Sarah said with a smile, glad the girls had found something to bond over, even if it was disgust over pickled beets.

Martha unscrewed the lid on the jar, then dipped a plastic fork in to spear a beet. "I guess it's a generational thing. I remember eating pickled beets all the time while I was growing up."

"Me, too," Sarah said, helping herself to one.

Audrey chattered with Lexie during the picnic, with Trina and Pru occasionally chiming in. Amy sat silent at the table, poking at her food with her fork but eating very little.

"I have a question." Audrey licked pink frosting off her thumb as she turned to Lexie and Pru. "Are you all sisters? Because you don't really look alike."

The girls laughed, then Lexie replied, "We're all cousins. My dad and Pru's dad are brothers."

"And my mom is their sister," Trina said.

"Cool," Audrey said. "We have cousins in Texas, but we don't get to see them very often. Our mom is an only child, so we don't have any cousins on that side of the family."

"Well, we all have brothers," Lexie said with a groan. "They're pretty horrible, too, so the three of us have to stick together."

"Now, Lexie," Martha said, "your brothers aren't horrible. They're very nice boys."

"You're just saying that because you're their grandma. You have to like them."

"Anybody want to go for a walk?" Lexie asked as she swung her legs over the bench.

"I will." Audrey took a last sip of juice, then set her cup on the table.

"Me, too," Trina and Pru chorused.

Martha turned to Amy. "How about you?"

"I think I'll stay here and shoot some baskets."

"Okay," Audrey said, "suit yourself." Then she and the other girls took off down the trail.

Sarah hated to see Amy isolate herself. "Are you sure you don't want to go with them? It could be fun."

"I'm sure," Amy said, grabbing her basketball and heading toward the court on the other side of the playground area.

After Amy was out of earshot, Martha turned to Sarah. "Is she all right?"

"Yes," Sarah replied. "She's just shy. Audrey tends to overshadow her at times since she gets along so well with everyone."

"Well, give it time." Martha pulled a crochet hook and thread out of her cloth bag. "I'm sure all the girls will warm up to each other."

Sarah pushed aside her plate, anxious to share her news with Martha. "I found another clue yesterday."

Martha looked up from her crocheting. "About Molly?"

Sarah nodded. "I spent four hours in the library, but it was worth it. I was researching Clayton Wiggins, who owned the house at 212 Elm in 1920."

"And?" Martha prodded.

"And he was an architect." She picked up her glass. "He designed Grandpa Noah's house."

Martha blinked. "That's an interesting coincidence."

"It also means he knew about the secret passageway. He'd know where to find Grandma Molly if she was hiding from him."

Martha twisted thread around her hook. "It sounds like the trail is getting warmer."

"I still need to figure out what happened to Wiggins. I don't know yet how long he lived in Maple Hill or anything about his family."

"At least now you know there's a connection to Molly."

"I feel like I'm getting closer to finding out what happened to her."

"Well, keep me posted. I could use some good news these days."

Sarah set down her cup. "What's wrong? Is Ernie still sick?"

Martha hesitated for a long moment. "He's better, I guess."

They'd known each other too long not to read between the lines. "Then what's bothering you?"

Martha stared down at her crocheting. "He's been different lately, Sarah. I hate to say it, but I'm worried about him. Really worried."

Her words made Sarah's heart clench. She remembered saying very similar words to Martha seven years ago, when Gerry had first noticed something was wrong. "Do you want to talk about it?"

Martha finally looked up at her. "If I don't, I think I'll burst. Ernie certainly doesn't want to talk about it. He thinks I'm imagining things."

"What kind of things?"

Martha set her crocheting on the table, proving to Sarah that this really was serious. "You know that broken-down recliner of his that he just loves?"

Sarah smiled. "The one he repairs with duct tape whenever it gets a tear?"

"Yeah, well, he doesn't sit in it anymore. He's had trouble getting out of it a few times and now he just avoids it altogether. I could understand if he were fat like me, but he's skinnier than ever."

"First of all, you're not fat."

"I'm pleasantly plump," Martha replied, "and proud of it. But despite my great cooking, Ernie is losing weight."

Sarah could see why Martha was concerned. These were all symptoms that could signal something serious. "Has he seen a doctor?"

"He won't go," Martha said. "You know how stubborn he can be. I'm about to drag him there myself and he's thin enough now I could probably do it."

"I think you should do whatever's necessary. I'm sure he's worried, too, even if he doesn't want to talk about it—especially if he doesn't want to talk about it."

"I know," Martha agreed. "I'm trying to remember how you handled it when Gerry got sick. He never liked going to the doctor either, did he?"

"No." Sarah stacked the empty paper plates in front of her. "But he finally went without telling me. That's when I knew it was really serious, before the doctor even gave us the diagnosis."

She didn't like to think about that time in their lives. Everything had changed so quickly. Gerry had always been such a strong man. He was an accountant by trade but loved to work with his hands. He'd created a woodshop in the cellar of their house and produced some beautiful furniture. Cradles for all the grandchildren. A rocking chair for the living room and the nightstand that stood by her bedside. Even the wooden spice rack in the kitchen. All things that made her feel close to him even today.

"I'm sorry," Martha said gently. "I didn't mean to bring up unpleasant memories."

That's when Sarah realized she'd been silent for several minutes, lost in her thoughts. She smiled at her friend. "There are only a few bad ones. Most of my memories of Gerry are good. Very good."

"I know," Martha said. "He was a wonderful man."

"So is Ernie. It's the not knowing that's the worst. We used to wait forever for Gerry's test results, hoping for the best and fearing the worst. It was a horrible roller coaster ride."

"I remember."

"That's because I kept calling to cry on your shoulder," Sarah said wryly.

"You're right. Not knowing is the worst. You wouldn't believe all the horrible illnesses I've imagined."

Sarah reached over to take her friend's hand. "Yes, I would. Just remember that God is watching over both of you. He'll always be there. And so will I."

Martha squeezed her hand, then forced a smile. "I think that calls for a cupcake. There's only one left, so we'll have to split it."

"Sounds good to me."

Sarah cut the cupcake in half, sending up a silent prayer for Ernie and Martha. She couldn't ask for better friends and entreated God to watch over both of them.

CHAPTER FIFTEEN

When Sarah pulled into Jason's driveway to drop the girls off after the picnic, her son came out to greet her.

"Thanks, Grandma," the girls chimed in unison as they climbed out of the car and headed for the house.

Jason walked over to the open driver's side window. "Hey, Mom, can I borrow Dad's belt sander?"

"Sure." Sarah shaded her eyes from the bright sun. "When do you need it?"

"Today would be good. There are a couple of warped steps on the staircase and I want to sand them down before somebody trips."

"Hop in," she said. "We'll run over to the house and get it right now."

"Great." Jason rounded the front of the car and got into the passenger seat. He buckled his seat belt, then leaned back and rested his elbow out the open window. "So how was the picnic?"

"Good, I think." She told him about their afternoon during the short drive to her house.

"Sounds like the girls had fun."

"I hope so." Sarah parked the car in the driveway, then headed for the back door. "All of your dad's tools are still in the cellar," she said as they stepped up onto the porch, "right where he left them."

Jason followed Sarah into the kitchen and through the cellar door. She flipped on an overhead light before heading down the stairs. The air smelled faintly of cedar and was much cooler than in the rest of the house.

One half of the cellar had been turned into Gerry's woodshop, complete with a table saw, planer, and a radial arm saw. A workbench stretched the length of one cinder block wall. It had dozens of drawers full of nails and screws of all sizes, along with other tools of the carpentry trade, such as sandpaper, varnish, and wood putty. Several pieces of wood still leaned against one wall, bought for projects Gerry had been unable to start.

The other half of the cellar belonged to Sarah. There were shelves filled with her home-canned goods, including plenty of pickled beets. There was also a large storage area containing some quilt frames she no longer used and a trunk filled with some of her early quilt-making attempts.

"Wow," Jason said, "this place brings back memories. I can't remember the last time I was down here, but it looks exactly the same."

Sarah chuckled. "I guess I've gotten set in my ways. I can't even bring myself to change your Dad's workshop. I like looking at it."

"So do I."

She walked over to the workbench, happy that Jason would be using some of Gerry's tools. "Now, what do you need again?"

"A belt sander," Jason said, looking around the shop. "There it is." He walked over to the shelf and grabbed the machine by the handle."

"Anything else?"

Jason thought for a moment. "I could use some wood putty." He opened a drawer and pulled out a jar. "Do you suppose this stuff is still good after all this time?"

"Only one way to find out."

She watched Jason unscrew the lid and dip the tip of his index finger in the putty. He rubbed it between his finger and thumb.

"Still good," he announced.

She looked around the woodshop. "What else do you need?"

"I think that's it."

He followed her back up the stairs. "I heard you found out about Maggie's latest boondoggle."

She winced at the word. "She told you?"

"Just last night." He walked through the cellar door and into the kitchen. "I couldn't believe she'd do something like that without telling me. The lease is unbreakable. I even offered to pay the landlord a penalty fee if he'd tear up the contract, but no deal."

"How did Maggie take your reaction?"

He sighed. "Not well. I don't support her dream of owning an antique store, she says." He rubbed a hand over his chin. "I support her, I just think her dream is going to turn into a nightmare."

She found herself coming to Maggie's defense. "It *is* a great location for an antique store. She might do quite well."

"The failure rate for small businesses is almost sixty percent, Mom. And now we're trying to start two of them. I don't know what she was thinking."

Sarah didn't say anything, certain this latest development wasn't reducing his stress. So she did what any good mother would do. "How about a slice of peach pie? I have some in the freezer I can thaw out."

"No, thanks." He set the belt sander on the bench. "I'm sorry, Mom. I didn't mean to go off on you. It's just been a little tense around the house lately."

She could imagine. Sarah walked over and laid a hand on his arm. "You and Maggie'll find a way to work this out."

"I know," he said, then walked over to the kitchen sink and washed the putty stain off his fingers. He plucked the dish towel off the counter, then said, "Hey, what's this?"

"What?" Sarah asked, walking over to him.

He picked up the folded newspaper he'd found under the towel and held it up to reveal the classified ad section. Several of the ads had been marked with yellow highlighter.

"Are you looking for work?" Jason teased.

Before Sarah could reply, Katie walked into the room. "No, I am."

Jason put the paper back on the counter. "Oh, sorry."

"Katie, this is my son, Jason," Sarah told her. "Jason, this is Katie, my new boarder."

"Nice to meet you." He shook her hand. "And please accept my apology. I wasn't trying to be nosy."

"No problem," she said, picking up the newspaper. "None of these jobs are right for me anyway. Most are full-time and I need something temporary."

"It's almost impossible to find a part-time job here in the summer," Sarah told her. "A lot of the college kids come home from school and snap those jobs up in early spring."

Katie sighed. "I guess I should have planned better."

Sarah wondered why she hadn't. If Katie was smart enough for graduate school, she should be smart enough to make a budget. Then again, she was only in her twenties. A baby, really. Maybe she'd never been out on her own before.

"What kind of work are you looking for?" Jason asked her.

"Anything," Katie replied. "I just need something to tide me over for the last few weeks of summer."

Sarah wondered if Liam could use some extra help at the Spotted Dog. She didn't want to take advantage of their friendship, but she'd noticed this morning that Katie's refrigerator shelf was empty and she sensed the girl was getting desperate.

"What was your last job?"

"I assisted a home improvement company, mostly painting and wallpapering. Do you think I could get a job like that around here?"

"Are you kidding?" Jason said. "If you can paint, I'll hire you myself."

Katie's face lit up. "Really?"

"Absolutely. My office needs painting and Maggie's been itching to paint the parlor so we can finally get some furniture in there. Now that she's busy opening her new shop, she'll need some help. The sooner we get our businesses off the ground, the better."

Sarah resisted the urge to give her son a hug. Despite his gruff talk earlier, he really did love his wife. And he had a touch of impulsiveness himself, if he'd only admit it.

"It sounds like serendipity to me," Sarah said. "If you're interested, Katie."

"Are you kidding?" Katie said. "It's like a dream come true. I love to paint and I'm good at it, too."

Jason leaned back against the counter and folded his arms across his chest. "How many hours can you work per week?"

Katie took a deep breath to collect herself. "Well, I'm pretty broke, so as many hours as possible."

Sarah sat down at the kitchen table. "What about your schoolwork?"

"I can afford to take a little time off."

"Are you sure?" Jason asked her.

"Positive," Katie said firmly.

Sarah wondered why Katie hadn't budgeted for spending the summer in Maple Hill. But perhaps an expense had come up that she hadn't anticipated, like car trouble. It could be anything.

Jason shifted on his feet. "Well, the next subject is, how much do you want to get paid?"

Katie hesitated. "My last job paid me fourteen dollars an hour. Is that too much?"

"Sounds fair to me," Jason said. "And you can start tomorrow as far as I'm concerned. Heck, you can even start today if you want."

"Actually, I might do that." Katie looked thoughtful. "Then I can figure out what supplies I'll need."

"Great." Jason pulled his cell phone out of his pocket. "If you don't mind driving me home, I'll call Maggie and tell her we're on our way. She'll be thrilled."

Sarah was thrilled, too. Happy to see her son trying to mend fences with his wife. One of them had to take the first step. After the phone call, Jason picked up the belt sander and followed Katie to her car.

Sarah watched them leave through the window, amazed at the transformation in Katie. Her face was actually glowing. Maybe her money problems explained her odd behavior these last few days. The prospect of paid work had certainly changed her.

Eager to work on the quilt, Sarah walked into her sewing room and picked up the seam ripper. She slipped into her chair, then used the small tool to carefully pick out the stitches around a moth-eaten square that was so badly damaged it needed to be replaced. She'd use matching thread to sew a new square in place.

When she'd pulled the original square free of the quilt, she recorded her work in the notebook.

Removed fabric piece #87 for replacement. Outline stitch in blue silk thread on all four sides.

Sarah placed the original thread in an envelope, then sealed it and wrote #87 on the front. As she began to pull the stitches loose from the next tattered square, her mind drifted to Clayton Wiggins.

He was just one small piece of the puzzle, but a vital piece. She needed to find more information or she might never solve Grandma Molly's case. Her next step would be researching the gravestone listings for the Maple Hill cemetery. The historical society had that information, but it was closed on weekends. Which meant she'd need to get a good start first thing Monday morning.

CHAPTER SIXTEEN

Thunder rumbled overhead as Sarah placed white daisies from her garden on Grandpa Noah's grave. She'd wanted to come to the cemetery yesterday after church, but heavy rain showers had kept her away. Now on this gray Monday morning, she stood alone in the damp green grass of the cemetery, having already visited the graves of her husband and mother. She'd saved Grandpa Noah for last. She needed some time here.

A few dandelion weeds sprang up at the base of his headstone and Sarah leaned over to pluck them. The black marble felt warm under her hand, thanks to the hot weather they'd been having the last few days.

That was about to change. A cool breeze wafted through the evergreen trees that lined the cemetery fence. Swollen, gray clouds filled the sky, casting a gloomy pall over everything. Even the birds seemed to have stopped singing.

Sarah tossed the weeds away, then brushed a few loose blades of grass off the stone. "Sorry I haven't been here for a while, Grandpa. I guess time gets away from me."

She'd been thinking about him often, though, and reliving so many memories. His life had never been the same after Grandma Molly's disappearance.

Sarah couldn't rest either, not until she found out what had happened to Grandma Molly. Finding her father's long lost quilt with the note inside had stirred up so many emotions for her.

Lightning flashed in the distance, directly over Mount Greylock. The wind picked up, blowing Sarah's hair into her eyes. She tucked it behind her ears, knowing she didn't have much time.

"Did you know about the secret passageway, Grandpa?" Sarah asked over the wind. "You didn't, did you? Otherwise you would have looked for Grandma Molly there and found the quilt."

Another crack of thunder sounded, rumbling the ground beneath her feet. "Dad couldn't have known it existed either or he would have told me about it."

"I'm not sure what to do next, Grandpa. I just don't want to let you down."

Fat raindrops pelted her, a prelude to what promised to be a downpour. Sarah brushed the moisture out of her eyes, reading the words Grandpa Noah had wanted on his headstone.

"Trust in the Lord with all your heart," she said aloud, as lightning flashed in the sky, "and lean not on your own understanding; in all your ways acknowledge him, and he will make your paths straight."

Her grandfather had lived that verse every day that she'd known him. That was the example she needed to follow while trying to find the truth.

"Oh my," Irene exclaimed when Sarah walked through the door of the historical society. "Looks like you got caught in the downpour."

"I sure did." She wiped her shoes on the mat, then ran her hand through her damp hair. "That will teach me to leave home without an umbrella."

She'd come straight from the cemetery, eager to continue the search that she'd planned to conduct there today. "I need the plot map of the Maple Hill Cemetery."

"I'll get it for you," Irene said, walking over to one of the file cabinets she kept behind the counter. A moment later, she returned with a book. "Are you looking for someone special?"

"Clayton Wiggins," she said. "If he's buried there, I can see if he's part of a family plot and possibly trace that to a living relative who can tell us something about him."

Irene smiled. "I wish I had your brain. By the way, thank you for telling me about Luther Endicott. He's a fascinating man. I've been spending every night with him."

"You found a book about him?" Sarah ventured.

"Yes. It's about the renovation of the Massachusetts State House, and Luther earned himself an entire chapter."

Sarah wondered if there might be something in the book that could help her. "I don't suppose it talks much about his time in Maple Hill?"

Irene frowned. "He acts like we don't even exist. What is it with people going out into the world and forgetting their roots?"

The front door opened and Martha's oldest grandson, Kyle Maplethorpe, walked inside. Kyle was a tall, gangly youth, who reminded Sarah of a Labrador puppy, with hands and feet that looked too big for his body.

"Hey, there," Kyle greeted them. "How's it going?"

"Just fine," Sarah replied. "How are you, Kyle? Happy to be home for the summer?"

He shrugged. "I guess. I really liked my first year of college though. It sure makes things around here seem boring."

Boring was a word she'd been hearing a lot lately, especially when she was around her granddaughters. "Don't you like working for the *Monitor*?"

"Oh, sure," Kyle said. "It's great. But they keep giving me the silliest stories to cover. I mean, who wants to know that two old ladies named Betty drove to Springfield for a meeting of the Betty Club?"

"I do," Irene exclaimed. "I think the Betty Club is a cute idea. I wish they had an Irene Club."

Sarah smiled. "I like the folksy stories in the *Monitor*. It's a good hometown newspaper."

"If that's what you want, I guess it's all right," he admitted, "but part of my internship is creating a portfolio to take back with me to college. I can't put the Betty story in there." He shuddered at the thought. "I'd be laughed right out of my journalism class."

"Well, summer isn't over yet," Sarah reminded him. "Maybe you'll get some hard-hitting newspaper stories that you can add to your portfolio before you have to go back to college."

"I hope so." Kyle rested his arms on the counter. "If you hear of any good news stories around Maple Hill, let me know. My goal is to get my own byline before this internship is up."

"I've heard there's a new antique store opening soon."

He sighed. "Great. Maybe I can write a story about the Betty Club touring the antique store."

Sarah laughed in spite of herself. Kyle's hangdog expression made him look even more puppylike. Something told her he wasn't as forlorn as he pretended, even if he was waiting for his big scoop.

"Thanks for your help, ladies," Kyle said, pushing himself off the counter. "I'd better go see if anything exciting is happening in town. I have a three o'clock deadline."

"Bye," Sarah called after him as he headed out the door.

"That Kyle can always make me laugh," Irene said as she closed the record book in front of her. "I probably should have asked him to investigate Clayton Wiggins."

"I hope he's in here." Sarah opened the paperbound book and saw a drawing of the cemetery with each plot numbered. Below the drawing was an indexed list of names.

"It's not in alphabetical order, is it?" Sarah said as she ran her finger down the list of names.

"I'm afraid not." Irene leaned in for a closer look. "They're listed in order of plot number."

Sarah's finger faltered when she came to Gerry's name on the list. She took a deep breath and moved on. "Wexler, Adams, Sawyer," she murmured, "Davis, Lawton, Maplethorpe, Maplethorpe, Cunningham, Turnquist, Turnquist, Bancroft..." She flipped to the back, noting that there were over twenty pages of names to go. "This may take a while. I think I'll take a seat before I read through the rest of them."

"Good luck."

Twenty minutes later, Sarah was back at the desk. "Clayton Wiggins isn't buried in Maple Hill Cemetery and neither are any other Wigginses."

Irene frowned. "So he either moved away, or died here but was buried somewhere else."

"Looks that way." Sarah handed her the book, remembering the Bible verse on her grandfather's headstone. "I guess I need to find another path."

"So now what?" Irene asked.

She glanced at her watch. "Now I have a date with my granddaughters."

An hour later, Sarah drove to Jason's house to pick up the twins. The girls had moaned and groaned when they'd learned Sarah had volunteered them to help Doris with her lawn. Even more so when they learned that they'd be working for free.

Sarah's cheerful determination had gotten them this far, but she knew they could revolt at any time. As the girls walked toward her Pontiac, Sarah noticed Katie's car parked in Jason's driveway. She'd started painting their parlor yesterday, as evidenced by the yellow paint in her hair when she'd come home last night. Katie had even shared a little bit about her life, telling Sarah about being an only child and a missionary kid from South America.

What a difference a paycheck makes, Sarah thought to herself as she drove to Elm Street.

"Do we have to go?" Audrey asked as she climbed into the front passenger seat. "I just did my nails last night." She held up both hands so Sarah could see the sparkly pink polish.

"I brought some gardening gloves for each of you," Sarah told her, "so your nails will survive."

Audrey slumped against the seat and reached for her seatbelt as her sister got in the back seat.

"Hi, Grandma," Amy said as she closed her car door.

"Hello, dear."

As Sarah pulled away from the curb, Audrey indulged in a silent protest by putting on a set of headphones connected to her MP3 player and turning toward the window.

Sarah glanced in the rearview mirror to see if Amy wanted to mutiny, too. But her other granddaughter sat with her head buried in a book.

"What are you reading, Amy?"

"It's a graphic novel about mutant earthworms. I got it at the library yesterday."

While she was thrilled Amy liked to read, Sarah wasn't up on the latest trends in young adult fiction. "What's a graphic novel?"

Amy looked up at her. "It's like a comic book, only longer. This is a really good one, Grandma. You can read it when I'm done."

Sarah wished Amy would be this open and friendly with everyone she met. It always seemed like her shyness was keeping people at arm's length, making it difficult for them to get to know her.

"I don't know," Sarah said, "I may never be able to garden again if I read a book like that."

"It has a good romance in it," Amy said. "If you're into that sort of thing."

"A mutant earthworm romance? I think I'll stick with the classics, like Jane Austen."

"Who's she?"

Sarah turned onto Elm Street. "A woman who wrote one of the greatest romances in literature called *Pride and Prejudice*. You might be a bit young for it now, but I'll definitely buy you a copy when you're older."

Audrey slipped off her headphones. "Are we there yet?"

"Almost," Sarah replied as she pulled alongside the curb in front of Doris's house.

"Is this it?" Audrey winced. "That yard looks horrible! We'll be here *forever*."

"Then we'd better get started," Sarah said cheerfully. "The rain softened up the ground, so that will make it easier to pull out the weeds."

"Yeah, Audrey," Amy said, opening her car door, "quit complaining. A little exercise won't hurt you."

"Go back to your earthworms," Audrey said.

Sarah handed a pair of cotton gardening gloves to each girl. "Come to the house first. I want to introduce you to Doris before you get started."

"Do we have to?" Audrey groaned. "That's just going to make it take longer."

"Enough with the whining," Amy said. "The sooner we start, the sooner we'll be done."

Sarah picked up her purse and joined the twins on the sidewalk. As they approached the house, Sarah noted that the lawn looked even worse than before. More weeds had popped up and twigs had fallen on the sidewalk during the morning's thunderstorm. The air was still damp with rain and a meadowlark trilled in the distance. When they reached the front porch, Doris opened the door before Sarah even had time to knock.

"I saw you pull up," Doris said, fiddling with her necklace. The turquoise beads complemented her brown knit top and matching slacks.

"Hello, Doris," Sarah greeted her, then turned to introduce her granddaughters. "This is Audrey and the one in the ponytail is Amy. I wanted them to meet you before they got started."

Before Doris could reply, the cat walked up to the open door and meowed.

"Oh, look at the kitty," Audrey said. "She is *so* pretty."

"Her name is Bianca," Doris told them as both girls bent down to pet the Persian. Bianca closed her eyes, enjoying the attention.

"Why don't you girls get started?" Sarah suggested, not wanting them to get distracted by the cat. She handed Amy her keys. "There are a couple of rakes in the trunk, along with some garbage bags."

"Okay," Amy said, turning toward the street. "Come on, Audrey."

"Bye, Bianca," Audrey said to the cat. "I wish I could stay here and play with you." Then she heaved a long sigh before following her sister.

"Do you want to come in?" Doris asked her.

"Sure." Sarah stepped inside, then reached in her bag for the envelope she'd placed there earlier. "Here's your historical landmark certificate. Thank you for letting me take it with me."

"You're welcome." Then Doris cleared her throat. "I know who you are."

Sarah blinked, confused by the statement. "What?"

"I knew the first day you came here. My aunt had pointed you out to me on the street. You're the granddaughter of that man who killed his wife."

"He didn't kill her," Sarah said softly, wondering how many other minds Cleo Turnquist and her father had poisoned with their lies.

"I believe you. Aunt Cleo said bad things about a lot of people, including me."

Sarah could imagine the type of verbal abuse Cleo would dish out to someone as reserved and unassuming as Doris. She didn't fit in with the rest of the Turnquist family.

Yet she'd taken care of her aunt until she'd died. Sarah thought about the way Doris had let her into her home and tried to help her, even after all the nasty rumors she'd heard about the Drayton family.

"I think you're one of the nicest people I've ever met," Sarah said honestly.

A rosy blush bloomed in Doris's cheeks. "I'm not sure many people would agree."

Before Sarah could reply, Audrey burst through the door. "Grandma!"

"What on earth?" Sarah said, turning around.

"Come outside—you'll never guess what we found!"

CHAPTER SEVENTEEN

Sarah and Doris followed Audrey around the side of the house to a large, weed-filled window well. Several of the weeds that had been close to the brick house had already been pulled up and sat in a pile near the cellar window.

"What's going on?" Sarah asked, when she saw Amy sitting on the ground. "Are you hurt?"

"No, I'm fine." Amy pointed to a brick by the cellar window. "Audrey and I were pulling weeds when we found this."

Sarah knelt down for a closer look at the brick. Someone had scraped the letter M into the brick, followed by other letters that had been scratched over, making them indecipherable.

Sarah looked from the cellar window to the brick and back again, noting how close they were to each other. Close enough that someone inside the basement could open the window and reach out to etch letters into the brick.

"We think M stands for Molly," Audrey whispered. "Maybe she was kept prisoner here."

Sarah was thinking the same thing. It was just wild speculation at this point, but she wasn't about to ignore any potential clues in this mystery. Just the thought of being imprisoned in that dark, dank cellar made her shudder.

She looked over her shoulder at Doris. "I'm sorry, Doris. I should have told you the whole story sooner." Sarah explained how she'd found the quilt and the note inside.

When she was finished, Doris grinned. "That's like something you'd see in the movies."

"It does sound far-fetched," Sarah admitted. She looked back at the brick, wondering why someone would etch letters into it. Then she surveyed the other bricks on that side of the house to see if any of them had been etched as well, but the brick by the cellar window was the only one.

"It still could have happened," Doris said. "If it did, my aunt sure never knew about it." Her brow crinkled. "It's funny that my aunt never saw it there. She worked in the yard all the time before she got sick."

Sarah shrugged. "It's probably not something you'd pay much attention to normally. The girls were with me when I found the quilt, so they knew about the note with this address on it and that Grandma Molly's disappearance might be connected to this house."

"Maybe Molly was kept prisoner in the cellar," Doris said, echoing Audrey's theory, "and was trying to write a message when Clayton Wiggins caught her and tried to scratch it out."

When she said it like that, it sounded preposterous. She shook her head, bemused by this turn of events. "The next thing you know, a mutant earthworm will pop out of the ground."

"A mutant earthworm?" Doris echoed, clearly puzzled.

"That's a book I'm reading," Amy said. "It's a really good graphic novel."

"I love graphic novels," Doris told her.

"I got it at the library if you want to check it out when I'm done."

"I'll do that. Spencer Hewitt is very good about sending me books as long as I pay the postage costs. I just look at the online catalog and then place my order."

Audrey pulled off her gardening gloves. "Grandma, I'm hot. Can we take a break?"

"Sure," Doris said, before Sarah had a chance to answer. "Come inside for a glass of lemonade."

Bianca bounded up to the girls when they walked into the house. They sank down onto the beige carpet to play with her while Doris fetched the lemonade.

Even if the M etched on the brick turned out to have nothing to do with Grandma Molly, the discovery had seemed to bring Doris out of her shell. Maybe it was as simple as sharing part of your life with someone else.

A few minutes later, Doris returned to the living room with a tray of lemonade glasses and set it on the coffee table.

"I really like your necklace," Audrey told her as she took a glass.

Doris's hand went up to her throat. "Thank you. I make jewelry and sell it online. This was one of my favorites, so I kept it for myself."

"You made that?" Audrey gasped. "It's so pretty."

"Making jewelry is fun," Doris said. "I make necklaces, bracelets, earrings, and brooches. I can teach you how to do it sometime if you'd like."

"That would be cool," Audrey exclaimed.

Amy walked over to the coffee table and picked up a glass. "Maybe you could give us lessons on the days we work on your yard."

Doris smiled. "That sounds like a great deal to me."

As Doris and the twins worked out a schedule, Sarah's mind drifted back to that brick by the cellar window. The letter M and another message partially scribbled out. The puzzle seemed to be getting harder instead of easier, but at least she was moving forward.

By that evening, Sarah's mind was so exhausted from examining the twists and turns of the clues she'd found that she decided to take a break. After tidying up the kitchen, she pulled a quilting book from her bookshelf and carried it into the living room. She still needed to find a way to stabilize that silk taffeta binding on Molly's quilt.

With a tired sigh, she sat down in the rocking chair that Gerry had made for her. It was a classic mission-style design, made of stained oak with a leather upholstered seat. She loved the wide armrests and the easy rocking motion that always soothed her.

Sarah heard a key turn in the lock and looked up at the front door to see Rita walk inside. "Hello, there."

"Hi," Rita said, holding a shopping bag in each hand. "I had the best time today."

"Where did you go?"

"To a little flea market in Pittsfield." Rita wiped her shoes on the floor mat. "I collect vintage cookbooks and they had some wonderful treasures that I just couldn't pass up."

"If you like antiques and collectibles, you should stop by my daughter-in-law's new store. It's called Magpie's Antiques and she's holding her grand opening Wednesday evening at seven o'clock."

"Well, I have a little money left after today," Rita said with a smile, "so I might have to stop by. Is it downtown?"

Sarah nodded. "Yes, right next to the Galleria."

"I've been there."

"I think Katie's going to the grand opening, too. She's been doing some work on my son's house so Maggie's told her all about it."

"Is Katie home yet?" Rita asked.

"She just got back and headed straight for the shower."

Katie had been working almost around the clock for Jason and Maggie. The money she'd already made had allowed her to reactivate her cell phone, and she'd told Sarah that she'd start paying her weekly rent instead of bartering for it.

"That's where I'm headed too. With all the wind and rain today, I feel like I brought half the dirt in Massachusetts home with me."

Sarah laughed. "Well, you don't look like it."

"That's good to know." She headed for the stairs. "Goodnight, Sarah."

"Goodnight." Left alone once more, Sarah turned back to her book. She read about different types of interfacing and fabric adhesives, but none really seemed to solve her particular problem. Soon her eyelids began to droop and she found herself nodding off in the chair.

A long yawn escaped her, another sign that it was time for bed. She closed the book, then reached over to turn off the lamp when a loud rap sounded on the front door.

"Who in the world?" she murmured, glancing at the clock. She wasn't used to receiving visitors this late at night.

When she opened the door, a stocky man she didn't recognize stood on the other side. His shaved head reflected the light of the full moon, but it was his eyes that unnerved her. They were smoky gray under dark, bushy eyebrows. Eyes that seemed to look right through her.

"Good evening," he said. "Sorry to bother you like this, but I'm looking for somebody."

She detected a faint New York accent and looked past him to see a black sedan with rental plates parked in front of the house. "Who?"

He held up a photograph of a pudgy young woman with long blonde hair and blue eyes. "Her name is Tori Monroe. Does she happen to be staying here?"

Sarah looked at the picture, then shook her head. "No, I'm sorry. I've never seen her before."

The man stared at her for a long moment. She shifted on her feet, tempted to close the door in his face and bolt the lock.

"Well, it was a long shot," he said at last. "Her family heard she might be in the Berkshires this summer so they hired me to check all the boardinghouses, hotels, and inns to see if I can locate her."

"Why?"

"Her sister needs a kidney and Tori could possibly be a donor. They're desperate to find her."

Sarah didn't believe him, but she wasn't about to challenge his story. She just wanted him off her front porch. "I'm sorry. I can't help you."

He pulled a card out of his wallet and handed it to her, along with the photograph of the missing girl. "Here's my card. I'll be traveling around the area for a few more days so if you do see her, could you give me a call?"

"Of course," she said.

"Thank you, ma'am. Goodnight."

Sarah closed the door and turned the dead bolt, then looked at the card in her hand. According to the card, the stocky man was Tony Rosen, Private Investigator. There was a phone number listed but no address, fax number, or e-mail address.

As she walked back to her rocking chair, she looked at the photograph again. There was something vaguely familiar about the girl, although she couldn't put her finger on it. She turned on the lamp next to the chair for a closer look.

Katie came down the stairs wearing her nightgown and robe. Her long, dark hair was still damp from the shower. "I'm going to make myself a cup of tea before I go to bed. Do you want one?"

"No, thank you," Sarah said, looking up at her.

As Katie disappeared into the kitchen, Sarah stared after her, the blood pounding in her ears.

Katie's brown eyes had turned blue.

She looked at the picture again, the resemblance now becoming clear. The girl in the picture definitely was Katie. Her hair was a different length and color now, and she was much slimmer than the girl in the photograph, but it was Katie. The blue eyes confirmed it.

Sarah's head was still spinning when Katie headed back upstairs with her tea. Was Katie Campbell actually Tori Monroe? Sarah figured she must be wearing colored contact lenses to conceal her blue eyes and had obviously forgotten to put them back in after her shower.

But did she really have a sick sister somewhere who needed her kidney? According to what Katie had told her last night, she was an only child. Something didn't add up. Either Tony Rosen had been lying about why he was trying to find her or Katie had been lying about her identity all along.

Or both.

"Lord, help me figure this out," Sarah prayed aloud. "You brought her to me. What do you want me to do?"

But even as she asked the question, she knew the answer. She had to confront Katie with the photograph and demand the truth. But not yet.

She had some investigating to do first.

CHAPTER EIGHTEEN

The next morning, Sarah retrieved Katie's rental agreement from her desk and dialed the number of the professor Katie had listed as a reference at Northwestern University. She could hear a radio blaring from upstairs, so she knew that Katie wouldn't overhear the conversation.

"May I speak to Professor Galloway, please?" Sarah asked when his secretary answered the telephone.

"I'm sorry," the secretary said, "but Professor Galloway isn't available."

"Is there a good time to call? I really need to speak to him."

"I'm afraid he won't be back in his office until school starts again in September. He's teaching a course in Greece this summer."

"Then perhaps you could help me," Sarah said. "I'm calling about one of his graduate students. She listed him as a reference and I need to verify her information on the rental agreement."

"No problem. I have a list of all his graduate students. What's her name?"

"Katie Campbell."

"One moment please."

Sarah waited, her stomach tied in knots. She wondered why Katie hadn't told her Professor Galloway was in Greece when she'd listed him as a reference on the rental agreement. She supposed it was possible Katie didn't know about his trip, but that seemed unlikely.

"I'm sorry," the secretary said at last, "but I've reviewed the list twice and Professor Galloway doesn't have a graduate student by that name."

Sarah's heart sank, although she wasn't really surprised. "How about a student by the name of Tori Monroe?"

"Hold on and I'll check."

Now she knew why Katie hadn't told her about the professor's trip to Greece. She'd probably been hoping Sarah wouldn't check her references, but even if she had, the fact that the man was out of the country made him difficult to reach.

A few minutes later, the secretary came back on the line. "Professor Galloway did have a graduate student by the name of Victoria Monroe, but she dropped out of the program a few months ago."

So there it was. That confirmed her suspicion that Katie really was Tori Monroe. And if she'd dropped out of graduate school months ago, then she hadn't come to Maple Hill to write a thesis about Nathaniel Bradford.

So why had she come here?

It was possible that Professor Galloway might know the answer to that question. As her former advisor, he'd probably gotten to know her fairly well.

"Is there any way I can reach the professor in Greece?"

"I'm sorry," the secretary replied, "but Professor Galloway is actually leading an archeological dig in a remote area of the country. If it's an emergency, he can possibly be reached by messenger."

Sarah sighed. "No, this isn't an emergency. Thank you for your help."

She hung up the phone, her thoughts whirling as she dialed the next number on Katie's reference list. The telephone at her former employer's rang only one time before Sarah heard an automated voice in her ear.

"We're sorry, but the number you're trying to reach has been disconnected."

"That's convenient," Sarah muttered as she hung up the phone. Neither reference that the girl had listed was available, which seemed like more than a coincidence. Sarah supposed she could try to trace Katie's parents in South America, but that seemed an impossible mission. Especially if she'd lied about them, too.

Sarah walked into the kitchen and rinsed out her coffee cup, then placed it in the dish drainer before heading back to her sewing room. She always did her best thinking while she was working on a quilt. Pulling back a chair, she sat down in front of her father's quilt and began to snip the loose threads from the new fabric pieces she was about to add.

Now that she had proof the girl had lied on the rental agreement, she could ask her to leave immediately. Or she could pretend that nothing had happened and hope that Katie would eventually confide the truth. Neither one seemed very palatable to her.

After twenty minutes, Sarah realized there was really only one option. She set down her scissors, then headed upstairs and knocked on the girl's bedroom door.

CHAPTER NINETEEN

hen Katie opened the door, she had brown eyes again. "Good morning, Sarah. I didn't mean to sleep so late. I'd better run if I don't want to be late."

"We need to talk first."

The girl blinked at her tone. "Is something the matter?"

Sarah handed her the photograph the man had given her last night. "Why don't you tell me, Tori?"

All the color drained from the girl's face and she took a step backward. "What?"

"I know your name is Tori Monroe," Sarah said calmly.

Katie pushed the photograph back into Sarah's hand. "You've got it all wrong. I knew a girl named Tori Monroe in grad school, but I'm not her."

"I checked with Professor Galloway's office," Sarah continued. "There is no Katie Campbell enrolled in graduate school at Northwestern."

Katie raked a hand through her hair. "He's my former advisor. I have a new one now. A woman. Her name is Sharon Shepherd, but I don't have her summer phone number with me. That's why I listed Professor Galloway as a reference instead."

Sarah might have believed this story if she hadn't done her homework. It embarrassed her to realize how easily she'd been duped. That was the price of trusting people, but she didn't want to live any other way.

"Why did you come here, Katie?" Sarah asked her. "Or should I call you Tori?"

"I already told you," Katie cried. "I'm not Tori! Please just leave me alone."

Sarah took another step into the room. "Not until you tell me the truth."

"You already think you know the truth," she snapped, her cheeks flushed. "I wish I had never come here. It was so stupid…"

Sarah steeled herself against the pain she heard in the girl's voice, not willing to be taken in again. "You might be able to get a ride home."

Katie's head shot up. "What do you mean?"

"A private detective named Tony Rosen came to the door last night looking for you. He's the one who gave me the photograph."

Panic flared in her eyes. "Why didn't you tell me?" Katie bolted for the closet, pulling her suitcase out and tossing it on the bed.

This was no act. The girl was terrified.

"What are you doing?" Sarah asked.

"I've got to get out of here." She pulled clothes out of her dresser drawers and tossed them into the suitcase.

Sarah walked over and took her gently but firmly by the shoulders. "Wait, there's no need to panic. I told the man that I'd never seen you before. I didn't recognize you when he first showed me the picture."

Relief washed over Katie's face and she sagged in Sarah's grasp. Sarah helped her over to the bed, then waited while the girl collected herself.

"Do you want to tell me what's going on?" Sarah said gently. "Maybe I can help."

The girl shook head. "I wish you could, but I'm afraid no one can help me."

"Do you have a sister who might need a kidney transplant?"

Katie looked at Sarah like she was crazy. "No, why would you think that?" Then understanding dawned on her face. "Oh, is that why he said he was looking for me?"

Sarah nodded. "But I didn't believe his story for a minute. It wasn't until you came downstairs last night with blue eyes that I figured out you were the girl in the photograph. It took me a while to get over the shock, especially when I realized you've been lying to me this whole time."

"I'm so sorry," Katie said, sounding sincere. "I never meant to involve you in all this. I thought I could pull it off, but it's exhausting keeping track of all the lies."

"Then tell me the truth."

She sucked in a deep breath. "Katie is my middle name. Short for Kathleen. My full name is Victoria Kathleen Monroe. Campbell was my mother's maiden name."

"Why did you come to Maple Hill?"

"Because I'd planned the trip almost a year ago, when I was still in graduate school and writing my thesis about Nathaniel Bradford."

"What made you drop out?"

She was silent for so long that Sarah feared she wasn't going to answer. A tear dropped onto the quilt. Then another.

Sarah reached over and placed her hand on Katie's shoulder, not saying a word until the silent tears subsided.

At last, Katie spoke. "The truth is I have an ex-boyfriend, Evan Gould, who doesn't want to let me go. He followed me to Chicago. That's why I had to suddenly drop out of school and disappear again."

"Why didn't you go to the police?"

"They can't help me," Katie said, "I've learned that the hard way. Evan's got money and connections. I keep changing my cell phone number, but somehow he's always able to get my new number. Probably through the private detectives he hires. When Evan calls me I know that it's time to run again."

"So you're just going to keep running? You had to give up graduate school and I'm guessing you had to cut ties with your family, too."

Another tear trickled down Katie's cheek. "You don't understand. I don't know what else to do. I thought I could start over here, but…"

"Maybe you still can," Sarah said gently.

"Not if he's found me."

"There's no reason to think he's found you. Tony Rosen said he had information you were staying in the Berkshires, so he was checking out all the boardinghouses and hotels in the area."

"You mean this was a random check? He didn't know I was here?"

"If he had, he probably wouldn't have left without trying to talk to you."

Katie gave a slow nod. "You're right, but he'll still be showing that picture around town."

"You're living in my house and I didn't recognize you when he first showed me the photograph. I doubt anyone else will either."

A spark of hope lit her eyes. "Really?"

Sarah nodded, still wishing Katie would go to the police. But the girl was so panicked and fragile now she didn't want to push the issue. "You can keep living here like nothing has happened."

Tears welled in her eyes again, but this time they were tears of gratitude. "I don't know what to say."

"Then don't say anything." Sarah rose to her feet. "Just take a deep breath, go wash your face and take it a day at a time."

Katie glanced at her suitcase, then looked up at Sarah. "Are you sure you don't mind if I stay?"

"Of course not."

"Okay," Katie said weakly. "I'll stay. At least, for a little while longer."

Sarah breathed a silent sigh of relief. Everything finally made sense. Katie's odd appearance and behavior when she'd first arrived, her desperation to move in right away. "Do you want me to call you Katie or Tori?"

"Katie," she said without hesitation. "Katie Campbell. Tori Monroe was a stupid girl who doesn't exist anymore."

"Don't you think you're being a little hard on yourself?" Sarah asked. "Everyone makes mistakes."

"I know," Katie wiped her face with her hands. "How will I ever repay you, Sarah?"

"You don't owe me anything," Sarah told her. "Just know that you can always confide in me. I'm on your side."

CHAPTER TWENTY

Sarah walked into Magpie's Antiques the next evening, amazed at the transformation Maggie had made in the place in just a few days. There were antiques and collectibles filling almost every foot of space in the store except the narrow aisles where people congregated to browse or talk.

She waved to the twins who were handling the refreshment table in the corner, then saw Jason standing near a shelf of vintage books. She made her way over there. "This is even nicer than I imagined."

"I hope it's more profitable than I imagine," he quipped, then his face relaxed into a smile. "Maggie did a great job getting ready for her grand opening, didn't she?"

"She sure did." Sarah turned in a slow circle, taking in the display cases of dishes and glassware and the tables filled with antique toys. There were small pieces of furniture scattered about, too, along with an assortment of chamber pots and a bureau full of antique linens.

The linens reminded her of the two pillowcases Grandma Molly had embroidered with morning glories. Grandpa Noah had used them on his bed until they'd practically fallen apart. It was the only thing he'd had left of his wife after she disappeared, other than some clothes and their wedding photo.

Sarah still found it strange that her grandmother had had so few personal possessions. No letters from friends, photos from her childhood, or even a family Bible.

It was as if she didn't have a past before coming to Maple Hill. Or else she'd wanted to keep it a secret. Like Katie.

Only there was someone from Grandma Molly's past that Sarah knew about—Charles Harrison—her first husband and Sarah's biological grandfather. That was a lead she hadn't followed yet. Maybe it was time she started digging into his past too.

"I'd better go check on the girls," Jason said, stepping away from the bookshelf. "They're in charge of refreshments and I'm in charge of them."

She'd been so lost in her thoughts that his voice startled her. Sarah took a moment to collect herself, then looked around the store. "Where's Maggie?"

His smile widened. "In the back room showing a customer an antique baby carriage that wouldn't fit in here."

"You mean she has more things in the back, too?"

"She's been busy. I told her not to buy any more inventory until she's sold at least half the stuff in here."

Sarah watched him move toward the refreshment table, then she waved to Irene Stuart across the room. Most of the residents of Maple Hill would pass through this store in the next week or two, always excited to welcome a new business in town. She just hoped they bought something while they were here, too.

That reminded Sarah that she wanted to make a purchase or two to support Maggie. She moved to the bin of vintage buttons, always eager to add some to her supply. Buttons are often used to embellish quilts, and Sarah liked to have a wide variety on hand.

As she sorted through them, Katie approached her. "Hello, Sarah."

She hadn't seen the girl since last night and could tell by the dark circles under her eyes that Katie hadn't gotten much sleep.

"Hi." Sarah picked some small brass buttons from the bin. "How are you feeling today?"

"A little embarrassed," Katie said, her gaze dropping to the floor. "I can't believe I'm still here."

Sarah wasn't surprised. Katie had been running for so long it might take a while for her to feel safe and settled. "Is there someplace else you'd rather be?"

Katie slowly lifted her gaze. "There's probably someplace else I should be, but I'm not strong enough to go there."

Her tone more than her words made Sarah lose interest in the buttons. "Where is that?"

Katie shook her head. "Forget it. I'm tired. I don't even know what I'm saying."

Sarah didn't want to let it go, but this wasn't the time or place to pursue Katie's meaning. "Did you tell Jason and Maggie about your problem?"

Katie nodded. "I didn't want to put you in the position of having to lie for me, so I told them my real name and why I've been hiding my identity. They were really nice about it. Nicer than I deserve."

Before Sarah could reply, Rita approached them through the crowd. "Be still my heart," she cried. "Is this place rocking or what?"

Sarah laughed, noticing that Katie couldn't help but smile at Rita's exuberance. "Definitely rocking. Have you found anything you want?"

"Honey, the problem is finding something I *don't* want." Rita slung her red leather bag over her shoulder. "But I've set a money limit for myself tonight so I don't go overboard." She turned to Katie.

"For three women living in the same house, we sure don't see each other very much, do we?"

"I guess we're all busy," Sarah said, and saw John Peabody—pastor of Bridge Street Church—making a bee-line for her. Sarah could guess his mission before he even reached their group.

"Hello, ladies," John said, his green eyes twinkling with delight. He was fifty-four, a widower, having lost his wife in a car accident ten years before, tall, with dark hair threaded with silver and beginning to thin at the crown. Sarah liked his gentle spirit and the easy smile that made everyone feel welcome in his church.

"This is my pastor, John Peabody," Sarah said. "And these are my boarders, Rita and Katie."

"It's nice to meet you," he said, reaching out to shake their hands. "Isn't this shop a nice addition to our little town?"

"It sure is," Rita said. "I'm leaving for Canada soon, so I'm glad I got a chance to see it."

"At least stick around until Thursday," John said. "That's the day of our church youth group's annual bake sale."

Sarah grinned. "I knew you were going to find a way to work that into the conversation."

"Well, I wouldn't want anyone to miss it."

"How are the plans for the bake sale coming along?" Sarah asked.

"Not too bad," he said. "Our list of baked goods is a little short, but I'm not worried. Congregation members always come through in the end."

"Martha and I are getting together with our granddaughters tomorrow to do some power baking," Sarah told him.

"Wonderful!"

"Can nonmembers donate baked goods too?" Katie asked.

"Of course," he replied. "All donations are welcome."

"What's the fund-raiser for?" Rita asked.

"We use the money we raise to send the church youth group on mission trips. Last year they helped out at a homeless shelter in Boston."

Rita nodded. "I've done that a few times myself. It's a great experience, no matter what your age."

Sarah saw Amy motioning to her from across the store. "Excuse me, please. I think my granddaughter needs something."

She wove her way through the crowd until she reached the refreshment table and saw the empty punch bowl. "What is it, girls? Do you need more punch?"

Audrey shook her head. "Dad's already getting some for us."

"I've got something for you, Grandma." Amy pulled her backpack from under the table and unzipped the top. "Doris waved me down when I was riding my bike by her house today. She asked me to give this to you."

"What is it?" Sarah asked, half expecting a piece of jewelry.

Instead, Amy pulled an envelope out of her backpack and handed it to Sarah. "Doris said you might want to read this."

Sarah looked down at the letter in her hands. The faded postmark read December 18, 1920.

CHAPTER TWENTY-ONE

The following afternoon, Sarah and her granddaughters stood in Martha's kitchen with Amy and Audrey on one side of the long pine table and Martha's three granddaughters on the other.

"What shall we make for the bake sale?" Martha asked them.

Pru pushed up her glasses. "Chocolate chip cookies. I found a great recipe on the Web last night."

"No, let's make brownies," Lexie said. "The more chocolate the better."

"Chocolate gives you pimples," Trina said. "How about snicker-doodles instead?"

Martha turned to the twins. "Audrey? Amy? Do you have any favorites?"

Sarah watched Amy slip her cell phone into the pocket of her jeans. She'd been texting almost nonstop since they'd arrived.

"Maybe peanut brittle?" Audrey looked around the table. "Or peanut butter cookies? Everybody likes those."

"Not me," Amy mumbled so softly that no one but Sarah could hear her.

"Pru is allergic to peanuts," Lexie announced.

"I break out in hives all over," Pru explained. "It's not a good look for me."

The girls giggled, breaking some of the tension in the room, as Martha looked over at Sarah and raised her hands in surrender. "We need to make a decision or we'll be baking till midnight."

"You girls can make more than one kind of cookie," Sarah told them. "There are seven of us, so we could bake up quite a variety."

Martha's granddaughters exchanged furtive glances with each other, then Pru cleared her throat and said, "Actually, we were talking earlier and decided we'd like to bake everything ourselves."

Martha blinked in surprise. "You don't want our help?"

"No." Trina straightened to her full height, which was a good two inches shorter than her cousins. "We're all old enough to do it."

"I think it's a great idea." Audrey's blue eyes flashed with excitement. "Besides, the kitchen will get too crowded if seven of us try to bake in here."

Martha smiled at Sarah. "She has a point."

"All right," Sarah said, "we'll let you girls do the baking, but let us help you get organized first."

"That's a good idea," Martha agreed. "Figure out what you want to make so I can be certain we have all the ingredients. Then you're on your own."

All five girls huddled together, exchanging lively whispers. A few moments later, they announced their choices.

"We're going to make chocolate chip cookies," Pru said, "and brownies."

"Caramel brownies," Lexie amended as the other girls nodded in agreement.

"Good choices," Sarah replied.

Amy cleared her throat. "I think we should divide into teams."

"You mean, like a cooking contest?" Trina asked.

Amy nodded. "If we have to bake, we might as well make it fun."

Lexie looked around the table. "I'm game, but there are five of us, so the teams won't be even."

"That's all right." Trina walked over to stand beside Amy. "The two of us will go up against the three of you."

"And our grandmas can be the judges," Amy added.

Martha clapped her hands together. "All my cookbooks are in the cupboard in the corner and you'll find all the ingredients you need in the pantry and the refrigerator."

Sarah watched the girls take opposite sides of the table. "Are you sure you girls can handle it?"

"Don't worry, Grandma," Audrey said, "our team will be fine."

"Yeah," Lexie said, "we got this."

"Okay, everybody ready?" Trina said, assuming a runner's stance.

Pru leaned toward the refrigerator. "Set."

"Go!" Amy shouted and then sprinted toward the pantry with the cookie recipe in her hand.

"We'll be in the living room," Martha said as the girls raced around the kitchen gathering their supplies. "Just give a shout if you need us."

Sarah and Martha exchanged wary smiles as they walked out of the kitchen and down the hallway, meeting Ernie in the hallway. At sixty-seven, he wasn't as spry as he used to be, but his thick black hair and neatly trimmed mustache didn't have a hint of gray. He wore lightweight tan coveralls that zipped up the front and protected his clothes from oil and grease when he tinkered with cars.

"Is it safe to go in the kitchen?" he asked as the girls' high-pitched chatter filled the air. "I was going to fill up my thermos before I head out to the shop, but it sounds like a henhouse in there."

"Enter at your own risk," Sarah warned him, glad to see he looked well. A little thinner, perhaps, but Gerry had always lost a few pounds every summer too.

He scowled. "I should probably cut down on caffeine anyway."

Martha patted her husband's arm as he passed by, then she and Sarah proceeded to the living room. The

Maplethorpes lived in a Cape-Cod-style house with Pennsylvania Dutch furnishings and artwork. The polished hardwood floors gleamed, a testament to Martha's diligence as a housekeeper. Sarah took a seat on the sofa while Martha retrieved her crocheting bag and settled into the recliner.

"I have to admit," Martha said with a chuckle. "I'm a little nervous leaving them in there alone." As if on cue, a large crash sounded from the kitchen.

"Don't worry," Trina shouted down the hallway. "That was just a baking sheet. Nothing is broken."

Sarah smiled. "This morning could be a little nerve-wracking, but the best way to learn something is to do it yourself."

"That's true." Martha set the ball of thread in her lap and began making a filet stitch around the edge of her tablecloth. "I certainly had my share of kitchen disasters after Ernie and I were married. It's a wonder he survived."

"How's Ernie doing?" Sarah asked her. "I think he looks pretty good."

"Do you?" Martha asked, relief flashing in her eyes. "That's good to hear. I finally decided to take matters into my own hands and made him a doctor's appointment for next Monday."

"Has he agreed to go?"

She sighed. "He grumbled quite a bit when I told him about it, so I don't know."

Sarah looked toward the kitchen, tempted to take a peek and see how the girls were doing. There hadn't been any crashes in the last two minutes, so maybe they had things under control.

"Any new information about your Grandma Molly?" Martha asked, picking at a knot in her crochet thread.

"That's what I've been wanting to tell you." Sarah reached into her purse and pulled out the envelope Amy had delivered to her last evening. "Doris Hatch found a letter from December 18, 1920, among her aunt's things."

"Oooh, read it to me," Martha leaned back in the recliner and put her feet up.

Sarah unfolded the fragile paper. *"Dear Cleo, I hope this letter finds you in good health. I hear you're doing well at boarding school. I just wanted to write and tell you there's a good chance your father will be a town selectman after all... Noah Drayton, the man who cheated your father out of the office, has misplaced his wife. She disappeared about a week ago and everyone suspects Drayton of doing her harm. Now some people are calling for his ouster from office...."*

Martha snorted. *"Some people.* She means the Turnquist clan."

"Exactly," Sarah replied, then continued reading the letter. *"Your father's already been suggested as his replacement since the election was so close. There are other reports about Mr. Drayton's violent temper, including a brawl that occurred between him and another man, Horace Lynch, just hours before his wife disappeared. Apparently, Mrs. Drayton's young son tried to stop the fight by throwing a baseball at Lynch but hit his father instead."*

"Why do you suppose they were fighting?" Martha asked.

"I don't know." Sarah set the letter in her lap, "but it certainly makes Lynch look suspicious. I intend to find out more about him." After she took the twins home, she was going to head straight to the historical society to scan the old newspaper archives once more.

"Does the letter say anything else?"

"Nothing important." She placed it back in her purse. "At least this..."

"Listen," Martha sat up in her chair. "Do you hear that?"

"I don't hear anything."

"Exactly." Martha set her crocheting aside. "It's awfully quiet in that kitchen. I wonder what those girls are up to."

The front door opened and Ernie walked inside carrying a silver thermos. "Is it safe yet?"

"That's what we're trying to determine." Martha rose from her chair. "Do you still want that coffee?"

"I can get it." As he turned toward the hallway, Ernie stumbled and fell, almost hitting his head on the stair rail.

"Ernie," Martha cried, moving toward him.

Sarah hurried over to them, hoping he wasn't hurt. She looked on the floor, but saw nothing he could have tripped on, not even a floor rug.

"Are you all right?" Martha asked as she helped her husband to his feet.

"I'm fine," he said gruffly, brushing her off him. "There's no need to fuss."

"What happened?" Martha asked, her brow creased. She pressed her lips together.

"I fell down," he said, shooing them away with his hands. "Must have lost my balance. I'm an old man now, you know."

Sarah didn't say anything, but she knew it was a bigger deal than he could admit. In high school, Ernie had been a talented, coordinated athlete. He still exercised every day by walking around town or, if it was too cold, climbing up and down the stairs in the house twenty to thirty times.

A man in his condition didn't just fall down for no reason. Something wasn't right.

"I'll be in the shop," he muttered, then walked out the front door without another word.

Martha turned to Sarah. "Do you see what I mean?"

"Yes," Sarah said softly.

"He's going to that doctor's appointment next week, even if I have to drag him there kicking and screaming," Martha said. "I need to know what's wrong with him before I go crazy."

Sarah couldn't argue with her, although she understood Ernie's trepidation. It seemed easier to ignore problems and hope they'd go away than to discover your life might be changed forever.

A few minutes later, Lexie appeared in the living room. She had flour dusting her hair and a spot of chocolate on her cheek, but other than that she was no worse for wear. Sarah hoped Martha could say the same about her kitchen.

"How are you girls doing?" Martha asked, recovering. "Almost done?"

"We sure are." She grinned. "Are you ready to declare a winner?"

"Maybe we should make it a tie," Sarah whispered to Martha as they followed Lexie back to the kitchen. "Otherwise, some of our granddaughters might stop speaking to us."

"Good idea." Martha whispered back.

When Sarah saw the kitchen, she breathed a sigh of relief. Flour dusted the counters and dirty dishes filled the sink, but it wasn't a total disaster. Two pans sat on the table with clean dish towels covering them. "Ah," Sarah exclaimed as she and Martha approached the kitchen table, "it looks like we're going to have an unveiling. I'm excited to see how it all turned out."

Audrey tried to stifle a giggle as she, Lexie, and Pru stood knotted together in front of their tray. Trina and Amy remained stone-faced on the other side of the table.

"Here are the caramel brownies," Pru announced, picking up the dish towel from the first pan. "What do you think?"

Sarah took one look at the fudgy brownies laced with golden ribbons of caramel. "Very nice."

"And a little crispy around the edges," Martha added, "but I happen to like my brownies crispy."

"So do I," Sarah said as Audrey cut a small portion for each of them.

Sarah took a bite of the brownie as the girls waited expectantly for her verdict. "Delicious. Nice and chewy in the middle, just like they should be."

Martha nodded her agreement. "You did a wonderful job."

They turned to the next tray, but neither Amy nor Trina made a move to unveil their cookies.

"Well," Martha said when they just stood there, "aren't you going to show us what you made?"

"Go on," Pru prodded, a hint of sympathy in her voice, "they're going to find out soon enough."

After a moment, Amy pulled the dish towel off the pan. Lexie and Audrey burst out laughing.

Sarah leaned closer to get a look at the melted golden brown mess on the pan. She touched the surface of it with her finger and found it hard as a rock. There was no way they could declare this contest a tie. "Did you make peanut brittle after all?"

The three other girls now doubled over, their giggles filling the air.

Trina lifted her chin in the air. "It's not that funny."

Martha tried to pry off a piece with a spatula but it was stuck solid. "It can't be peanut brittle. I see chocolate chips in there."

"It's *supposed* to be chocolate chip cookies," Amy burst out. "We followed the recipe exactly, didn't we, Trina?"

"Exactly! Maybe the recipe was wrong."

"There has to be an explanation," Sarah said, looking around at the kitchen.

The flour and sugar canisters were sitting out on the counter, along with clear plastic bowls of brown sugar and powdered sugar.

"Here," Martha said, finally prying a small piece loose with the edge of a knife. She handed part of it to Sarah and popped the rest in her mouth.

Pure sugar. It was so sweet Sarah found it difficult to swallow as she watched Martha spit her piece into a napkin.

Sarah cleared her throat, "I think I know what happened." She walked over and picked up the bowl of powdered sugar. The bowl wasn't labeled, but anyone familiar with baking would recognize powdered sugar.

That ruled out Amy.

"I'm guessing you two used this as your flour," Sarah said.

"No way," Trina cried, then turned to Amy whose face had turned bright red. "Or did we?"

"We did," Amy said. "I thought it was flour. It looks like flour—I mean, they're both white and powdery." She dropped her head. "Okay, I'm really stupid."

Sarah reached out to give her shoulders a comforting squeeze. "You're not stupid, dear."

"Yeah," Trina said, "I didn't realize either."

Pru nibbled off a bite of brittle cookie. "I don't think it's all *that* bad." Then she coughed and spit it out. "Okay, it's bad."

The other girls started laughing again and, after a few moments, even Amy smiled a little.

Sarah looked up at Martha and saw her friend glancing toward the window. She followed her gaze and saw Ernie walking across the backyard toward the dumpster. He faltered in his steps once but steadied himself before continuing on.

Sarah's heart went out to her friend, well aware of the kind of worry that was nibbling at Martha and testing her faith to trust God in all things.

"Lord, please watch over Ernie and Martha," she prayed silently. "Give them the guidance and strength they need to face whatever may lie ahead."

CHAPTER TWENTY-TWO

An hour later, Sarah was enjoying the quiet serenity of the historical society as she sat in front of the microfilm machine. It was fun spending time with the twins, but a little exhausting. Pru had invited Audrey and Amy to help with the church bake sale tomorrow and the girls had accepted; Sarah had been wanting to get them involved with the church youth group and this seemed like the perfect opportunity.

She leaned back in her chair, waiting for the old issues of the *Maple Hill Monitor* to load onto the machine. After giving it some thought, she'd decided to start with January 1921 and go from there. If Horace Lynch had fought with Grandpa Noah only hours before Molly disappeared, he had to have been a suspect in the case. Even if the police had eventually cleared him, there might be something they'd missed. She just hoped the newspaper reporters hadn't been so focused on implicating Grandpa Noah that they'd ignored everyone else who might have been involved.

A headline jumped out at her, making her sit up straight in her chair. *LYNCH CLEARED IN DISAPPEARANCE OF MOLLY DRAYTON.*

Sarah checked the date on the newspaper. January 14, 1921, which was approximately one month after Grandma Molly vanished without a trace.

She leaned forward to read the article. "*Horace Lynch,*" she whispered under her breath, "*formerly of Maple Hill, has recently been found and cleared as a suspect in the disappearance of Mrs. Noah Drayton. Her husband, Mr. Noah Drayton, had been demanding police question Lynch about Mrs. Drayton's disappearance.*

Drayton claimed he hired Lynch, a handyman, on December 12 to do repair work on his house, but when he discovered Lynch rifling through his desk, the two men scuffled. Drayton bound Lynch with rope, but claimed he let him go after the man pleaded financial hardship.

Authorities have just learned that Lynch was arrested for public drunkenness in nearby Savoy, Massachusetts, that same evening and spent the next three days in jail, giving him an irrefutable alibi for the time in question. According to police, Mr. Noah Drayton remains the prime suspect in his wife's disappearance."

She looked up from the computer to see Irene approaching her. "Find what you were looking for?"

"Yes and no," Sarah said, trying to tamp down her disappointment. "I found the information I wanted, but it doesn't get me any closer to discovering what happened to my grandmother."

"It's quite the puzzle, isn't it?"

Sarah nodded, as she calculated her next move. So far, she wasn't having any luck finding out what happened to Grandma Molly after she disappeared from Maple Hill. Maybe she needed to research Molly's life *before* she arrived there. And that meant looking for information about her first husband, Charles Harrison.

She glanced up at Irene. "What's the best resource to find information about soldiers who served in World War One?"

"Soldiers from Maple Hill?"

"No," Sarah said, "Boston." That was about all she knew about Grandma Molly's first marriage, that they'd lived in Boston before Charles Harrison had gone off to France to fight in the war. He'd been killed in battle in November of 1916 and been buried in France, leaving his young wife and two-year-old son behind to fend for themselves.

"We've got a military database on the computer." Irene led her over to the computer workstation. "There's an icon for it on the desktop. Just click on it and you'll see more information about World War One than you ever imagined." She breathed a wistful sigh. "I love those doughboys."

Sarah sat down as Irene walked off to help another patron. She opened the database, then scanned all the links until she found the one she wanted. "Massachusetts casualty lists," she said softly. "World War One. 1916."

She clicked on the link, which produced a long, sobering list of casualties for that year. Not only soldiers who had been killed in battle, but those who had been captured, wounded, or reported missing. Amazingly, the list also included the next of kin for each soldier, as well as his hometown.

She typed the name Charles Harrison into the search box, then waited for a hit. It took only a second.

Corporal Charles James Harrison. Wounded. October 16, 1916. Bridgeport, Connecticut.

Sarah blinked. That couldn't be right. He'd been killed in November, not wounded in October. And he'd been from Boston, not Bridgeport. Unless there was more than one Charles James Harrison. That was certainly a possibility, but why weren't both of them on the casualty list?

She closed the Web site, staring at the screen as she pondered this latest development. Then something caught her eye.

"Irene," Sarah called out as the director walked by.

"Yes?" Irene moved toward her, shifting the books in her arms.

"What's this?" She pointed to another icon on the computer screen.

Irene's eyes widened. "Oh, that's fun! The board of directors just approved the funds for a monthly subscription to an online genealogy site. It's pretty pricey, but for the data it provides, it's well worth it."

"How does it work?"

"Just input a name, along with any vital statistics you know about the person, like birth date or date of death. It will search literally thousands of genealogy Web sites, both public and private, and list all the hits on that name."

Sarah's heart fluttered. Could it be that simple? Grandma Molly had been twenty-four years old when she disappeared, which meant she'd been born in 1896. As she typed *Molly Hollis Harrison Drayton* into the search box, she tried not to get her hopes up, but her fingers still trembled.

Then she waited. And waited. The small hourglass on the screen told her the computer was still searching for a match. *Thank you, God, Sarah prayed, for giving us this wonderful technology.*

Like most things in life, there were both good and bad things about the Internet, but her grandfather and father had never had access to this kind of information, literally at the click of a button. Maybe if they had, they would have found Molly.

At last, a lone link appeared on the screen. *Harrison Family Forest.* Sarah smiled—her smile widened when she reached the Web page and found not only Grandma Molly and Charles Harrison on the family tree, but her father as well.

Charles James Harrison was born on June 28, 1892, in Scranton, Pennsylvania. He died on November 2, 1916, in Bridgeport, Connecticut. Spouse: Molly Hollis. Children: William James Harrison.

"Weird," Sarah breathed, realizing the Charles Harrison from Bridgeport listed in the military database had to be the same one listed here. But he'd died in France, not Connecticut. At least, that's what Grandma Molly had told Grandpa Noah.

Sarah noticed a way to e-mail the owner of the Web site. She clicked on the e-mail button, then wrote a short message.

Hello, my name is Sarah Drayton Hart. I'm looking for any information you have about Charles Harrison and Molly Hollis Harrison, who were married in 1914. Please call me as soon as possible. Then she listed both her cell phone number and home phone number on the e-mail before hitting the send button.

Now all she could do was wait.

When Sarah returned home that evening, she stopped by the mailbox to pick up the mail, then thumbed through the envelopes on her way to the house. There was nothing urgent, so she could put them aside for now and spend the rest of the evening working on the quilt. That, more than anything, would help her sort out all the puzzle pieces swirling around in her head.

She carried the mail into her sewing room and set it on the desk, pulling a new quilting magazine from the stack. The articles in this particular magazine helped her stay current on the newest quilting techniques, and it even had a special section on quilt restoration.

She walked over to the table to assess the progress she'd made so far. The six irreparably tattered fabric pieces had been carefully removed, leaving gaping spots of yellowish white foundation fabric. Now she was ready to begin the process of adding the new pieces. She'd already selected them from her closet, matching the new fabrics as closely as possible in color and texture to the original ones.

Now the trick was to maintain the vintage integrity of the quilt. New fabric would stick out like a sore thumb on the ninety-year-old quilt top. The fabric needed to be aged, and she knew just the technique to do it.

Gathering the new fabric remnants she'd chosen, Sarah returned to the kitchen and set them on the counter near the stove. Then she filled a pot with water and placed it on a burner to boil.

When the water bubbled in the pot, she added three tea bags and let them steep for about five minutes. Then she moved the pot off the burner and reached for the yellow cotton fabric that sat at the top of the stack. Sarah dropped it into the pot, using a wooden spoon to stir it so the fabric was fully submerged.

Tea-staining was a simple and inexpensive way to age new fabrics. Because different colors could bleed in hot water, it was impossible to soak all the fabrics together. Sarah knew the longer she left the yellow fabric soaking in the tea, the darker it would become. She'd even soaked fabrics overnight to achieve a desired effect.

Thirty minutes ought to do it, she thought, reaching out to set the stove timer. Once the yellow fabric looked aged enough to match the original piece, she'd rinse it in cool water several times, then hang it on the clothesline to dry.

While she waited for the stove timer to go off, Sarah returned to the sewing room and sat down at the table. There were several squares on the quilt top with small holes that could be repaired. Sarah would use fusible web to apply a piece of new fabric to the back of the original square, matching the color and texture closely enough to make the repair undetectable.

Sarah's gaze went to her first challenge, a two-inch square of striped blue and white silk. She was fairly certain the fabric had come from an old campaign ribbon and the hole in the piece was centered right on a blue and a white stripe. She'd have to piece together some white silk and some blue before carefully positioning the patch and fusing it to the back of the original piece. Otherwise the stripes would be crooked.

Reaching for her seam ripper, Sarah began to take out the stitches holding the silk square in place. As the fabric piece loosened, she glimpsed something unusual in the half-inch seam allowance that had been hidden before. It looked like part of an election slogan, confirming her earlier guess that this piece of fabric had come from a campaign ribbon.

When Sarah removed the last stitch, she pulled the silk square closer to read the words. *MAYER FOR MAYOR! He'll bring new hope to New Hope.*

Interesting. She flipped the square over. There was no date on it or any indication of where the town of New Hope was located. Curious, she retrieved the oversize atlas from the desk and opened it to Massachusetts. All the towns and their populations were listed along the bottom edge of the page, but the print was so tiny she had to lean over the desk to read it.

Newbury, Newburyport, New Lenox, New Marlboro. Sarah straightened. No New Hope.

So where had the campaign ribbon come from? Had Grandma Molly included the fabric in the quilt because it was special to her? Perhaps the Mayer campaigning for office was a good friend or relative. Someone she might go to in a time of trouble...Picking up the silk square, Sarah began to look at it in a new light. She might have just found another clue.

According to Grandpa Noah, Molly had been orphaned as a teenager and had no other family. But what if that hadn't been true? What if she hadn't always lived in Boston, but somewhere else?

Like New Hope.

Sarah sat down with the atlas, turning to Connecticut first. If Charles Harrison really came from Bridgeport, perhaps the town of New Hope was close by. But a quick scan of the towns invalidated that theory. There was no New Hope, Connecticut.

The next logical step was to find all the towns called New Hope in the United States. For that, she'd have to go state by state. Starting with the A's. She reached for her clip-on magnifying lenses, then turned to Alabama and began searching through the list of towns.

There it was. New Hope, Alabama. Population 385. Located in Madison County. She used the grid numbers to find the town on the map, then used a yellow highlighter to mark it.

Sarah searched through four more states before finding another New Hope, this one was located in Colusa County in northern California, population 5,580. She found that town on the map and marked it, too.

Four states later, she found a New Hope, Iowa. Only thirty-five states to go.

The stove timer dinged, making Sarah jump. She'd forgotten all about her aging fabric. She hurried into the kitchen and used the wooden spoon to lift the tea-stained yellow fabric out of the pot.

"New Hope," she said aloud, feeling closer than she ever had before to solving the case. "How fitting."

CHAPTER TWENTY-THREE

The next morning, Sarah picked up the twins and drove them to Bridge Street Church. The pastor and the youth group had already set up several of the long tables from the church basement in the parking lot and erected a hand-painted sandwich board near the street that read: *Bridge Street Church Bake Sale, Help Us Help Others.*

"Wow," Audrey said from the back seat as they parked next to the church. "There are a lot of kids."

Sarah glanced at Amy beside her, who looking apprehensive as she searched the crowd. "I don't see Lexie or Pru or Trina. Maybe we should stay in the car until they get here."

"I'm sure they'll be here soon," Sarah said, picking up the tub of cookies she'd made. "One of you girls needs to carry that box in the back seat."

Katie had done some baking last night, long after Sarah had gone to bed. She'd left a small box of assorted cookies on the counter this morning with a note asking Sarah to take them to the bake sale. Sarah had taken a peek inside at the white truffles and dark chocolate cookies.

"I've got it," Audrey said, as she pulled the box onto her lap.

"Some of the kids are starting to stare at us." Amy shrank down in her seat. "Okay, now they're *all* staring."

"They're probably just curious because they haven't seen you before." Sarah knew Jason and Maggie wanted to attend services at Bridge Street Church, but they'd been so overwhelmed by the move that they hadn't made it there yet. "This is a small town, so anyone new is bound to generate some excitement."

Audrey unbuckled her seatbelt. "I think they're staring because we're just sitting here like a couple of idiots. Come on, Amy, let's go." They all climbed out of the car and walked over to the tables, Amy trailing a few feet behind Sarah and Audrey.

John walked up to them, a smile wreathing his face. "Hello, Sarah. These must be the twins I've heard so much about."

Some of the other kids edged closer as Sarah made the introductions. "This is Amy," she said, placing a hand on the girl's shoulder, "and this is Audrey. Girls, this is Pastor Peabody."

"I'm so happy to meet you," he said, shaking each one's hand in turn. "We'd love to have you stay and help us with the bake sale today if you're free."

Neither girl said anything, so Sarah answered for them. "Martha's granddaughters have already invited them to help, so they're planning to spend the day here."

"Wonderful," he said and turned around to call one of the boys to him. "Cody, come over here please."

A gangly boy who looked about fourteen ambled over to the table. "Yeah?"

"Cody, this is Amy and her sister Audrey. They just moved to town, so I'd like you to introduce them to everybody."

He shrugged. "Okay."

She watched Cody take the twins over to the group of kids waiting by the tables. It was tempting to move closer so she could hear what they were saying.

"They'll be just fine," John said. "I'll keep an eye on them for you."

"Thank you."

"Now may I interest you in some baked goods?"

"You certainly may," Sarah said, walking over to peruse the offerings. "That's the advantage of showing up at a bake sale early. You get to choose from the widest selection."

The cookies and bars cost a quarter each, and the youth group supplied paper plates and plastic wrap so customers could pick a variety of goodies. Sarah filled three plates, one for herself, one for Jason, and one for her father.

Martha walked up to her as Sarah waited in line to pay.

"We finally made it," Martha said as her granddaughters placed their baked goods on the table. "Pru is always running late. I had to honk the horn three times."

"Amy will be glad to see them. She was a little worried your girls might not show up."

Martha grinned. "If there are teenage boys around, my girls won't be far away." Sarah glanced over at the clutch of young people. Audrey and Amy stood on the perimeter of the circle, both looking a little uncomfortable. "I'll take the twins home after the bake sale," Martha said. "I have to pick up my gang anyway, so there's no reason for both of us to make a trip."

"Sounds good to me."

"I'll see you later," Martha said, heading for the cookie table.

"Bye," Sarah called after her, finally reaching the front of the line. She finished making her purchases, then headed back to her car.

Five minutes later, she walked into Jason's office, greeted by the scent of fresh paint. Sarah took a moment to admire Katie's neat handiwork. "Very nice. I love the color."

"Thanks," Jason said, swiveling his office chair toward her. "What brings you here?"

She held up the cookie plate in her hand. "I come bearing gifts," Sarah edged around the maze of stacked boxes that led to his desk, then pushed a pile of file folders off one corner to make room for the plate. "It looks like you could use a break."

He sighed. "It's going to take me a month just to go through all of these files. I didn't realize when I took over the guy's practice that he was so disorganized."

"Here," Sarah said, removing the plastic wrap, "have a brownie."

He laughed as he took the brownie from her. "Just like old times."

"I know," Sarah said with a sigh. "Your father always said I was spoiling you kids, but I hated to see either you or Jenna hurting. I never said I was a perfect mother."

"Hey, I'm not complaining."

"Audrey helped make these," Sarah told him as he took a bite of the brownie. "Amy's batch of cookies didn't turn out too well."

"They told us all about their baking adventures at the Maplethorpe house. It sure is nice to hear them laughing again."

"They're meeting more kids at the bake sale today. That should help them with their homesickness as much as anything."

Sarah turned around to move a box from a chair so she could sit down. "What's in all these boxes anyway?"

Jason rolled his eyes. "Anything you could possibly imagine. I don't think the guy ever threw anything away."

"Do you mind if I look?"

"Help yourself," Jason said, reaching for another brownie. "But if you find a legal document, like a prenuptial agreement or a will, let me know. I've found a few of those mixed in with the junk, otherwise I'd just throw it all out."

Sarah spent the next hour digging for treasure. Among other things, she found a Maple Hill telephone directory from 1954, a book of green stamps, and a gift certificate to a store that had closed fifteen years before.

"It looks like a lot of these things belong in Maggie's store," Sarah said as she pulled out a *TV Guide* dated 1972.

"No way," Jason said. "We'd have to rent another storage unit to hold all this stuff."

As she dug deeper into the box in front of her, Sarah's gaze fell on a folded, yellowed document.

She lifted it out of the box. "Look at this."

Jason walked over to take a closer look. "What is it?"

"It looks like a plat map of Maple Hill." She carefully unfolded the map, aware of how easily the brittle paper could tear. Then she saw the date in a corner of the map. "It's from 1915."

"Maggie would love this," Jason said as he perused the map. "I wonder if it's worth anything."

"She could put it in her shop and find out," Sarah replied, "but we should check with Irene at the historical society first. She might like to add this to their collection."

Jason frowned down at the map. "Something about it doesn't look quite right."

She followed his gaze. "What?"

"There's no highway, for one thing." Then Jason pointed to a square on the map. "And it's not very accurate. It lists our house address as 114 Bristol Street. We live at 106."

Sarah felt a wave of excitement. "Memorial Drive Highway."

"What?"

Sarah paused. "A few years after World War One, the town put in a new highway that cut straight through the center of Maple Hill. They named it Memorial Drive in honor of war veterans."

Jason gave a slow nod. "They probably had to remove some houses to make room for the highway and the right-of-way on each side of it. It intersects with Bristol Street, so it makes sense the addresses would change."

"It intersects Elm Street too." Sarah turned back to the map, her finger trailing along the grid until she found Elm Street. "The house that stands at 212 Elm Street on this map," she said, "is actually 204 Elm Street now. Do you know what that means?"

"It means the address you found in that quilt *wasn't* the house where Doris Hatch lives?"

"That's right. I've been looking for Grandma Molly in all the wrong places."

CHAPTER TWENTY-FOUR

Hattie Hepperson was the oldest person in Maple Hill. At 102 years of age, she still lived in the house on Elm Street where she'd been born. She'd never married, but had plenty of nieces and nephews to keep her busy. Sarah had known Hattie all her life, having accompanied her mother countless times to Hattie's beauty shop in the basement of 204 Elm.

When Sarah pulled up to the house, she saw Hattie out on her front lawn, a small canvas sack attached to her walker. Hattie reached inside, scooped up a handful of birdseed and tossed it to the waiting robins and chickadees that surrounded her. Sarah lingered on the sidewalk in front of the house until Hattie finished feeding the birds, not wanting to scare them away.

"Are you here for a haircut?" Hattie called out, a wide smile on her face, "I might be a little shaky with the scissors these days, but I'm willing to risk it if you are."

Sarah laughed as she approached her. The birds didn't even seem to be aware of her arrival. They were too focused on searching for any remaining seeds on the ground. "No haircut for me today. I've come for a completely different reason."

"Well, I'm happy to see you again, whatever the reason," Hattie told her. "I don't get much company these days other than family. Most of my friends are dead and waiting for me to hurry up and join them. This rickety old body doesn't seem quite ready to go yet."

Hattie was incredibly spry for her age and still attended Bridge Street Church every Sunday, thanks to the church van that drove around town and picked up those too old or infirm to drive themselves.

"You look great," Sarah told her. "How do you feel?"

"Pretty good for an old gal. How's your dad doing?"

"He's well," Sarah said, "although his memory isn't too reliable anymore."

"I don't mind when the bad memories get fuzzy," Hattie told her. "It's the good ones I don't want to forget."

Sarah prayed that Hattie's memories about Grandma Molly would be clear. "I came here today for more than a visit. I'm hoping to solve a mystery."

Hattie raised a thin white eyebrow. "I can't wait to hear it."

"Would you like to go inside?" Sarah asked her. "I don't want to make you stand out here in the sun."

"I don't mind at all," Hattie told her. "The warmth feels good on my creaky bones, and at my age I can use all the vitamin D I can get."

Sarah smiled, figuring a little vitamin D wouldn't hurt her, either. She'd been spending a lot of time cooped up in her sewing room lately.

"I'm looking for information about my grandfather's wife, Molly Drayton," Sarah said. "Do you remember her?"

Hattie nodded. "It was a terrible thing, her disappearing. I was eleven years old when it happened and I remember having nightmares about it. For a while there were rumors that a madman was roaming Maple Hill and snatching young women out of their beds."

Sarah could only imagine the terror that must have struck in a young girl's heart. Back in those days there were no twenty-four-hour news channels to keep you updated on all the latest kidnappings and crimes that were happening across the world. This had made Molly's mysterious disappearance big news in a small town like Maple Hill.

"I recently found my father's old quilt that disappeared the same night she did," Sarah told her.

"Really?" Hattie slowly shook her head. "People believed she was buried in that quilt. Where did you find it after all these years?"

Sarah told her about the secret passageway in Jason's house and how there had been a note stuck inside the quilt with 212 Elm Street written on it.

"But this was 212 Elm back in 1920," Hattie said, looking perplexed. "They changed our address after they built Memorial Drive Highway."

"I know. That's why I'm hoping you might be able to tell me why my grandmother would have put your address in that quilt."

Hattie was silent for several minutes. At last, she spoke. "I'm sorry, Sarah, I can't think of any reason at all. My mother, Clara, was a nodding acquaintance of Molly, but they weren't friends. My papa passed away in 1916, before Noah and Molly were even married, so he didn't know her at all."

Sarah wondered if there could be some other connection to the house. "Did anyone else live with you here, even a servant that she might have known?"

"After my papa died, we didn't have enough money for servants. It was just my mother and my little sisters and me. Ma did some seamstress work for extra money, but I don't think Molly was ever one of her clients."

Judging from the quality of the quilt she was restoring, Sarah could tell that Molly had been an excellent seamstress in her own right. Something didn't make sense. If Clara Hepperson was the only adult living in the house back in 1920, she had to be the reason Molly had written the address on the note. The question was: Why had she written it? If Clara and Molly had been friends, Molly would have known where to find her without writing it down. If they were merely nodding acquaintances, as Hattie believed, it was more likely that Molly would need an address to find the house. She'd just moved to Maple Hill after her marriage and wouldn't be familiar with the town and its residents.

Sarah reached up to rub her temple. A headache was starting to form there as she tried to work out the knots in this thread. "Do you think it's possible your mother might have helped her without your knowing about it?"

"I suppose it's possible," Hattie replied. "Parents didn't share much with kids back in those days. Not like today, parents trying to be their kid's best friend. But I'm as sure as I can be that Ma didn't help Molly."

"What makes you say that?"

Hattie's pale blue eyes looked into Sarah's. "Because she believed Noah Drayton killed his wife. I'm sorry, Sarah, but she was convinced of it until her last breath. She'd even cross the street to avoid passing him on the sidewalk."

The words hurt, but Sarah appreciated Hattie's honesty. She supposed it was possible that Clara Hepperson was expecting Molly to show up at her house that night. Maybe when she didn't arrive, Clara became convinced that Noah had prevented her from coming.

"Thank you, Hattie," Sarah said at last. "I appreciate your help."

"Good luck," Hattie told her, "and stop by again if you have more questions. Hopefully, I'll be more help than I was today."

"You were a big help," Sarah said. And it was true. Hattie might not have provided the answers she wanted to hear, but they would keep her from continuing down the wrong path. "At least I'm not snooping around 212 Elm Street anymore. I even thought an M etched in a brick by the cellar window might have been put there as a cry for help from Molly."

Hattie's brow crinkled. "An M on a brick? Now that sounds vaguely familiar."

"It does?"

She nodded. "I seem to recall something…" Her voice trailed off as she gazed into the distance. A moment later, she snapped her fingers. "I know how that M got there."

"You do?"

"Sure. I've lived in this neighborhood my whole life. Mary Wiggins lived at what's now 212 Elm, right down the block, and we used to walk to school together. She had the biggest crush on Caleb Henry, a boy who used to mow their lawn, so she scratched Mary loves Caleb in that brick, hoping he'd see it."

"And did he?"

"As soon as he saw that brick, Caleb scratched through those letters. The M was the only thing left by the time he was through. Mary got the message and never talked to him again."

"What ever happened to the Wiggins family?" Sarah asked.

"Mary eloped with a boy when she was sixteen. Her folks were so ashamed they packed up and moved away. I never heard from any of them again."

So *that* was why there had been no further information to be found about Clayton Wiggins and his family. After all the time Sarah had spent searching the library's archives, the Web, old Chamber of Commerce records, and the cemetery map, she'd finally come to a dead end. Well, that was one mystery solved, though it just wasn't the mystery Sarah was most interested in. After her initial thrill at finding the plat map in Jason's office, Sarah now felt a little deflated.

After she left Hattie's house, Sarah drove around town to sort out her thoughts. There had to be something she was missing. She was finding some answers, but was still no closer to discovering what had happened to Grandma Molly.

Sarah glanced in her rearview mirror, noticing a black minivan traveling close behind her. She stepped on the gas to put a little distance between them. Too many drivers got distracted with cell phones and text messages these days to pay attention to the road.

Her thoughts drifted back to the clues she'd found so far. She was still waiting for the phone call from the owner of the Harrison family genealogy Web site, hoping to find some new information. If Charles Harrison hadn't died in the war, then that meant Grandma Molly had lied to her new husband. But for what reason? To protect Charles? To protect herself? Maybe he'd divorced her and she'd been too embarrassed to admit it.

Sarah shook her head. She needed facts, not speculation. As she turned onto Memorial Drive, she noticed the van behind her turning too, still following a little too closely. She checked her speed, not wanting to risk a ticket.

Then she steered her car closer to the shoulder to allow the minivan to pass her. She even slowed down, hoping that would encourage the driver to go on his—or her—merry way. Instead, the minivan slowed down too.

Now Sarah's full attention was on the van behind her. Her hands tightened around the steering wheel as she kept one eye on the road and the other on the rearview mirror. When she changed lanes, the van changed lanes.

"What's going on?" she muttered, wondering if it was some teenagers playing road games.

As she approached the next intersection, the light turned yellow. She sped through it, hoping to lose the van, but it careened through the intersection. Sarah told herself it couldn't be following her, but when it turned onto her street right after she did, she was too unnerved to pull into her driveway. Her heart thumped against her chest as she drove past her house, wondering what to do next.

There was something menacing about the minivan. The windows were all shaded, making it impossible to see the driver or any passengers. When she sped up, it sped up. When she slowed down, it slowed down.

Should she go to the police station or Jason's office?

Her first thought was that it might be the man who had showed up at her door the other night looking for Tori Monroe. He'd been driving a black car too, but it had been a sedan, not a minivan.

Just as she decided to head for the police station, Sarah saw the minivan turn off on another road. She breathed a sigh of relief, telling herself she'd been imagining things. She continued down the street, intending to circle the village green and head back home. Maybe by the time she got there her heart would have resumed its normal pace.

She reached out to turn on her radio, hoping some music would calm her nerves. Then she saw a flash of black in her mirror and realized the minivan was behind her once again.

Sarah drove downtown and parked in front of Maggie's store. Maggie's red Tahoe was parked outside, so she knew her daughter-in-law was there. She got out of the car and was almost to the door when she turned to look at the minivan.

It drove right past her, not slowing down a bit. No doubt she was overreacting, Sarah told herself. There were no plates on the car, only an In Transit sign in the back window. The driver was probably new to the area and simply lost.

Or maybe it was Katie's ex-boyfriend trying to track her down.

Sarah pulled her cell phone from her purse and dialed Katie's number.

A moment later, Katie picked up. "Hello?"

"Hi, Katie, this is Sarah. Where are you?"

"I'm just leaving the paint store. Jason met me here to pick out a color for the file room in his office. We're just headed back there now. Did you need something?"

Sarah hesitated, not sure what to say. She didn't want to scare Katie unnecessarily and it did make Sarah feel better to know that Jason was with her. "No, I was just checking up on you."

"Okay. I'll probably be home late tonight. Pastor John invited me to the Spotted Dog to join the church singles' group for coffee. I really shouldn't go, but ..."

"I think you should go," Sarah said, happy to see Katie go out. That girl spent way too much time working and not enough time socializing. The only way to get Katie over her self-imposed exile and her fears about her ex-boyfriend was to expand her social circle. Sarah also hoped spending time with the pastor would encourage her to open up to him about her problems.

"All right," Katie said, laughing, "I'll go if you insist. Don't wait up for me."

After Sarah hung up the phone, she looked up and saw the black minivan make another cruise around the village green, only this time it stopped in front of the pizza parlor. The car doors popped open and two women emerged just in time to corral the four young children spilling out of the back of the van.

Heat crawled up Sarah's face at her foolishness. They were sightseers, not stalkers. Sarah shifted her car into reverse and pulled out of the parking spot.

She'd never been the paranoid type. Maybe she was dwelling too much on Grandma Molly's mysterious disappearance. That, along with Katie's troubles with her ex-boyfriend, had fired up Sarah's imagination in ways she'd never experienced. Now she needed to put that imagination to good use and solve this mystery once and for all.

CHAPTER TWENTY-FIVE

A warm afternoon breeze fluttered the lace curtains in the window of Sarah's sewing room.

On her desk was the list she'd compiled of all the towns called New Hope. There were fourteen of them spread out all over the country.

Might as well start at the top. Sarah clicked on her computer, and then searched the Internet for an online directory page for Alabama. She typed the words: *Madison County clerk* in the search box, then waited for the result.

A moment later, she picked up the telephone and dialed the number listed on the screen.

"Madison County clerk's office," said a woman's voice with a thick southern drawl. "May I help you?"

"I have a rather unusual question," Sarah said. "I need to know if someone by the last name of Mayer, M-a-y-e-r, ran for mayor of New Hope, Alabama, in the early twentieth century."

"You want to know if Mayer ran for mayor?"

"Yes," Sarah said. "I have one of his campaign ribbons and that was his slogan: Mayer for Mayor."

"Hold on, Hon. I'll see what I can find."

Sarah knew it might take a while, so she carried the phone over to the ironing board in the corner of the room and plugged in the iron.

She'd finished tea-staining all her replacement fabrics, but they were stiff and wrinkled after drying out on the clothesline. As soon as she pressed them, she could start adding them to the quilt.

"Ma'am?"

"Yes, I'm still here." Sarah moved back to the desk.

"I searched our election records, but there's no one by the name of Mayer who ever ran for any office in this county."

"All right," she said, "thank you for your help."

Sarah hadn't expected to succeed on the first try, although it would have been nice. She called the clerk of Colusa County in California with the same question. Twenty minutes later, he gave her the same answer.

Then she moved on to the New Hopes in Iowa, Maine, Minnesota, and North Dakota, ironing the fabric pieces while each clerk looked up the information, which sometimes took up to twenty minutes, but the answer was always no.

She still had eight more states to go. One of them had to be the right New Hope. Looking up the next phone number on the computer, Sarah dialed the number and repeated her request once more. Then she used her index finger to spit-test the heat of the iron before pressing it over the yellow cotton remnant.

By the time she reached Wyoming, the last state on her list, she'd pressed, measured, and cut all the replacement fabric pieces. According to the clerk of Goshen County, no Mayer had run for office in the town of New Hope.

Sarah hung up the phone, her hope of finding the information she needed fading. The only possible explanation for coming up empty was that the New Hope she wanted to find no longer existed. Which meant she'd come to another dead end.

Later that evening, Sarah made a trip to Bradford Manor to deliver a cookie plate to her father. After all the futile phone calls this afternoon, she needed someone to cheer her up.

"Hi, Dad," Sarah said as she walked into his room.

His face brightened when he saw her, but he didn't say anything.

She set the cookie plate down on his desk, then knelt by his wheelchair so he didn't have to look up at her. "I'm Sarah, your daughter."

His brow crinkled. "When did your hair start turning gray?"

She smiled, then reached out to give his hand a reassuring squeeze. "Oh, it's been that way for a while now."

He looked out the window. "It's getting dark and I still have letters to deliver. Have you seen my mailbag? I can't find it anywhere."

"Dad, you're retired," she said gently. "So you don't have to worry about the letters. They've all been delivered."

"Does your mom know I retired?"

Sarah nodded as she rose to her feet. "Yes, she knows. She threw you a party and made you a strawberry cream cake."

He glanced over at the desk. "Did you bring me a piece?"

"I don't have cake," she said, walking over to retrieve the paper plate. "But I have some cookies and bars here. Your great-granddaughters, Amy and Audrey, baked some of them. Do you remember when they came to visit you the other day?"

He thought about it for a moment, then asked. "Do they have gray hair, too?"

"Not yet," she said, setting the cookie plate in front of him. "They're only twelve."

"So they're still young whippersnappers," he said, then began fumbling with the plastic wrap covering the plate and she reached out to help him.

"Which one should I eat first?" he asked, looking over the assortment in front of him.

Sarah studied the selection, which she'd chosen from several different trays at the bake sale. "This is one of the caramel brownies the girls made." She picked it up and handed it to him. "Do you want to try it?"

"Okay." He took a bite of the brownie, a few of the crumbs spilling onto his light blue shirt. "Hey, that's pretty tasty."

"I'll tell them you like it," Sarah said, although she wanted to bring back the girls for a visit soon.

She watched him eat the brownie, then got up to pour him a glass of water. "Here you go, Dad," she said, setting the cup in front of him.

"Thank you," he said, smiling up at her. "You're one of my favorite nurses."

She sat down in the chair beside him and watched him finish the brownie, then wash it down with a long sip of water. "How about another one?"

"Don't mind if I do." He picked a dark brown cookie up off the plate. It had come from Katie's box. He took a bite, then an odd expression came over his face as he chewed.

"Doesn't it taste good?" Sarah asked him.

Tears gleamed in his eyes and the cookie dropped from his hand, crumbling into pieces when it hit the floor.

"Dad," she cried, half rising out of the chair. "Are you all right?"

He blinked in rapid succession. "Where is she?"

"Where's who?" Sarah asked, growing more concerned.

"Where's my mama? I want to see her."

Sarah sank back into her chair. "Your mama's not here, Dad. I'm here with you, though. I'll stay as long as you want tonight."

He stared down at the broken cookie on the floor for so long that Sarah finally leaned over and swept it into her hand.

"When did she make these cookies?" He pointed to the crumbled pieces in her hand.

"These cookies came from the church bake sale," she explained. "My boarder, Katie, made them."

"Did Mama give her the recipe?"

"Dad, Katie didn't know your mother," Sarah said gently. "She was gone before Katie was born." She hadn't seen him this animated about something for a long time. "I'll ask her for the recipe," she promised, hoping that would soothe him. "If she gives it to me, I can make these cookies for you anytime you want them."

"Okay." He reached over and patted her shoulder. "You're a good girl."

Sarah got up and brushed the cookie crumbs into the wastebasket, then searched the plate for another cookie just like it. When she found one, she broke it in two, then took a small bite. She tasted chocolate, cinnamon, and a touch of anise. It was an unusual flavor combination, and one she'd never tasted before.

"It's good, isn't it?" Dad said, watching her. "Mama makes the best cookies."

"Very good." Sarah handed him the other half of the cookie. It might not even be the same recipe, for all she knew. After all, ninety years had passed since he'd last tasted his mother's cookies and many people's palates changed as they grew older.

He chewed slowly, closing his eyes for a moment, then opening them again. "Are you sure Mama didn't make them?"

"I'm sure, Dad."

William nodded, trusting her answer. Then he looked out the window. "It's getting dark already. The mail can't wait all day."

When she got home later that evening, Sarah found Katie eating a sandwich in the kitchen. She had a thick book open in front of her.

"What are you reading?" Sarah asked as she poured herself a glass of tea.

"A book about Revolutionary War generals." She looked up at Sarah. "I was talking to Pastor John and he told me not to give up on my studies, even if I'm not in school anymore."

"Does that mean you told him about your problems?"

Katie nodded. "He promised me that anything I told him would be confidential, so I told him about Evan and everything else."

Sarah was glad to hear it. Katie needed some kind of counseling and Pastor John could offer her good, commonsense ideas. "It sounds like he gave you good advice."

"He did." Katie brushed some bread crumbs off her book. "I've let Evan take too much away from me, so I've decided to start taking some things back."

"Like Nathaniel Bradford?"

She nodded. "I've fallen behind on my research. I might not be able to go back to graduate school for a while yet, but I want to be caught up when I do."

When I do.

It was nice to hear Katie talking about a future for herself, especially after taking such desperate measures to escape from Evan. Dropping out of school, moving to a strange town, and changing her identity had proved just how much he scared her. Katie had found sanctuary in Maple Hill, but not freedom. She was imprisoned by her fear, and she was the only person who could break those chains.

Sarah headed for her sewing room, then turned around, remembering the promise to her father. "I'd love to get the recipe for those chocolate cookies you donated to the bake sale."

She brightened. "You liked them? I wanted to try something a little different."

"They were very good. They reminded my dad of the cookies his mother used to make."

"That's sweet. I searched through so many Web sites last night, I'm not sure which one I found that recipe on."

"Didn't you print it?"

She shook her head. "No, I just brought my laptop down to the kitchen and read it off the screen." She rose out of her chair. "I can try to find that recipe again."

"You don't have to do it right now," Sarah told her, not wanting to take her away from her reading. "Just sometime in the next few days would be great."

"Okay." Katie sat back down. "I'll see what I can do."

The telephone rang and Sarah walked over to answer it. "Hello?"

"Is this Sarah Drayton?"

"Yes," she replied, hoping it wasn't a telemarketer. She walked into her sewing room so she wouldn't disturb Katie.

"My name is Paula Castellano. You sent me an e-mail through my genealogy Web site asking about Charles and Molly Harrison."

"Oh, yes." Sarah sank down in her chair, her heart skipping a beat. "Thank you so much for calling."

"Well, I'm sorry it took so long."

"That's okay." Sarah pulled the spiral notebook toward her and turned to a blank page. "I was so excited to find the Harrison family tree on the Internet."

"I'm something of a genealogy buff," Paula explained, "so when I married my late husband, I took on the challenge of researching all his ancestors."

"I'm so glad you did. I've been looking for information about Charles and Molly. They're my paternal grandparents."

Paula gasped. "Well, isn't that something? I'd given up on ever finding out more about that particular branch of the family tree. It was such a tragedy..."

"Tragedy?" Sarah's gaze fell on the quilt in front of her. She sensed Paula wasn't talking about the war.

"Yes...didn't your grandmother tell you?"

"I never met her." She gave Paula a very brief history of Grandma Molly's disappearance, eager to find out what the woman knew.

"Now that *is* strange," Paula said after Sarah had finished her story. "Because Molly disappeared after Charles's memorial service, too. At least, that's what I gathered from reading old family letters and journals. My late husband was a cousin to Charles, although he'd died before my husband was born."

"Can you tell me how he died?"

"In a fire."

The words made Sarah's heart sink. So Grandma Molly *had* lied to Grandpa Noah. "Are you sure?"

"I'm positive. Their home burned to the ground one night. Molly and her baby barely made it out alive, but Charles didn't make it—probably because of his leg."

"Leg?"

"He'd lost it in battle," Paula said. "He'd only been back in the States a month when the fire happened."

Sarah took a moment to let it all sink in, the pen idle in her hands. "Can you tell me anything about Molly? Where she came from or if she had any family?"

"No, nothing," Paula replied. "I did learn that Charles's parents were devastated when she disappeared with little William. They had no other grandchildren."

Not quite. Sarah started jotting notes on the paper in front of her, although she wasn't about to forget what Paula had told her. "Maybe I can finally fill in some of the blank spaces on that branch of the family tree."

"Would you?" Paula exclaimed. "I'd love to list all of William Harrison's descendants."

"His name is William Drayton now. I'll send you an e-mail with names, dates, and other details," Sarah promised. "It's the least I can do after the help you've given me."

"It's been my pleasure."

"Oh, one more thing," Sarah said. "Did Charles ever live in Boston?"

Paula hesitated. "As far as I know, he never left Bridgeport, except to go to war, of course."

They chatted for a few more minutes, then Sarah hung up the phone. She pulled the quilt closer to her, her fingers tracing her father's initials on the corner block. "Why did you lie, Grandma Molly? What did you have to hide?"

CHAPTER TWENTY-SIX

This is amazing." Vanessa stared at Grandma Molly's quilt spread over a table in the Wild Goose Chase. "From this distance, I can't tell the new fabric pieces from the old ones."

"I'm glad to hear it." Sarah had driven to the store first thing Monday morning, eager to get Vanessa's opinion. She hid a yawn behind her hand. She'd stayed up half the night to finish her work on the quilt top.

"You're doing a great job, as usual. Your father is going to love having his quilt back."

"I hope so." After she'd finally gone to bed last night, Sarah's scattered thoughts had kept her awake. She'd wondered if the twins had made friends with anyone at the bake sale, worried about Katie's situation, and kept replaying her father's strange reaction to those cookies over and over in her mind. Even now, thinking about the way he'd asked to see his mom made her throat tighten. She hoped giving him the quilt would give him some measure of comfort.

"I know he will," Vanessa said, her gaze still focused on the quilt. She leaned down close to it, then picked up a handheld magnifier from the table beside her to peer at one of the squares. "Wow, you did a great job patching the hole in this striped fabric. How did you get the blue and white stripes so straight?"

"Trial and error," Sarah said wryly. "It took me a good two hours before I finally got it right. It was worth repairing though. That's actually part of an election campaign ribbon. I thought the name on it might be a clue in Molly's case, but that lead petered out."

"That's too bad." Vanessa set down the magnifier. "So what do you have left to do on the quilt?"

"The quilt top is done, and I've pieced the new backing, so now I need to find fabric to replace the blue binding." Sarah held up one side of the quilt. "It's made of silk taffeta, so after ninety years there's a lot of fraying."

Vanessa nodded. "It won't hold together much longer if your dad uses the quilt."

"Exactly." Sarah walked over to the rows of fabric bolts lining the back wall. "I want to find a color that matches as closely as possible to the original binding."

"I've got some blue silk taffetas right over here," Vanessa walked over and pulled a couple of bolts off the shelf.

"This shade looks just about right." Sarah picked up one of the bolts and held it next to the original binding. "It's just dark enough to give the binding an aged look so it matches the rest of the quilt."

Vanessa nodded her approval.

"That was easy." Sarah couldn't contain her smile. "I can't wait to get started. It's going to look so much better with the new binding."

"Then why wait?" Vanessa pulled a seam ripper out of her pocket. "You've been my only customer so far today, so I'm not busy. While you remove the old binding, I'll start cutting strips for the new one."

Quilting was always more fun with a friend. "You've got a deal." Sarah sat down at the table and pulled the quilt to her. Then she carefully inserted the pointed end of the seam ripper into one of the small stitches on the binding.

"How wide do you want the bias strips?" Vanessa asked from the cutting table.

"Two and a half inches." As Sarah removed more stitches, the original binding started to shred in her hands. That's what she'd feared might happen when she'd first looked it over. Now she could see the silk taffeta was in even worse condition than she'd thought.

"How's it coming?" Vanessa asked as she carried strips of blue silk taffeta over to the table.

"The bottom edge is almost off," Sarah said as she began to loosen the binding and pull it away from the quilt. Something caught, and she looked closer to see that she'd missed a couple of stitches, keeping that portion of the binding attached to a white triangle piece.

Sarah gently peeled back the triangle to loosen the stitch when she noticed something unusual on the underside of the white fabric. "What's this?"

Vanessa stepped closer. "What?"

Sarah picked up the magnifier, the faint lines now enlarged. "It looks like the letter R."

"I hope it's another hidden note from your grandmother."

"No, this is some kind of machine printing." Sarah set down the magnifier, then picked up the seam ripper. She began to carefully cut through the stitches around the piece. After a few moments, she'd freed it completely.

Vanessa held the magnifier up against the fabric. "You're right, there is an R."

Sarah looked at the quilt. "I wonder..."

"What?"

She looked up at her friend. "I think Grandma Molly used fabric from the same source for all these triangle pieces." She pointed to the triangle in front of her. "If this one has a letter on the back, maybe some of the others do too."

Vanessa's eyes lit up. "Do you think so?"

An hour later all ninety-six of the white triangle pieces were sitting on the table, turned face down. Each one had been marked with a fabric pencil to indicate exactly where it came from on the quilt.

"You were right," Vanessa said, moving the magnifier over the triangles. "A few of these pieces do have printing on them. Too bad we can't read it."

"You like word scramble puzzles, don't you?" Sarah said, pulling a notepad and pen from her bag. "This is the same thing."

"Some of the letters have faded too much to read."

"Then tell me the ones you can read," Sarah said, pencil in hand.

"Okay." Vanessa moved the magnifier to the piece closest to her. "We've got a Y." She moved to the next one. "This piece has a B and an L. Then over here are P and N. This triangle has D U R, so that's part of a word. The next piece has C and M and some other letter I can't see. The last one I can make out has F, L, and another faded letter."

"Is that it?"

Vanessa lowered the magnifier. "That's it. What have we got?"

Sarah looked down at her notepad. "Y, B, L, P, N, D, U, R, C, M, F, and L."

Vanessa laughed. "In other words, a big mess."

"Now just wait," Sarah said, studying the letters. "We've only got one vowel and we already know that goes between the D and the R." She started another line on the notepad. We've obviously got more than one word here."

"But how many?" Vanessa asked.

"Well, I'm thinking this fabric had to come from a feed or flour sack. They used to recycle everything back then." She started rearranging the triangle pieces, trying to figure out how they went together."

"Here," Vanessa said, pointing. "F and L probably spell flour."

A thrill shot through Sarah as she put three of the other triangles together. "And C, M, P, N, Y, stands for Company."

"Something Flour Company. So now all we have left are one triangle with the letters B and L, and another triangle with D, U, and R."

Sarah put those two pieces next to each other. "D-U-R-B-L"

"Durbl?" Vanessa said.

"E is the most common vowel. Maybe it's Durble?"

"Durble Flour Company?" Vanessa shrugged. "Maybe the owner's last name is Durble."

"No, that can't be right." Sarah studied the pieces in front of her. "There are two faded letters here. One before the B and one after the L." She wrote it out on her notepad, leaving space for the two missing letters.

"Too bad we don't have an answer key for this puzzle."

Sarah agreed. "We'll just have to use trial and error. The last letter has to be a vowel."

She wrote out the possible combinations, leaving a space between the letters R and B: *Dur_bla, Dur_ble, Dur_bli, Dur_blo, Dur_blu.* Sarah studied the partial words in front of her, trying to make sense of them. If the word was a surname, there could be a huge number of letter combinations. But if it was an adjective . . . "Could it be Durable?" she asked at last. "Durable Flour Company?"

"It fits," Vanessa replied with a wide smile. "And it sounds like a flour company you can depend on." She walked over to her computer. "Let's see if we can find it on the Net."

Sarah leaned over her shoulder as Vanessa typed the words Durable Flour Company into the search engine. A moment later, only one link came up.

Vanessa clicked on it, then read the information aloud. *"The Durable Flour Company began in 1898 in Latham, Kansas. It was owned and operated by P. L. Holden and his descendants until it closed in 1968."*

"Latham, Kansas," Sarah looked over at the quilt. "It's come a long way."

"How did Molly get flour sacks from Kansas to make her quilt?"

"I don't know." Sarah's head was spinning. If Grandma Molly had flour sacks from Kansas, maybe that's where she'd gotten the campaign ribbon, too. "But I'm going to find out."

When Sarah arrived home, she looked up Kansas in the atlas. First, she located Latham, a town of 3,800 people in south central Kansas, and marked it with her yellow highlighter. Then she rechecked the list of towns to make certain she hadn't missed New Hope when she'd done her atlas sleuthing a few days ago, but it still wasn't there.

"Relax," Sarah told herself. "You can figure this out."

She'd boxed up Molly's quilt, the loose triangle pieces, and her new binding before leaving Vanessa's store. Now, she unloaded the box on the sewing room table, spreading out the quilt and placing the triangle pieces back in their original spots. She'd sew them in later, when her hands weren't shaking from the excitement of finding another clue.

But what did New Hope and Latham have in common other than finding their way into Molly's quilt? If she could figure that out, she might be another step closer to solving this case.

Sarah turned to her computer and found the Web site for the city of Latham, Kansas. There was no historical society listed among the community links, but there was a library. She clicked on the link, then punched the phone number into her cell phone.

Three rings later, a woman picked up. "Latham Public Library. This is Nancy."

"Hello, Nancy." Sarah paced across the floor, too nervous to stand still. "My name is Sarah Hart and I'm calling from Maple Hill, Massachusetts."

"My, that's quite a distance."

"Yes it is. I'm looking for some information and hope you can help me."

"I'll do my best."

Sarah started with the question nearest to her heart. "Is the name Molly Hollis familiar to you at all? She would have been born in 1896."

"No, I'm sorry, it doesn't ring a bell."

She suppressed a sigh of disappointment. "How about a town called New Hope?"

"Oh, yes," Nancy replied. "New Hope was just south of Latham. About ten miles away."

"Was?"

"A tornado destroyed half the town in 1925. Most of the homes and businesses were never rebuilt. The town limped along for a while, but the Great Depression drove the few remaining residents out."

"So it doesn't exist anymore?"

"There are a few vacant buildings there, but nothing else.

A ghost town. Sarah pondered that for a moment.

"If you're interested in New Hope," Nancy continued, "there is a section about it in the Latham Centennial Book."

"Centennial book?"

"Latham celebrated its centennial about twenty-three years ago. Several members of the community put together a history of the area and the people who settled here."

That sounded promising.

"Most of the families in the area added their own story," the librarian continued, "and several included old photographs and journal entries. It's possible you might find out something about Molly Hollis in there."

"Can I buy one from you?"

"They're not for sale, but I can send it through interlibrary loan. I just need the name and address of your local library."

"It's Maple Hill Library." Sarah hurried over to the drawer to retrieve the phone book, "and the address is...1416 Pilgrim Avenue."

"Got it. These interlibrary loans usually take a couple of weeks..."

"Would you mind shipping it by priority mail?" Sarah asked, not sure she could wait that long. "I'll pay for it. The Maple Hill librarian, Spencer Hewitt, is a friend of mine. I know he'll vouch for me."

"I guess I can do that."

Sarah assured her that it would be okay. "I'll pay whatever it takes."

"All right," Nancy said. "The mail's already gone out today, but I can send it tomorrow."

"Oh, one more thing," Sarah said. "Do you have an Elm Street in Latham?"

"We sure do. It runs right past the school."

"Thanks for all your help. I really appreciate it."

Sarah hung up the phone, feeling like she was finally on the right track. She headed for the door. She needed some fresh air to clear her head after these latest developments. That's when she saw Martha's green minivan heading toward her house.

Sarah waited on the sidewalk. Ernie's doctor's appointment had been today. Martha pulled into the driveway, then slowly emerged from the car. One look at her friend's face told Sarah it wasn't good news.

CHAPTER TWENTY-SEVEN

Sarah got Martha settled on the front porch with a glass of iced tea and a slice of lemon bread, then took a seat on the Adirondack chair beside her. Martha's hands shook slightly as she raised the glass to her mouth and took a small sip.

Sarah remembered the state of shock she'd been in when she'd learned about Gerry's cancer, so she let Martha sip her tea and nibble on the lemon bread until she was ready to talk.

"Thank you," Martha said, brushing some bread crumbs from her fingers. "I haven't eaten a thing since we got the news, and I was feeling a little dizzy."

"You probably need something more substantial than lemon bread." Sarah rose to her feet. "Why don't I make you a sandwich?"

Martha shook her head. "No, I'm fine now. Really. I don't have much of an appetite."

240

Sarah was unnerved by Martha's ashen face. She wasn't used to seeing her friend this way. Martha always found something to smile about, even in times of trouble.

"We don't have all the tests back yet," Martha said at last, "but the doctor is fairly certain of the diagnosis. Ernie has Parkinson's Disease."

Sarah sat back in her chair, trying to absorb the news.

"That's the reason he's been stumbling around so much. Loss of balance is one of the symptoms."

"Oh, Martha, I'm sorry. I know this must be hard for both of you."

"He's already got tremors in his left hand. I didn't notice for a while because he's been keeping that hand in his pocket, trying to hide it from me." She sighed. "And probably from himself." Trying to deny anything was wrong—that wasn't uncommon, especially for men. Sarah knew that from personal experience.

Angry tears gleamed in Martha's eyes. "These are supposed to be our golden years. They just got pretty tarnished."

"I know." Sarah couldn't think of what else to say.

Martha sucked in a deep breath. "And I know I'm whining. Other people have it worse than us. I just don't know how to fix this."

"How is Ernie handling it?"

"Not well." Martha brushed a fly away from her glass. "He didn't say a word on the way home, then he went into his shop to work on his car. You know how much he likes to tinker with his cars. What if he can't even do that anymore?"

Sarah didn't know what to say.

"The doctor told us we'd have to learn to *adjust* to the disease." Martha jutted her chin out. "I'd rather kick its butt." That sounded like the Martha she knew. Her family always came first and she'd battle anyone who tried to hurt them. Only this was a different kind of battle, and one Sarah knew Martha would have a hard time fighting.

"Then he started telling us what might happen down the road," Martha continued. "A wheelchair. Paralysis. Dementia." She shuddered. "I stopped listening after that."

"*Might happen*," Sarah reminded her. "I know this sounds trite, but you have to take it a day at a time. Right now, Ernie doesn't have a wheelchair or paralysis or dementia. He can still work on his cars and play with your grandchildren and drive you crazy."

Her mouth twitched. "Isn't that the truth?"

"Even the Bible tells us not to worry about the future. *'Therefore do not worry about tomorrow for tomorrow will worry about itself. Each day has enough trouble of its own.'*"

Martha raised her eyebrows. "You have that one memorized."

Sarah smiled. "When Gerry was sick I'd spend so much time worrying about what was going to happen. Whenever I'd get really anxious about it, I'd recite that verse. It helped me remember that God was in charge."

"If God's in charge…" Martha paused. "Ernie is a good man. He doesn't deserve this."

"No one does," Sarah said softly.

They sat in silence for several moments, then Martha set her glass on the wicker table between them. "I guess we really don't have any choice, do we?"

"No," Sarah said honestly. "We have to play the cards we're dealt."

"The good news," Martha said, "if you can call it that, is Parkinson's can take years to progress." A wry smile tipped her mouth. "When the doctor told Ernie he might be around for another twenty years, Ernie said, 'Do I have to wait that long?'"

Sarah laughed. "That sounds like the Ernie we know and love."

Martha's smile faded. "That's what scares me the most. What if I lose the Ernie I know? What if he changes so much..." Her voice trailed off and she stared into the distance.

This roller coaster of emotions was so familiar to Sarah. Fear. Humor. Anger. Sadness. She'd been in Martha's shoes, but there was no one-size-fits-all approach to news like this. Everyone handled it differently.

"You just found out about his illness today," Sarah said. "You'll have plenty of time to figure everything out."

Martha leaned back in her chair, not saying anything. Sarah sat with her in silence for several minutes, watching a hummingbird hover above one of her hanging flower baskets.

"Thanks for letting me vent," Martha said at last. "I didn't want to do it in front of Ernie. I'm trying to stay positive for his sake." She sighed. "They say laughter is the best medicine, but nothing seems very funny right now."

"Even if you can't laugh today, don't give his illness so much power that it robs you of the joy of living."

"You're right." Color crept back into Martha's cheeks. "Ernie and I have a lot of years ahead of us. I intend to enjoy every moment of them."

Sarah reached over to hug her. She knew it wouldn't be easy for them, but Martha's sunny disposition would help more than anything. Sarah would help too, in any way that she could. They sat quietly on the porch, and Sarah began to pray.

Dear Lord, please give Ernie and Martha the strength they'll need to face this disease and the changes it will make in their lives. Grace them with your healing spirit. Help me to be a good friend to them and let all their friends and family surround them with love and fill them with hope. Amen.

After supper that evening, Sarah sat down in her sewing room and began reattaching the triangular pieces she and Vanessa had removed that morning.

She still needed to document it all in her quilting notebook, but she'd do that later. Right now, sewing soothed her as she reminisced about the tumultuous day. She made a note to check in with Martha tomorrow, just to make sure she was all right.

Sarah picked up her scissors to snip the thread from the needle, then looked at her handiwork. The quick beep-beep of a horn outside made her look up from her quilt. Her first thought was of Katie, who had plans to work late at Jason and Maggie's house tonight. Unless she'd come home early. *Maybe Evan was following her. Maybe the honking was a cry for help.*

Sarah rose from her chair and headed for the door. When she stepped onto the front porch, she saw a shiny red convertible in the driveway and Rita sitting behind the wheel, her brown hair peeking out from beneath a Red Sox cap.

She beamed at Sarah. "Want to take a ride in my midlife crisis?"

"Wow! That is some car." Sarah walked over for a closer look. The silver chrome trim gleamed in the sun and the white leather seats looked as soft as butter.

"Get in," Rita urged.

Sarah hesitated. "It's tempting, but I'm working on a quilt right now."

"Come on," Rita said. "We'll just take a quick spin around town and let the wind blow in our hair. You can't stay cooped up in the house on such a beautiful summer evening."

She had a point. Sarah opened the car door. "Okay, I can't resist."

"Buckle up and we'll be on our way."

As they traveled down the tree-lined streets, Sarah felt like a teenager again. Gerry had owned a convertible in high school and they'd spent their Saturday nights driving slowly up and down the main drag to see what all their friends were doing.

"What do you think?" Rita asked.

"It's a great car. Where did you get it?"

"At a used car lot near Pittsfield. My old car was starting to act up. Probably from tooling around Massachusetts for the last two months. I had a mechanic check out this beauty, then made a trade-in."

Sarah leaned back against the headrest, enjoying the way the warm breeze caressed her face and hair. "Thanks for inviting me for a ride. I needed a break."

"Well, if you want to know the truth, I had an ulterior motive."

Sarah turned to look at her. "What's that?"

"I want to take back my two-week notice. I know I'm supposed to leave for Canada in two days, but you see, I've met this guy…"

Sarah started laughing. "Oh, Rita. Is that all?"

"I thought you might already have someone lined up for my room. I've been gone so much lately that we haven't had much time to talk."

"I'd love for you to stay on," Sarah told her. "Now tell me about this guy."

She grinned. "Well, we met at a bird-watching workshop in Springfield on Monday and got into a spirited debate about the Yankees and the Red Sox. He called me the next day to debate some more, then asked me out to lunch." She breathed a happy sigh. "We have another date tomorrow."

They drove past Patriot Park and the aroma of grilling hot dogs filled the air. Sarah turned to watch the kids playing on the swings, then sat straight up in her seat.

Was that Amy shooting baskets with Cody from youth group? Trina was there, too, but standing off to the side watching them.

"Is something wrong?" Rita asked, slowing the car down.

"I don't think so." Sarah smiled. "Just the opposite, in fact."

By the time they returned to the house, it was almost dark.

"Thank you for the drive," Sarah said, "The best part was learning that you plan to stay on for a while."

"I'm so glad it's not a problem," Rita told her as they walked inside the house. "Now I'd better get my beauty sleep." She winked as she headed for the stairs. "Or maybe I'll brush up on my debate skills first."

"Goodnight."

Sarah walked into the kitchen and made herself a cup of decaffeinated coffee, then returned to her sewing room. Too tired to sew, she sat down at the table and opened her quilting notebook to a blank page.

Where to start?

Sarah took a sip of coffee, then set the cup on the table as she pondered the question. So much had happened with the quilt and Molly's case today. Maybe she should just start writing and organize it later.

Picking up a pencil, she began describing the condition of the blue silk taffeta binding she'd removed from the quilt. Then she moved on to her first glimpse of something unusual on the underside of one of the white triangles.

She'd filled two pages when her head began to droop. Sarah crooked her arm on the table, then rested her head there as she wrote. Only a few more paragraphs and she'd be done. The next thing she knew, she heard the sound of glass shattering. Sarah's eyes flew open. She lifted her head from the table, her neck stiff. It took her a moment to realize she'd fallen asleep in her sewing room.

The door to the room opened and Katie stepped inside wearing the shorts and T-shirt that served as her pajamas. "Sarah! Are you all right? I heard something break in here."

Sarah looked down at the floor where her favorite coffee cup now lay in pieces. At least it had been empty. "I'm fine. I must have dozed off."

"I thought you were already in bed when I got home. That was five hours ago."

Sarah blinked. "What time is it?"

"Two o'clock in the morning."

She glanced at her watch, certain that couldn't be right. But it was. She'd been asleep in her sewing room all this time. Her joints groaned their displeasure as she slowly rose out of the chair, careful to avoid the broken cup by her feet.

Katie disappeared for a moment, then came back with a broom and a dustpan.

"Here," Sarah said, holding out her hands. "I can do it."

"I've got it," Katie told her as she swept the shards into the dustpan, then dumped them in the wastebasket.

"What are you still doing up at this hour?" Sarah asked as she followed Katie into the kitchen.

"I couldn't sleep." She set the broom back in the closet, then shut the door.

That's when Sarah noticed the dark circles under her eyes. They reminded her of the way Katie had looked when she'd first shown up at her door. "Are you all right?"

"I just have a touch of insomnia. Nothing for you to worry about."

Before Sarah could reply, Katie bid her goodnight and walked out of the kitchen. Sarah stared after her, still feeling a little fuzzy-headed from her impromptu nap. Hopefully, everything would look clearer in the morning.

CHAPTER TWENTY-EIGHT

The next day, Sarah sat hunched over her sewing machine. She didn't realize that Jason had entered the house until she looked up from her sewing machine and saw him standing in front of her.

Her hand flew to her chest. "You scared me! Why didn't you knock?"

"I did," he said, walking over to pat her shoulder. "I'm sorry, I didn't mean to startle you, but I was little scared myself when you didn't answer your door."

"I guess I couldn't hear the knock over the sound of my sewing machine."

"How's it coming? I've heard you've been working night and day."

"I'm almost finished." She lifted the presser foot on the machine, then carefully pulled out the strip of blue silk taffeta. "I'm working on the binding now. Once that's done, I'll just have trim work to do."

He walked over to the table for a closer look. "It's a beautiful quilt and, I have to admit, it's got an entertaining history."

"That it does," she said, then filled him in about New Hope and the flour sack puzzle that had led her to Latham, Kansas. "I'm hoping the centennial book will arrive today. I told Spencer to put me on speed dial so he can let me know when it gets here."

Jason pulled out a chair and sat down. "Listen, Mom, maybe you should let this go for a while."

She stared at him. "What do you mean?"

"Katie told me what happened last night. You could have been hurt."

Sarah waved away his concern. "I just nodded off at the table. That could happen to anyone."

"Maybe so, but most people don't work with sharp objects on a regular basis. What if you'd drifted off with a needle in your hand or a pair of scissors? You could have been injured."

She reached out to cup his chin. "Now who's the worrier in the family?"

"I'm serious, Mom. I think between restoring the quilt and trying to solve the mystery of Molly's disappearance, you're pushing yourself too hard."

"Nonsense," Sarah said gently. "I'm almost done with the quilt and I've got a big lead now."

"A name on a flour sack doesn't seem like that big of a lead to me. Grandma Molly could have gotten it anywhere."

"I think the New Hope campaign ribbon makes it more than a coincidence."

"They're still not definitive evidence."

Sarah suppressed a smile. Her son didn't like to lose an argument—which was one reason he'd been so successful as an attorney in California. But she could be stubborn, too. "She vanished ninety years ago—I don't think there's any definitive evidence left." She leaned across the table to pat his hand. "Don't worry about me. I'll be fine."

Jason wasn't ready to give up yet. "You could take a trip or join a bridge club. Maggie's mother volunteers at an animal shelter and walks ten to twelve dogs every day."

"That's wonderful," Sarah replied, "how *is* Maggie's mom?"

He shook his head. "You always change the subject when you know I'm right."

"I just don't happen to agree with you this time." Sarah told him.

He sighed. "I just don't want you to be disappointed if you can't find out what happened to Grandma Molly. You've already put so much time and effort into it."

So that was it. Jason was worried about her feelings. "Do you remember when you tried out for the high school basketball team?"

He blinked. "Yes. Why?"

"You were the brightest boy in the class, but not very athletic. On top of that, a lot of your classmates had been playing basketball since they were in grade school. I was certain you wouldn't make the team and tried to discourage you from trying out."

"And you were right. I guess I should have listened to you."

"No, I was wrong." Sarah smiled. "You were disappointed about it for a day or two, then you joined the jazz band and entertained the crowd at the games. You tried and failed, then moved on. That's how it's supposed to be. Failure isn't something we should fear."

"So you won't be disappointed if you don't solve the case?"

"Of course I'll be disappointed, but I've learned a lot of interesting things along the way. Some have been difficult, like the articles about Grandpa Noah in the newspaper, but others have been wonderful. I've gained insight about my father's life and feel closer to Grandma Molly than ever before."

He smiled. "You do seem to be having fun. Like the day you discovered that plat map in my office."

"And meeting Doris Hatch," Sarah continued. "I got to see the beautiful ceiling in her home." She laughed. "I even discovered the story of a jilted romance, thanks to a brick."

He joined in her laughter. "I know the girls will never forget the day all of you entered that secret passageway and found the quilt."

"That's what this journey is really about," Sarah told him. "Cherishing old memories and making new ones."

He held up both hands. "Okay, I give up. I'm glad I never had to litigate against you. Just promise me you won't take any more naps around sharp objects."

"I promise." Then she gave him a little push toward the door. "Now scoot. I need to finish this binding."

"You also need to take a break once in a while. You're invited to dinner at our house tonight. Maggie wants to show off the parlor."

"I'd love to see it." Sarah also wanted to hear about Amy's new basketball buddy. "How is the shop coming along?"

Jason shrugged. "Maggie tells me it takes a while to build a good client base."

"I'm sure that's true."

"We'll see," he said, and Sarah suddenly regretted bringing up the subject.

"So, what time should I be there?"

"We'll eat about seven. Katie's been invited too."

"Can I bring anything?"

His expression relaxed. "Well, now that you mention it, I hear your pickled beets were a big hit at that picnic the other day."

She laughed. "The twins wouldn't even try them!"

"Pickled beets weren't exactly my favorite as a kid either."

"I guess they're an acquired taste. Why don't I leave the pickled beets at home and bring something else instead. I have some ripe tomatoes and cucumbers in the garden. I could make a salad."

"Sounds perfect." He headed toward the door. "See you tonight."

~~~~~

That evening, Sarah arrived at Jason and Maggie's house just in time to see the unveiling of the parlor.

"Are your eyes closed?" Maggie asked both Jason and Sarah as she steered them toward the parlor door.

"Mine are," Sarah said, reaching out one hand to find the door frame.

"So are mine," Jason said. "I might want to keep them closed when I see how much all these renovations are going to cost."

"We'll worry about that later," Maggie said. "For now, let's just enjoy the moment."

Sarah smiled at their bantering. "How much longer do I have to keep my eyes closed?"

"You can both open your eyes on the count of three," Maggie said. "One ... two ... three!"

Sarah opened her eyes. For a moment, it was if she had stepped back in time. The parlor looked exactly like it had when she was a little girl. The walls were painted a sunny yellow and white lace curtains framed the bay window. Two wing chairs and a matching gold velvet divan stood in front of the fireplace.

Then her gaze moved to the far corner of the room, where she saw Audrey sprawled on a pale blue camelback sofa. She wore a vintage gown from the 1800s and held a book in one hand and a fan in the other. She slowly waved the fan back and forth as she read, pretending no one else was in the room.

Jason laughed when he saw his daughter. "You must be the lady of the house."

"We thought it would be fun to have the girls dress up for the unveiling," Maggie said. "This is just how it might have looked one hundred twenty years ago when the house was built."

Sarah looked around the room. "Where's Amy?"

"She's right here," Katie said as the two of them appeared in the doorway, "or should I say, *he's* right here."

Sarah smothered a laugh when she saw Amy in a pin-striped suit. The pants were too long for her, the cuffs dragging on the floor as she walked to the fireplace. She wore a fake beard and mustache too.

Sarah watched Amy pick up the antique humidor on the mantle and offer it to Jason. "Care for a cigar, sir?" she asked, lowering her voice a few octaves.

"Don't mind if I do." Jason opened the humidor. "Hey, it's empty."

"Dad," Amy said, dropping her persona. "We're just pretending!"

Katie moved next to Sarah. "Doesn't the room look great?"

Sarah nodded, still overwhelmed by how familiar it all was. She half expected Grandpa Noah to walk through the door and offer her a licorice pipe.

"Well," Maggie asked Sarah. "How did we do?"

"It's amazing." She tilted her head toward the ceiling. "Even the chandelier looks the same."

"I searched for that forever," Maggie replied. "I finally found a company online that specializes in vintage light fixtures. It cost more than I'd planned to spend, but I think it's worth every penny."

Jason turned to Maggie. "You've been saying that a lot lately. Have we ever gone *under* budget?"

"This dress was under budget," Audrey said, shedding her role as a Victorian lady in repose. "We found it at the thrift store for only twelve dollars."

"Those are great costumes," Sarah said. "Where did you find the suit?"

"I have a bunch of old costumes in a trunk in the storage unit. It was pretty wrinkled when I finally dug it out, but Katie ironed it for me."

"We should have a costume party," Audrey said, her blue eyes wide with excitement. "Wouldn't that be fun?"

"Who would we invite?" Amy asked.

"How about your new boyfriend?"

Amy blushed. "He's not my boyfriend. We both just like basketball."

"Trina said you let him win."

"I did not!"

"Did too."

"Enough," Maggie said, holding up both hands to ward off the impending squall. "We need to get dinner on the table, so you two should go upstairs and change clothes."

"How can I help?" Sarah asked.

"You can relax. You and Katie are our guests tonight. Jason and the girls will probably be more help than I need."

"Well, if that's the case," Jason began, but Maggie stopped him with a kiss.

"You're not getting out of helping me that easily." She pushed him toward the kitchen. "Let's go." Katie followed after them.

Sarah found herself alone in the parlor. She walked slowly around the perimeter of the room, remembering all the times she'd played in here as a child. Grandpa Noah had taught her checkers and let her win most of the time. Her parents had taken her picture by the fireplace once, and every December a Christmas tree had stood in the corner by the window.

Grandma Molly had once sat in this room, too, Sarah thought to herself. She'd warmed herself by the fire and stood at the window to watch people stroll by the house. Then she'd disappeared without a trace.

Her family deserved to know the truth about what had happened to her, no matter how ugly. And Sarah didn't intend to stop until she found it.

CHAPTER TWENTY-NINE

Spencer Hewitt sat on the library steps when she pulled into the library parking lot the next day. He held a cup of coffee in one hand and the remains of a pecan roll in the other.

"Good timing." Spencer popped the sweet roll into his mouth, then washed it down with coffee. "I'm just finishing my morning break."

"I came as soon as I got your phone message," Sarah said as they walked inside. "I must have been out in the garden when you called."

"It's right here," Spencer said as he rounded the circulation desk. "I haven't even opened it yet."

Sarah watched him tear open the priority box, then pull out a light blue book that was about two inches thick.

"Here you go," he said, handing it to her.

"How much do I owe you?"

He checked the postage label on the box. "Ten dollars and seventy cents."

"That's certainly a lot cheaper than flying to Kansas," Sarah said as she reached for her billfold.

Spencer pulled a stamped envelope out of the box. "It looks like the Latham librarian included a self-addressed envelope to mail the postage money in."

"That's handy," she said, giving him the money.

"It's been a pleasure doing business with you," he said, placing the money in the envelope and sealing it. "I'll make sure this goes out with our mail today."

"Thanks, Spencer." She picked up the book. "I really appreciate it."

"Anytime, Sarah."

She turned around and walked to the nearest table, not wanting to wait another moment to look at the book. Pulling out a chair, she sat down, then read the title on the front cover: *A Centennial History of Latham County, Kansas, 1887 to 1987.*

She opened the front cover and saw a dedication to the original settlers of Latham County.

To the men and women who faced great hardships traveling here and settling this land. They built homes and schools and churches so that they and their families could have a better life. We dedicate this book to them and hope that we may carry on their legacy.

She turned the page to the table of contents, noting that the first half of the book was filled with information about the early settlers and the railroad. It also featured articles about local businesses and had an entire chapter dedicated to the Durable Flour Company. In the middle of the centennial book was a section about New Hope and the tornado that had leveled half the town.

The second part of the book was about the families that lived in or near Latham. She turned to that part of the book first, eager to find Molly.

The families were listed in alphabetical order. Some of the family sagas were several paragraphs long, full of specific details about their ancestors. The Bell family, for instance, had a separate article about the life of each one of their thirteen adult children, taking up more than ten pages in the book. Other family sagas were just a few brief sentences, giving the most basic information. There were also vintage photographs throughout the book that seemed to span almost every generation.

Sarah quickly thumbed through the pages until she got to the H section of the families. "Haber, Halstead, Hampton, Healy, Hill," she whispered as she slid her index finger over the pages. "Hiatt, Himmelberg, Holden, Hollis..."

She stopped, a thrill shooting through her. There *was* a Hollis family from the area. Several branches in fact. The original Hollis family was headed by Carl and Bertha Hollis. According to their biography, they'd traveled with their eight children from Willow Grove, Pennsylvania, to Latham County, Kansas, in 1886. They bought farmland there and raised six children to adulthood.

One of the surviving sons listed had to be Molly's father. But which one? Frank, Harold, Walter, or Fred?

Sarah turned to the next page and found the story of Carl and Bertha's oldest son, Frank Hollis. It was accompanied by a family photograph circa 1905. The heavily bearded Frank Hollis and his portly wife, Helen, were seated in chairs with their three children standing behind them.

Sarah ran her index finger along the small caption at the bottom of the photograph. *The Frank Hollis family of New Hope. Left to right: Dena, George, and Molly.*

Sarah froze. She'd found her. After all this time, she'd finally found her. Her gaze moved to the young girl in the grainy photograph. She couldn't have been more than ten years old when the picture was taken. She wore a wide bow in her hair, a long dress with a lace collar, and high-top shoes. Her expression was solemn, like the rest of her family, but it was hard to make out her features due to the poor quality of the photograph.

Sarah's throat tightened and she was surprised by the emotion that welled up inside of her. This was her grandmother as a young girl. She took a deep breath, trying to collect herself, then began to read the Hollis family history.

Frank Hollis moved to Latham County, Kansas, in 1886. There he met Helen Mayer..."

"Mayer," Sarah breathed, recognizing the name from the campaign ribbon. The man running for mayor had been Grandma Molly's relative.

She turned back to the story. She was so close to solving the ninety-year-old mystery. *Frank and Helen were married in New Hope, Kansas, in 1890. To this union were born three children: Dena, George, and Molly. Two children survived to adulthood. The youngest child, ten-year-old Molly, became ill with diphtheria and died in 1906 ..."*

The rest of the words blurred as Sarah sat back in her chair. That couldn't be right. She read the sentence again, just to make sure she'd understood it. But there was no mistake. Molly Hollis had died in 1906.

CHAPTER THIRTY

Sarah sat in her chair, shell-shocked, trying to make sense of it. This couldn't be possible. All the clues fit. The New Hope campaign ribbon in the quilt, along with the flour sacks from the Durable Flour Company. An Elm Street in Latham. A girl from New Hope by the name of Molly Hollis. Even the dates were right. If she'd been ten in 1906, that would make her twenty-four when she disappeared in 1920.

Only, Molly couldn't have disappeared if she was dead. She couldn't have married Grandpa Noah either, or made her special cookies for her son.

Or sewn the quilt Sarah had found in the secret passageway.

Spencer Hewitt walked up to the table. "Did you find what you were looking for?"

"Yes," Sarah replied, her mind reeling, "and no."

Spencer raised an eyebrow, but Sarah didn't know how to explain the strange twist her investigation had just taken. She rose from her chair and picked up the book.

"I'll tell you about it later," she promised. *As soon as I figure it out myself.*

When Sarah arrived home a few minutes later, she carried the Latham Centennial Book into the living room. Taking a seat in her rocking chair, she opened the book on her lap and read the Hollis family story again. Then she thoroughly checked the other branches of the Hollis family from that era, but none had a daughter named Molly.

So why had Grandma Molly used old campaign ribbons for someone named Mayer in the quilt? There had to be a connection. Sarah turned the pages of the centennial book until she found the family name she was looking for, only there was no photograph with this story.

Paul and Charlotta (Koch) Mayer settled on a farm near Latham, Kansas, in 1855. Dates of birth and death unknown. They had three children: Helen Mayer Hollis (see story on pg. 141), Ruth Mayer Sanderson, and John Mayer.

Ruth Mayer was born on April 11, 1877, and married Abner Sanderson in Latham in 1894. She passed away from a brain hemorrhage in 1917. She and her husband had one daughter, Adele Sanderson, born November 29, 1895, who succumbed to consumption in August 1921. Ab Sanderson, undone by the grief of losing his family, was later committed to the Kansas State Insane Asylum until his death in 1929.

John Mayer was born in 1890. He worked as a supervisor at the Durable Flour Company and, after moving to New

Hope, ran an unsuccessful campaign for mayor of the town. He married Julia Crane, of Latham, in 1920. He drowned during a camping trip in 1928. The couple had no children.

Sarah leaned back in her chair. Now she knew that Molly Hollis's uncle, John Mayer, had run for mayor of New Hope. That meant the Molly Hollis in the photograph had to be her grandmother. Perhaps the person who'd written the Hollis family biography had been mistaken. The more Sarah thought about it, the more she liked that theory. Stories often changed over time, through miscommunications or simple mistakes. If Molly had left the area shortly after reaching adulthood, she wouldn't have any direct descendants living in Latham, Kansas, to set the story straight.

But maybe her siblings did.

She turned to page 141 in the centennial book to read about Dena Hollis Bosley.

Arthur and Dena (Hollis) Bosley were married in 1915 in Latham, Kansas, where Arthur worked for the Durable Flour Company until his death in 1947. Dena taught Sunday school for 20 years and sang in the church choir. They adopted a son, Andrew Bosley, on August 10, 1921.

That was it for Dena's story, with no descendants listed for Andrew and no way to know if he was even still alive. She'd put him on the back burner for now, hoping to find a faster way to answer her questions.

Sarah turned to the story of Molly's brother, George Hollis. She quickly scanned it, thrilled to find a long list of descendants. According to George's family history, his grandson, David Hollis, had owned a farm south of Latham with his wife, Susan, when the book was written. Of course, the centennial book had been written over twenty years ago. She hoped the farm, and David, were still there.

It took only a minute for her to access the online phone directory for Latham, Kansas, on the computer. Then she searched for David Hollis, hoping he hadn't moved some-time after the book was published.

She was in luck. There was a listing for David and Susan Hollis. Sarah reached for her cell phone and dialed the number on the computer screen, trying to formulate exactly what she was going to say.

"Hello?" a woman's voice answered.

"Is this Susan Hollis?"

"Yes, it is."

"My name is Sarah Hart and I'd like to talk to you about…"

"I'm sorry," Susan said politely, "we're not interested."

Click.

Sarah blinked, realizing the woman had hung up on her. Obviously, she'd thought Sarah was trying to sell her some-thing. She dialed the number and tried again.

"Hello?"

"Please don't hang up," Sarah said. "I'm not trying to sell you anything. This is about one of your husband's relatives. Her name is Molly Hollis."

For a moment, the woman didn't say anything. "He doesn't have any relatives living here by that name."

"She was his great-aunt, born in 1896, if my math is correct," Sarah told her. "Molly was the youngest sister of your husband's grandfather, George Hollis."

"Who are you again?"

"Sarah Hart. I know this is really strange, but my grandfather was married ninety years ago to a woman named Molly Hollis."

"I really don't think…" Susan began, her voice laced with irritation.

But Sarah pushed forward, wanting to get her story out before the woman hung up on her again. "Molly disappeared a year after their wedding, and no one ever knew what happened to her. Recently, I came across a quilt that had reportedly disappeared with her. Inside was a note…" Her voice trailed off when she realized it would take too long to explain it all.

"And?" the woman asked, her tone more curious now.

"And I've been trying to find some answers," Sarah finally concluded. "My search eventually led me to Latham, Kansas, and to you."

"I remember my mother-in-law talking about an aunt named Molly who died as a young girl, but that couldn't be the same person who married your grandfather."

Susan had just confirmed what Sarah had read in the centennial book, but she couldn't give up yet. "Is it possible there was another Molly Hollis living in the area during that time?"

"I don't believe so," Susan said. "David's the last of the Hollis clan around here and he's never mentioned another Molly as far as I know."

All of the loose threads in this mystery were unraveling. Sarah wasn't sure what to do next. "Thank you for your time," she said, trying not to let the disappointment show in her voice. "If your husband does remember another Molly Hollis or if you think of anything that might be pertinent to my search, could you please give me a call?"

"Of course," the woman replied, sounding much more sympathetic now. "What's your number?"

Sarah gave it to her, then said, "Please don't hesitate to call for any reason, no matter how small."

"All right," Susan told her. "I hope you find what you're looking for."

She didn't hold out much hope as she hung up the phone. She'd been counting on the Latham Centennial Book to lead her to Molly Hollis. Instead, she found herself, quite literally, at another dead end.

CHAPTER THIRTY-ONE

The next morning, Sarah slept late, having stayed up half the night trying to figure out another angle to pursue in Grandma Molly's disappearance. At last, she'd fallen into a fitful sleep, dreaming of her Grandpa Noah and a sweet little girl with a wide bow in her hair.

She arose with a pounding headache and walked slowly downstairs. The house was quiet, which meant Katie and Rita had already left for the day. Her headache drove her to the kitchen. She retrieved a small bottle of aspirin from the cupboard, popped two of them into her mouth, and then washed them down with a glass of water.

After putting on a pot of coffee, Sarah sat down at the table and reached for *Country Cottage* magazine, hoping to get her mind off her headache. As she flipped through the pages to a popular column on antiques, a soft thud rattled the back door.

"Sarah?" Martha called out. "Can you open the door for me? I've got my hands full out here."

She combed her fingers through her unruly hair as she rose from the chair, then tightened the sash of her robe. Even though it was ten o'clock in the morning, she was in no shape to receive visitors. Then again, Martha was more like family.

"Well, look at you," Martha said when Sarah opened the door for her. "Did you just roll out of bed?"

"About ten minutes ago," Sarah said. "I hope you don't mind seeing me in my jammies."

"Mind? I'd put on jammies myself if I had them with me." She held up two take-out cups from the Spotted Dog. "Jammies are the perfect outfit for drinking chai lattes with extra whipped cream."

"What's the special occasion?" Sarah asked, as she walked over to the counter and turned off her coffee machine.

Martha set the cups on the table, then turned around to face her. "It's my way of saying thank you for providing such a wonderful shoulder to lean on when I needed it. I can't tell you how much I appreciate it."

Sarah reached out to give her a hug. "You don't have to tell me. I was just following your good example."

Martha gave her an extra squeeze before releasing her and taking a seat at the table. "I was going to pick up some cinnamon buns to go with our drinks, but I've recently started a diet."

"I thought you didn't believe in diets."

"That's only when I don't *want* to diet," Martha said. "To tell you the truth, Ernie's diagnosis made me take a second look at my own health. I figure it won't hurt me to eat better and start exercising."

"We could start taking walks together."

"I'd like that," Martha said, then took a sip of her drink. "How many calories do you suppose a beverage like this has?"

"You don't want to know," Sarah said.

Martha laughed. "I suppose you're right. I'm not about to give up the really good stuff. I'll just add a few more vegetables and try to climb the stairs a few more times a day. Maybe if I put all the sweets in the attic, I can burn off the calories before I eat them."

The visual of Martha climbing two flights of stairs every time she wanted a cookie was so funny that Sarah almost choked on her drink. Martha was just the medicine she needed right now to bring her out of the doldrums. Sarah told Martha as much, then explained how the investigation into Molly's disappearance had come to a grinding halt.

"That's too bad," Martha said. "I know how much time and energy you've put into this. Maybe something new will come up soon."

"I don't know what it could be. I think I've finally run out of clues." Sarah cradled her cup in her hands. "Now tell me how Ernie is doing."

"He has his ups and downs. It seems every time he drops something or forgets something he blames the Parkinson's."

"I'd probably do the same thing."

"Me, too." Martha took a sip of her latte. "He's taking a prescription drug to help ease his symptoms, but I wish they'd invent a pill to help us accept what's happening to him."

"Acceptance will come," Sarah assured her. "It just takes a while."

Martha drew up her shoulders. "In the meantime, I've decided it's my job to make him laugh at least once a day. Ernie's always liked a good joke."

Sarah smiled at her. "Then you should tell him your plan to hike up to the attic for cookies and cake whenever you get a craving."

Martha chuckled as she reached for her crocheting bag. "Maybe I will."

Sarah watched her pull out her latest project and felt life fall back into place again. Martha was on the road to accepting Ernie's illness with her usual good humor and grace. Sarah knew there would be some bumps on the path ahead, but it was better to face them with laughter than with fear.

"How's Katie doing?" Martha asked. "I saw her in church Sunday, but didn't get a chance to talk to her."

"I can't tell," Sarah replied honestly. "Some days she seems fine, and other days..."

"What?"

She shrugged. "I'm not sure how to describe it. I guess withdrawn is the best word to use. Like she's on the outside looking in."

"Is she still working for Jason and Maggie?"

"Yes, but she'll be finished at the house today. She's just got some touch-up work left to do. Jason, Maggie, and the twins are planning to go to Springfield this morning to do some school shopping, so Katie won't have any distractions."

Martha shook her head. "I can't believe school will be starting again in a couple of weeks. Kyle can't wait to go back to college. He says Maple Hill is too boring."

Sarah held up her chai latte. "How can anyone say Maple Hill is boring when you show up at the door with chai lattes?"

"And catch you in your pajamas."

Sarah sighed. "Something tells me I'm not going to live that down for a while."

"Hey, it gives me a great excuse to stay in my pajamas all day. I'll just say I'm following your example."

"Okay, I get the hint," Sarah rose from her chair. "I'll get dressed."

"Don't do it on my account. You know I'm just teasing."

"I know, but it *is* almost..." She glanced over at the stove clock, wondering where the morning had gone. "Eleven? Yikes. My day's almost half over and I haven't done a thing."

"Is it that late already?" Martha packed up her crochet supplies. "I'd better get home and start making a healthy lunch."

Sarah walked her to the door. "Thank you for the latte and the company. They were just what I needed this morning."

"Me, too," Martha said, then gave her a wave. "See you soon."

Sarah closed the kitchen door and headed upstairs to shower and change, trying to ignore the layer of dust she saw on the sitting room furniture. She'd let the house fall by the wayside again, too involved in restoring the quilt and investigating Grandma Molly's case to get much cleaning done.

When she reemerged from her bedroom thirty minutes later, she felt much better. Her headache was gone and she was ready to face the day. She might be stymied in solving Grandma Molly's case, but she could finish her quilt. It had provided some of her most intriguing clues so far and brought her closer to her long-lost grandmother. It was as if Grandma Molly was trying to point her in the right direction and now Sarah just needed to figure out which way to go.

She headed downstairs to her sewing room and walked over to the table. She'd already pinned the new blue taffeta binding around the edge of the quilt. Now it was time to attach it permanently.

Sarah carried the quilt over to the sewing machine, where she carefully stitched the binding onto the top of the quilt. As she turned the first corner, she thought about the stories she'd read in the Latham Centennial Book, feeling like she was missing something.

When she'd finished, she removed the quilt from the machine and carried it to the table. She folded the narrow binding over the raw edge of the quilt and pinned it neatly in place on the back. Then she threaded a needle and deftly blind-stitched the binding to the backing.

There was only one more thing she needed to do.

Sarah walked over to her desk and opened the top drawer. Inside was the note Grandma Molly had written the night she disappeared. Sarah picked it up and carried it back to the quilt. She'd left a tiny seam opening between two of the fabric patches on the quilt top. She slipped the note inside, then took a threaded needle and closed the seam opening. The note was part of the quilt's history and Sarah always tried to remain as true to a quilt's history as possible. In her opinion, that was the primary duty of any good vintage quilt restorer.

Tears filled her eyes as she looked at the finished quilt. Restoring it had been a long, painstaking process, but worth every moment.

She'd give the quilt to her father this evening and take along a picnic supper with all his favorite foods. It was too bad she'd forgotten to ask for Katie's cookie recipe. She'd loved to bake him those chocolate spice cookies. That seemed especially fitting on the day she presented him with the quilt his mother had made for him.

Excited about the day ahead, Sarah picked up the phone and dialed Katie's number, but after five rings it went to voice mail. "This is Katie, please leave a message."

"Hi, Katie, this is Sarah. I know you're busy painting, but when you get a chance could you let me know if you ever found that cookie recipe? I want to do some baking this afternoon. Thanks."

Sarah rang off, then headed upstairs to do a little dusting while she waited for Katie to call her back. She needed to do some grocery shopping for the supper she planned to make, but first she needed a list of ingredients for the chocolate spice cookies.

As she ran a dust cloth over the top of the bookcase, Sarah began to sing one of her favorite hymns. *"Sweet hour of prayer, sweet hour of prayer, that calls me from a world of care. And bids me at my Father's throne, make all my wants and wishes known…*

An odd buzzing sound distracted her. She stilled, trying to figure out the source. As the buzzing continued, she followed the sound, all the way into Katie's bathroom.

That's where she found Katie's cell phone. It was sitting on the marble vanity top, half hidden beneath a cosmetics bag. By the time Sarah picked it up the buzzing had stopped. She was about to set it back on the sink when she noticed the name on the Caller ID screen.

CHAPTER THIRTY-TWO

As Sarah turned onto Bristol Street, she was dismayed to see a road construction crew in her path. Barriers had been set up for the entire block, forcing her to turn into the narrow alley that ran behind Jason's house.

She parked her car on the side of the alley, then hurried to the back door. It was locked, which surprised her. Sarah assumed Katie had probably locked the doors since she was working here alone. That made sense for a girl from the big city, especially one with a crazy ex-boyfriend.

She knocked once, but there was no answer. A radio blasted country songs from the open window on the second floor, meaning Katie probably couldn't hear her.

Fortunately, Jason had given Sarah an extra key shortly after they'd moved to Maple Hill. She retrieved the key from her purse, then let herself into the house.

She walked quickly past the persimmon walls, granite countertops, and stainless steel appliances as she made her way to the back staircase. She inhaled fresh paint fumes as she climbed the stairs, the steps squeaking under her feet just as they had when she was a child. When she reached the second floor, Sarah checked each room until she found Katie. The girl stood on a ladder with her back to the door, applying taupe paint along the blue painter's tape edging the ceiling. Oblivious to Sarah's presence, Katie sang along to a raucous country song on the radio.

Sarah leaned down to turn off the radio. "We need to talk, Katie."

Katie gasped as she turned around. "Oh, Sarah, it's you! I didn't know you were here. How did you get in?"

"I've got a key."

Katie stared at her. "Is something wrong?"

Sarah stepped farther into the room. "There's something you need to know."

"What?" Katie cried. "Has something happened to Jason or Maggie? To the girls?"

It touched Sarah to know her family meant so much to Katie. "No, it has nothing to do with them. It's about Evan."

The color drained from Katie's face. She set the paint-brush aside, then climbed down the ladder. "What about him?"

Katie's reaction surprised her. She looked apprehensive instead of scared. Like she was about to be caught in another lie.

Sarah reached into her pocket and pulled out Katie's cell phone. "He called you."

"That means he's found me again," she said, her voice hollow. Then she looked up at Sarah. "I couldn't find my phone this morning, so I left the house without it. I was starting to feel safe ..."

"You left it in the bathroom," Sarah told her. "I heard it buzzing and when I picked it up I saw Evan's name on the Caller ID."

Katie froze. "I need to run again."

Sarah moved closer to her. "That's the last thing you should do."

Katie met her gaze. "If he's not in Maple Hill yet, he soon will be. If he knows my cell phone number, that means he can track me through my cell phone's tower signal." She reached for a rag and frantically wiped the wet paint off her hands. "I don't have much time."

"Let's go to the police," Sarah said. "You can't let Evan keep terrorizing you this way."

"No," she cried, dropping the rag on the floor. "You don't understand ..."

Sarah understood that panic was driving Katie at the moment, and she needed to find some way to calm her down. "Then let's go for a drive. We can figure something out."

"I knew I never should have come here," Katie said, slowly shaking her head. "You've all been so nice to me and now you're in danger."

Before Sarah could reply, the sound of breaking glass made them both jump. Katie hurried over to the window and looked outside.

Then she turned to Sarah, her face etched with fear. "It's Evan."

ori?" a man's voice shouted. "I'm through playing hide-and-seek with you. Come out, come out, wherever you are."

He was inside the house.

Sarah dialed 911 on Katie's phone, then shielded the mouthpiece with her hand when the operator answered. "This is Sarah Hart," she said in a low voice. "There's an intruder at 106 Bristol Street. We're in danger here. Please hurry."

As she clicked off the phone, Sarah could hear the man talking to himself as he roamed around the first floor looking for Katie. She hoped the police got here soon.

"I know you're here, Tori. I've been watching you."

A chill ran down Sarah's spine. No wonder Katie had been so terrified of this man. Just the sound of his voice was enough for Sarah. She didn't even want to imagine the abuse Katie must have suffered when they were together. It probably explained a lot of things about her.

Katie grasped her arm. "You have to get out of here. He's dangerous. I don't know what he'll do if he finds you here."

"I'm not going anywhere," Sarah whispered, "unless you come with me."

"No, please," Katie cried, a sob escaping her. "It's my fault he's here at all. I should never have put you and your family in this kind of danger."

Sarah considered their options. They couldn't risk going down either the front or the back staircase. Those squeaky stairs announced every move.

Just like they were doing now. Katie clutched her arm as they both heard the stairs squeak under the weight of Evan's footsteps. Katie's grip tightened on Sarah's arm. "What are we going to do?"

"Hide," Sarah whispered, then led her to Amy's bedroom. She hurried into the closet and lifted the loose floorboard. She turned the crank just far enough to allow them to slip inside the secret passageway. She replaced the floorboard, then followed Katie into the narrow, humid passageway. She closed the door behind her, entombing them in darkness. A dank, dusty odor invaded her nostrils as she tried to steady her breathing. She reached out one hand, trying to find Katie in the darkness.

The girl jumped when she touched her, then gripped Sarah's hand. Her fingers were ice cold. Sarah gave Katie's hand a reassuring squeeze, praying that God would keep them safe. "Tori?" Evan called out, his tone brisker now.

"Don't make me look for you. I've been looking for you for months and I'm tired of your games."

Katie's grip tightened on Sarah as she moved closer to her. Goose bumps covered Sarah's arms even as tiny drops of perspiration ran down the back of her neck.

"You've got to be here somewhere, Tori. I'm not leaving until I find you."

When Katie whimpered, Sarah put her arm around the girl and whispered, "We have to be quiet."

Katie gave a shaky nod of her head.

A hard thump sounded on the wall a few feet away from where they stood. "I'll knock down this entire house if I have to," he warned. "So stop messing with me."

Sarah closed her eyes. Lord, help us!

Was this how Grandma Molly had felt the night she disappeared? Had she been hiding here, too, hoping someone wouldn't find her?

"Let me go out there, Sarah," Katie whispered in the darkness. "He doesn't know you're here. We'll leave and you'll be safe."

But Katie wouldn't be safe, and that was all that mattered to Sarah right now.

Katie started to move toward the panel door.

"No," Sarah hissed, pulling her closer. "I'm not going to let you disappear too."

"Are you hiding in the closet?" Evan shouted. "Under the bed? Am I getting warm?" He was so close Sarah could hear his heavy, uneven breathing through the wall.

Our Father, who art in Heaven, she prayed silently, *hallowed be thy name...*

A siren sounded outside the house.

"You called the cops on me?" Evan shouted in disbelief. "That wasn't very smart."

A stampede of footsteps pounded on the stairs and a moment later, Nate Webber, the chief of police, barked out a command. "Stop right there! I said stop! Hands up!"

Evan muttered an oath, which was followed by the sound of glass shattering and the scrape of heavy furniture being dragged across the floor. Sarah could picture him trying to barricade himself behind Amy's large oak dresser. What if he had a gun?

"I'm just looking for my girlfriend, officer," Evan shouted. "We had a fight."

"Move away from the dresser," Chief Webber ordered. "Hands up. I said up!"

A heavy thud sounded against the wall, followed by a loud groan. "Hey, watch what you're doing!" Evan cried. "This is police brutality."

Sarah heard the sound of metal clicking, then Chief Webber saying, "You have the right to remain silent. Anything you say can and will be used against you in a court of law. You have the right to an attorney. If you cannot afford an attorney, one will be appointed to you. Do you understand these rights?"

"Yeah," Evan spat out. "Now loosen these cuffs."

"Take him away, officers," Chief Webber said.

Feeling safe now, Sarah pulled open the panel door, wincing at the sudden brightness. She walked out of the secret passageway with Katie right behind her.

"Mrs. Hart!" Chief Webber said, moving toward her while his officers escorted a combative Evan down the stairs. "Are you two all right?"

"We're fine," Sarah assured him, still feeling a little shaky. "You've got great timing."

He looked past her into the closet, where the door to the secret passageway still stood open. "And it looks like you had a great hiding place."

Sarah nodded, wondering what she and Katie would have done if Amy hadn't found the secret passageway.

"I'll need you two to come down to the station house when you're ready and give us your report," he said as he headed out of the bedroom and down the hallway. "We've got the guy on breaking and entering, but I'd love to add more charges."

"We can come right now," Sarah started to follow him when Katie grabbed her arm.

"Wait, Sarah." Her voice wobbled as she stood rooted to the floor.

Sarah turned to face her. "What is it?"

Katie met Sarah's gaze. "There's something I have to tell you."

CHAPTER THIRTY-FOUR

Two hours later, Jason and Maggie arrived at the station house and were escorted into one of the interview rooms. A table and four chairs stood on the faded green linoleum, surrounded by four gray walls that made the room seem small and cramped.

"What's going on?" Jason asked his mother. "Where's Katie? Is she all right?"

"She's fine," Sarah assured them as they all took a seat at the table. "She's in the other room with Chief Webber. He's taking her witness statement."

Maggie breathed a sigh of relief. "We couldn't believe it when we got your call about that man breaking into our house. I'm so glad you and Katie are all right."

"Where are the girls?" Sarah asked.

"We dropped the girls off at Pru's house when we got back to Maple Hill," Jason explained. "Her parents were kind enough to offer to keep them until we get this all sorted out."

"It's a mess," Sarah admitted. "And you don't even know the half of it."

"Then why don't you tell us?" Jason moved his chair closer to the table, the metal legs scraping against the floor.

"Katie needs a lawyer." She looked over at her son.

He shook his head. "She doesn't need a lawyer to obtain a restraining order. Hopefully, that ex-boyfriend will be in prison long enough to learn his lesson, but we can find ways to protect her when he gets out."

"I don't think he'll be getting out any time soon," Sarah replied. "He's just been charged with larceny on top of the other charges."

Maggie's brow wrinkled. "I don't understand."

Sarah sighed. "Neither did I until Katie confessed to possessing stolen property."

Maggie almost fell out of her chair. "What?"

"I'm afraid it's true," Sarah said. "Katie's been on the run not only from Evan but from the police."

Jason's face darkened. "This is why you should've checked her references right away, Mom."

She hadn't checked Rita's references either, but decided now wasn't a good time to admit it. Sarah had given her rental form a cursory glance, her instincts telling her Rita was a good woman. Besides, Rita had listed her father as her only reference on the rental form. It was doubtful he'd say anything negative about his daughter even if she were a master criminal.

"You trusted Katie," Jason said. "You let her into your home."

"So did we." Maggie looked between Jason and Sarah. "Could there be some kind of mistake?"

"No," said a voice from the doorway. They all turned around to see Katie standing there. Her eyes were red-rimmed, and her face pale and drawn.

Jason rose to his feet and, for a moment, Sarah didn't know how he would react. Then he pulled out an empty chair. "Please sit down, Katie. I think it's time we heard the whole story."

Katie walked slowly into the room, then sank into the chair next to Sarah. "Where do you want me to start?"

Sarah turned to her. "Tell them what you told me."

Katie placed her hands on the scarred wooden table and knotted her fingers together. "Well, first I want to say that I feel like a complete idiot for falling for a guy like Evan Gould."

"How did you meet him?" Maggie asked.

"He worked with me at a home improvement company in Chicago. In fact, he was the owner's stepson. We'd go out on jobs together. He was funny and nice. We started dating, and he was always flashing money around, taking me to expensive restaurants." A flush crept up her face. "I didn't realize until too late that it was money he'd stolen from our clients."

Jason kept his gaze directly on Katie. Sarah knew he'd represented hundreds of clients, both the guilty and the innocent, honing a razor-sharp intuition about which ones were telling the truth. "How did you find out?"

Katie swallowed. "One of our clients had security cameras hidden in the house we were painting. Evan smoked, so I didn't really question it when he left the room we were painting to take a cigarette break. It turned out he was scoping out the house so he could burglarize it later."

"And the cameras caught him casing the joint," Jason concluded, "and since you worked with him, the police thought you were partners in crime."

"Even worse," Sarah said. "He hid evidence in my apartment—small, but expensive items stolen from their clients. Then he told Katie he'd frame her for those thefts if she ever left him. That's when she saw the real Evan Gould and it terrified her."

"So you ran away," Jason said, still staring at Katie. "And you've been running ever since."

"That's what happened." Katie got up from her chair and walked over to the barred window. "I told you I was an idiot."

Sarah shifted in her chair, feeling uneasy. Something was niggling at her again about Grandma Molly's case, triggered by something Jason had said earlier, but she couldn't put her finger on it.

"So why isn't Gould in jail?" Maggie asked. "They got him on tape, didn't they?"

"Only for that one incident," Katie clarified, "and since nothing was actually stolen, he got off with a hefty fine and probation. The police suspect him in the other burglaries, too, but they had no proof until today."

A moment later, the door to the interview room opened and Chief Webber entered. Sarah straightened in her chair, forcing herself to focus on him instead of trying to remember what Jason had said.

Chief Webber looked over at Jason. "Are you her lawyer?"

"No," Katie said, moving back to the table.

"Yes," Jason said, rising to his feet. He looked at Katie. "Believe me, you need a lawyer and I'm a good one, if I do say so myself."

"I don't have any money."

He reached out to pat her shoulder. "Don't worry. I represent friends for free." Then he looked over at Chief Webber. "Can we have a few more minutes in here?"

"Sure," he replied and left.

Katie breathed a sigh of relief. "I don't know what to say."

Maggie got up to hug her. "You don't have to say anything. We understand."

Her words made Katie dissolve into a torrent of tears. Sarah reached out and pulled her into her arms. She let the girl cry on her shoulder, gently rubbing Katie's back as all the tears and pain and fear drained out of her.

At last, Katie's sobs quieted until they were just small hiccups.

"Feel better?" Sarah asked gently.

"I do," Katie said. "A lot better. I'm glad you all finally know the truth. The whole truth. I never planned to stay in

Maple Hill so long. I was going to move on soon, but it was almost like having a family again."

"I'm glad you stayed," Sarah told her.

Katie sniffed. "Me, too." Then she turned to Jason. "What do you think is going to happen to me?"

"I don't know," he said honestly. "Do you have a criminal record?"

"No, nothing," Katie replied. "Not even a traffic violation."

"Well, that should work in your favor," Jason said. "The first thing we need to do is talk to a judge about bail."

Maggie turned to her husband. "She won't have to go to jail, will she?"

When Jason didn't answer right away, Sarah's heart contracted in her chest. Just sitting in this gray, cramped room was bad enough. She didn't want to think of Katie locked in a jail cell.

"I'll do my best." Jason walked to the door, his hand resting on the knob. "I can't promise anything more at this point. These are serious charges and I'm going to have to hear all the facts before I can figure out the best move."

"I'm sorry to put you in this position," Katie told him.

"Don't be sorry," he told her, his concern shining in his blue eyes. Eyes that reminded Sarah so much of her father. "My courtroom skills have gotten a little rusty since we moved here. This will help me polish them up."

"What should I do next?" Katie asked.

"I'll pay your bail," Sarah told her. "And you'll come home."

Katie sighed as she turned to Sarah. "How will I ever re-pay you for everything? I don't think bailing me out is part of our rental agreement."

"You can repay me with your chocolate spice cookie recipe."

Katie blinked. "I've never made chocolate spice cookies."

Sarah wondered if she'd called them by the wrong name. "The cookies you made for the bake sale," she clarified.

"You mean the white chocolate truffles?"

Sarah started to wonder if all the stress had affected Katie's memory. "You made white truffles and dark choco-late cookies. I saw them in the box you left on the counter."

"I only made the white truffles," Katie insisted. "Rita made the chocolate cookies. She told me it was an old family recipe."

Sarah stared at Katie, confused for a moment. Then ev-erything started falling into place.

CHAPTER THIRTY-FIVE

When Sarah arrived home, she saw Rita's red convertible in the driveway. Katie had gone to Bridge Street Church to talk to Pastor John, feeling the need for some spiritual counseling.

Once inside, Sarah headed straight for her sewing room and grabbed her notebook and the Latham Centennial Book before sitting down at her desk. Her head buzzed with all the information she'd gathered since finding the quilt. Now it was time to put it all together.

The key had been in this room all the time, but it wasn't the quilt. It was Rita's rental form. She opened the file drawer to search for it, remembering the way she'd barely looked at the form after Rita had filled it out. Now seemed like the perfect time to check Rita's references.

Twenty minutes later, Sarah hung up the phone. She took a few moments to gather herself. When she was finally ready, she headed upstairs.

"Hey, there." Rita reclined on the love seat with the latest edition of the *Maple Hill Monitor* open on her lap. "Are you looking for the newspaper?"

"Actually, I'm looking for you." Sarah sat down in a chair, still a little shaken by her discovery. "I'm pretty sure you're my cousin."

Rita lowered the newspaper. "What?"

She took a deep breath. "Maybe I'd better start from the beginning. You see, my grandmother mysteriously disappeared ninety years ago and I've been trying to find out what happened to her. The clues eventually led me to Latham, Kansas, and a woman named Adele Sanderson."

Surprise dimmed Rita's smile. "But that's ..."

"Your grandmother," Sarah finished for her. "I know, although it took me a while to figure it out even when the clues were right in front of me." She held up Rita's rental form. "Adele is your middle name."

"I was named after my father's birth mother, Adele," Rita murmured as she stared at Sarah. "He was adopted."

Sarah leaned back in her chair, feeling a little better now that she'd gotten this much out. "I read about his adoption in the Latham Centennial Book, although the information didn't seem significant to me at the time. I should have connected Andrew Bosley's adoption in August 1921 with Adele Sanderson's death in the same month and year, but I was looking for Grandma Molly, not a baby."

"Grandma Molly?" Rita echoed.

Sarah nodded. "Your grandmother—*our* grandmother—used her dead cousin's name as her alias when she left Latham and came east. It made sense in a way, since she didn't want to be found. Adele and the real Molly had been only a year apart in age, and of course Adele knew all about Molly's life."

Rita still looked confused. "It's been ninety years since your grandmother disappeared. Why did you start looking for her now?"

Sarah told her about finding the quilt in the secret passageway, along with the note and address hidden inside.

"212 Elm Street?" Recognition flashed in Rita's eyes. "That was my grandparents' address in Latham. I used to write them letters once a month when I was growing up."

"Arthur and Dena Hollis Bosley lived at 212 Elm Street and when Adele, Dena's cousin, died, they adopted your father, right?"

"Yes, they were my grandparents. Adele died in childbirth," Rita said. "Sick after being locked in a house with her crazy father for seven months."

Sarah listened quietly as Rita stitched together the last pieces of this family quilt.

"And he was definitely crazy," Rita said, "Adele had been able to escape from him for a few years, but he'd eventually found her and dragged her back again." Understanding dawned on her face. "So that's why she used Molly Hollis's name when she left, in the hope that he couldn't track her down?"

Sarah nodded. "Only he did find her." She could almost envision the scene since she'd just hidden in the secret passageway herself. "Maybe Grandma Molly saw her father outside her house in Maple Hill. Perhaps she planned to go outside and try to reason with him."

"There was no reasoning with him, from what I've heard." Rita suppressed a shiver. "Ab Sanderson was suspected of starting several fires in Latham County. She had reason to be worried about what he might do to her family."

No doubt the house fire that had killed her first husband, Charles Harrison, had spooked Grandma Molly, too. It was probably the reason she'd disappeared after Charles's memorial service.

"When Ab found his way into the house," Sarah said, "she hid from him for a while, until she became afraid of what he might do to her husband and son. So Grandma Molly hid the note in the quilt hoping someone would find it, then come and find her."

Both of them grew quiet as the implications of that fateful night sunk in.

"Grandma Dena said no one even knew her cousin Adele was back in Latham until she was in labor," Rita said softly. "Ab Sanderson finally fetched his sister-in-law, Grandma Dena's mother, to help deliver the baby. By that time, Adele was barely breathing. She never regained consciousness after my dad was born."

Sarah's heart ached at how much Grandma Molly must have suffered. To be snatched from Maple Hill, away from her husband and son, with no way to contact them. Then to discover she was pregnant…

"No one knew who the father was," Rita said. "The family kept it pretty hush-hush, even convincing the doctor to list her cause of death as consumption."

"And they sent Ab Sanderson to the Kansas State Insane Asylum?"

Rita nodded. "They certainly couldn't let Ab near Adele's baby. My grandma and grandpa couldn't have children of their own, so they were thrilled to take in the baby. My dad's life might not have started out well, but they were wonderful, loving parents and grandparents."

Sarah was glad to hear it. God had provided parents to love Grandpa Noah and Grandma Molly's baby even in the midst of all the chaos and heartache of his birth.

Rita blinked back her tears. "This is amazing. What made you decide to look at my rental form? I've been living here for over two months."

Sarah grinned. "It all comes down to a cookie."

"A cookie?"

"You made chocolate spice cookies for the church bake sale, right? I didn't even realize you'd donated anything until Katie told me she didn't make them."

"I was in a hurry that morning," Rita said, "so I just stuck them in the box Katie had already set out for you. Those cookies are an old family recipe. I thought they'd be a big hit."

Sarah clasped her hands on her lap. "They're the same cookies Grandma Molly used to make. My father never tasted another cookie like them until he ate yours. I thought it was just a coincidence, until my son said something to me today about the danger of not checking references. That's when I finally realized that I'd seen the name Andrew Bosley twice recently—in the Latham Centennial Book and on your rental form. And then I remembered seeing your middle name, on the form, too. That's when all the pieces started to fall into place."

"I need to call my dad," Rita said, rising off the loveseat. "He'll be thrilled to hear we found his father's family."

Sarah held up a hand to stop her. "I already called him using the number you listed on the form. I wanted to verify a few things before I talked to you." When she'd spoken to Andrew Bosley, he'd sounded so much like Grandpa Noah that her heart had confirmed the discovery before her head. "And I wanted to tell him about my dad, his big brother. I hope you don't mind."

"Not at all," Rita assured her. Then she bounded over to give Sarah a big hug. "Have I said yet how happy I am that we're cousins?"

"I feel the same way," Sarah said, giving her a warm squeeze. "Since you're family now I probably should stop charging you rent."

Rita laughed. "Isn't it amazing how God brings people together? When I moved in here, I had a good feeling about you."

"I felt the same way." Sarah grinned playfully. "Does this mean I can borrow your convertible?"

"Anytime," Rita said. "I think we're going to take a lot of trips in that car. One of the places I want to go is Bradford Manor to meet my uncle."

"He's going to love you."

EPILOGUE

BURGLAR APPREHENDED IN MAPLE HILL
By Kyle Maplethorpe

E van Gould, of Chicago, Illinois, was apprehended during a break-in at 106 Bristol Street in Maple Hill. The new owner of the house, attorney Jason Hart, stated that Gould was caught thanks to the quick thinking of his mother, Sarah Hart. Mrs. Hart was secluded in a secret passageway with her boarder, Katie Campbell, during the break-in and called for help.

Campbell is an alleged accomplice of Gould and has agreed to a plea deal in return for testifying against him. According to her attorney, Campbell will receive a suspended sentence in return for performing five hundred hours of community service under the direction of Reverend John Peabody.

Stay tuned next week for another exclusive report from Kyle Maplethorpe entitled: THE TRUE STORY ABOUT THE DISAPPEARANCE OF MOLLY DRAYTON.

Sarah watched her father set the newspaper in his lap. "Well, Dad, the truth about Grandma Molly's disappearance is finally going to come out."

Tears gleamed in William's blue eyes. "I wish my father was still alive so he could finally tell all those busybodies they were full of manure!"

Sarah smiled. The shock of hearing the truth after all these years had seemed to temporarily clear the cobwebs from his head. It was also the closest her father had ever come to swearing. "I don't think that was Grandpa Noah's style."

"That's probably right." Her father's gaze moved past her to the box on the bed. "Did you bring more mail for me to deliver?"

"No, Dad," she said gently, removing the newspaper before placing the box in his lap. "It's a present."

"Is that right?" He lifted the lid, then a small gasp escaped him. For a moment he just stared at the quilt, then he slowly reached out to touch it. His thin, blue-veined fingers lightly brushed over the velvet, silk, and cotton squares, pausing briefly on the embroidered animals Grandma had sewn with such loving care. "My blanket."

"I thought you might like to sleep with it again," she said, watching him reverently lift the quilt from the box.

He placed it against his face, rubbing it softly against his cheek, then inhaling deeply. "It smells like buttermilk."

"That's a special soap I used to clean it. I hope you don't mind."

"Mind?" He looked up at her in amazement. "It smells like my mother."

His words brought a lump to her throat as she watched his frail hands struggle to spread the quilt over his legs.

"Do you want me to put it on you?" she asked.

He nodded, unable to speak. Tears shone in his eyes.

She walked over to spread the quilt over his lap, then leaned down to kiss his cheek. "I love you, Dad."

"And I love my little girl," he said, reaching out to squeeze her hand.

She reached up to brush a stray hair off his brow. "You look sleepy. Would you like to take a nap?"

He nodded. "A nap sounds pretty good right now. The sergeant made us run five miles in the snow today. It was so cold."

"You'll be warm tonight," she promised him.

He met her gaze. "Will you come back soon?"

"I will," she promised him. "And I'll bring you more of those cookies you like so much, along with some very special people."

But he was already drifting off, unaware he'd be meeting his brother and niece tomorrow.

As Sarah walked to the door, William's eyes were closed and his head was already starting to nod. She watched his weathered hands grasp the quilt, pulling it more tightly around him. Sarah knew deep down that each stitch Grandma Molly put in that quilt represented the deep, abiding love she felt for her son.

And that was a family pattern Sarah intended to keep.

ABOUT THE AUTHOR

Kristin Eckhardt is the author of more than thirty books, including eight books for Guideposts' Mysteries of Sparrow Island and Home to Heather Creek series. She's won two national awards for her writing and her first book was made into a television movie. Kristin and her husband raised three children on their farm in central Nebraska and are active in their church and community.

HERE'S A SNEAK PEEK AT THE NEXT
PATCHWORK MYSTERY BOOK!

TIME TO SHARE

BY JOANN BROWN

CHAPTER ONE

C louds slid away from the peak of Mount Greylock just as Sarah Hart and her twin granddaughters, Audrey and Amy, reached the summit. The valley below, squeezed between the Berkshires to the south and the Green Mountains to the north, was a patchwork pattern of emerald fields and gray rooftops.

"Just in time," Sarah said. "I don't think I know any more 'mountain' songs we can sing."

As her granddaughters laughed, Sarah looked up at the Veterans War Memorial Tower set on the mountain's highest point. The white granite monument, over 90 feet tall, had been invisible only seconds before, but as they emerged from among the bent and gnarled trees edging the open area at the summit, it was awash in sunshine.

"It looks like a giant pepper mill," Amy said with a twelve-year-old's perception. Like her twin, Audrey, she was wearing blue jeans, a Red Sox cap, and a white t-shirt with HAWTHORNE MIDDLE SCHOOL in bright red letters across the front.

"More like a pawn on a chessboard," Audrey said. "What's the glass ball on top for?"

Sarah paused, glad to catch her breath after the climb up the mountain. They had taken one of the easier trails, but even so, the route had been four miles of steady rise. She took a bottle of water out of her red paisley bag, opened it, and drank.

"That's the beacon," she replied. "It's lit at night during the summer and winter. Not in the spring and fall when the birds are migrating, because it confuses them." She playfully wagged a finger at Audrey. "I thought the war memorial was the subject of your class project on unsung heroes. Are you trying to get me to do your homework for you?"

Audrey laughed, her freckled nose crinkling. "Grandma, I was just checking to see how much you know."

"Uh-huh." Sarah laughed too. Every minute she had with her granddaughters was a treasure; since they moved to Maple Hill during the summer, she had looked forward to special moments like this with them. There had been too few when they lived across the country in California. "But remember that I won't be the one standing up to give your presentation."

"We know, Grandma," Amy said. She grabbed her cap as a gust of wind tried to pull it off.

"It won't be that bad," Audrey said. "We only have to do a three-minute speech."

"Not that bad for you. My knees are shaking just thinking about it. You'll get up there and ace it."

"It's easy. You've just got to have a few tricks."

"Don't tell me you imagine the audience in their underwear," Sarah said.

The girls stared at her. "Ewww. No way."

Sarah laughed and walked along the dirt path toward the war memorial. The girls followed, still talking about the upcoming presentations that they would be delivering on Open House Night at Hawthorne Middle School next month.

"Who will be your unsung heroes, Amy?" Sarah asked.

"Hikers."

Sarah smiled. Trust Amy to find some athletic connection for her project. "OK, tell me. How can hikers be unsung heroes?"

"Not all of them. Just the ones who make sure they don't leave any litter along the Appalachian Trail. The ones who make sure they carry everything with them to where it can be disposed or recycled." Amy's eyes twinkled with her grin. "People complain about hikers who leave a mess, but never talk about the good ones who don't."

"Like us."

Amy laughed. "I could interview you for my project."

"Both of you are looking for the easy way out." Sarah draped her arms around the twins' shoulders.

About two dozen people were on the grounds of the memorial. Some sat on the base or on the stone wall by the edge of the mountain, enjoying the spectacular views of the valley and the mountains beyond; a few stood with their arms stretched out as if they expected the wind to lift them and let them soar over the valley; and more were bent like trees, waiting for the wind out of the west to die down again. Children raced across the small grassy area and toward Bascom Lodge, a two-story stone building built low to withstand the strong winds and snow. The mountain was closed to visitors in the winter, but Sarah had seen pictures of its trees enveloped in ice.

Fortunately, this late September afternoon was blustery but beautiful. With the trees just beginning to change from their summer green to brilliant oranges, subdued yellows, and fiery reds, it was like standing in a perfect photograph.

"Why don't you girls get your cameras out?" Sarah remembered to ask. The twins slipped off their backpacks. Amy pulled out a still camera and Audrey, a video one.

"There's the Rosenthals!" Amy called out, leading the way around the war memorial toward the summit road.

"Let's wait here," Sarah said. "Once they've parked, they'll find us."

"You're so lucky to be working with Emma and Cole," Audrey said as she fiddled with the video camera.

"Who are your partners?" Sarah asked.

"Tracy Witherspoon." She didn't look up.

"And who else?"

"Just Tracy. My team is the only one with two because we've got twenty-three kids in class. Seven teams of three and one team of two, and I got stuck with only one partner. I wouldn't mind, except that it's Tracy."

Sarah frowned. Audrey was having a difficult time adjusting to the move from California and it showed in her bitter tone. But Sarah said nothing—she knew the twins' parents were doing their best to help the girls. She didn't want to interfere, though she would mention the conversation to her son, Jason, when they returned home.

"Hi!" Amy yelled, her voice breaking Sarah free of dreary thoughts. Amy ran to meet a girl and a boy her age, who were walking from the summit parking lot, both in the same jeans and shirts as the twins. Behind them came a woman who must have been the boy's mother, because she had the same dark brown curly hair. She waved.

Audrey continued to watch the vehicles coming in a steady parade up the road to the parking lot. The summit was always busy on weekends once the leaves started turning.

"I'm sure Tracy will be along soon," Sarah said.

Audrey didn't say anything as Amy returned with her friends.

"Cole, Emma," Amy pointed to her classmates. "This is my Grandma Hart. She's really cool because she solves mysteries."

Sarah didn't want anyone to get the wrong impression. After greeting the children and the woman, whose name was Diane, she said, "It was only one mystery, Amy, and I don't think Sherlock Holmes has anything to worry about."

"But it was cool anyhow." Without stopping to take a breath, Amy asked, "Can we get to work now?"

With a smile, Sarah nodded. "Just stay where I can see you. If you need to go somewhere else, check with me first."

"Wait!" cried Audrey. "Where's Tracy?"

Cole shrugged.

Emma said, "She called and told me to go ahead without her. I guess her folks are bringing her up." She pulled out her cell phone. "Do you want me to call her if I can get a signal here?"

"I don't think you'll have a problem." Sarah pointed to the cell tower that rivaled the war memorial.

Emma dialed the number and handed it to Audrey.

They stood around while Audrey waited for Tracy to pick up. Finally Audrey spoke. "This is Audrey. I'm on top of Mount Greylock. Where are you?" She stabbed the button to end the call and kicked at the ground. "I'll just start without her, I guess."

"That's a good idea," said Sarah, stroking Audrey's hair. She could feel her granddaughter's tension; even though Audrey was acting outwardly nonchalant, she was upset. But was it just because her project partner was late? Audrey was clearly not thrilled about being paired with Tracy Witherspoon, so there might be more to the situation than the kids were letting on.

"Hey," Sarah said, "there are several hikers coming along the Appalachian Trail right now. Why don't you give Amy the video camera so her team can start their interviews? You can get some photos of the war memorial while you wait for Tracy."

"Go on, kids," Cole's mother said. "Get your footage and interviews and whatever else you need. We've got to leave in an hour."

The four ran past the tower, pausing to pet two pugs walking with their owner.

Diane turned to Sarah. "Do you want to get a cup of coffee? They brew a pretty good cup in the lodge."

"Go ahead. I'd like to keep a close eye on Audrey while she's on her own. Also I want to do some sketches."

"You're an artist?"

Sarah shook her head. "Only by the greatest stretch of the imagination. I'm doing some very rough sketches to help me remember the colors and shapes for a wall quilt I'm making."

"Good luck holding onto the paper," Diane replied as another gust of wind blew over the mountaintop. She hunched her shoulders and hurried toward the lodge. To the west, the sky was clear; they should have some time before the summit vanished into mist again.

Sarah walked down to the half wall about thirty feet away from the memorial. She sat on the dry stone wall, finding a spot where the slope allowed her to put her feet on the ground and where she had a clear view of both the valley and the trail. There, Amy's team was now interviewing two hikers only a few years older than the kids, and Audrey was getting photos of the war memorial from every possible angle.

Sarah drew out the sketch pad and her colored pencils and set them next to her. She could have borrowed the camera to take a panoramic shot of the hills, but drawing the scene herself, selecting the colors, and feeling the contours of the land as the picture grew on the page would help her remember the nuances.

She was planning on making the wall quilt from scraps left over from other projects. She wanted to hang it above the mantel in the living room, where she could enjoy it when she sat in the rocker her late husband, Gerry, had made for her. An heirloom painting of Mount Greylock had been displayed there since she was a young bride. When her son bought the house that once had been her parents', she had been happy to return the painting to where it once had hung.

She bent to her work, but an hour later, she had only the beginnings of a sketch. She'd spent more time watching the twins and their friends than drawing. Yet it was enough— each time she checked to make sure they remained safe and in sight, she took in the wondrous panorama of the mountaintop, and after guiding her pencils along those same splendid lines, she had the basic image she needed.

Audrey and Amy ran to her after the other children left to explore the war memorial. Amy bounded up eager as a pup, and Audrey trailed behind. Tracy had never shown up, but Audrey shrugged off Sarah's attempts at consolation.

"Can we go up into the monument with Emma and Cole?" Amy asked. "They're going up before they leave. We can get some good pictures of the Appalachian Trail from there."

Sarah gave her consent and started packing her sketch pad and pencils in her bag. Amy handed her the digital camera and ran along the wall to look at the view stretched out below. Sarah put it in her bag and asked the twins about the information they had gathered for their reports. Both girls talked at the same time, eager to share, and Sarah did her best to pick out each girl's words.

They entered the war memorial, the girls ran up the stairs, calling for their grandmother to follow. At the top, about four stories above the ground, windows cut into the granite offered an amazing 360-degree view of the mountain's summit. The twins, giggling, joined their friends and took turns taking movies out the windows any time other tourists stepped aside and gave them a clear shot. The window closest to Sarah offered her an eagle's-eye view of the valley. From here, she could see the ponds in the valley. She'd add them to her wall quilt.

Soon, though, another cloud crept by, obscuring everything in cottony white.

"Grandma!" called Audrey. "Come look! It's so weird!"

Sarah took a single step, but her cell phone jangled in her bag. She edged aside to allow people to go down the stairs, and she groped in her bag for the phone. From across the room, she heard Audrey's laugh and saw Amy holding the camera up against one of the windows. The view was being consumed, bit by bit, by the clouds.

Her fingers found the phone. She pulled it out and flipped it open. "Hello?"

"Oh, Sarah, thank goodness you had your phone on. I didn't know what I'd do if I couldn't contact you." It was Maggie, her daughter-in-law and the twins' mother. "Jason drove over to Pittsfield on an errand, and I'm not getting any answer from him." Sarah knew how bad the reception could be in the mountains.

"Maggie, what's wrong?"

"I think someone broke into the store."

"What?" A hundred questions bounced through her head, but that was the only one that escaped her lips. Maggie's antique store in Maple Hill had only been open a few weeks.

"When I got here, the back door was open."

"Broken open?"

"No, just open. But that means it's been open all night." Sarah took a breath. "Are you OK?"

"I'm fine."

"And the store?"

"I don't know. I haven't gone in yet." Her words spilled out in a rush. "I didn't want to go inside alone." Maggie paused. Then, her voice dropping to a whisper, she said, "Just stay on the line until I make sure everything's OK. OK?"

"Fine," Sarah said, even though it wasn't. A chill crept down her spine. If an intruder was still in the store....

Silently, she prayed, *Dear Father, protect Maggie. Help me to say the right things to strengthen her and comfort her.*

"I'm going inside now."

"Keep talking." The noise around Sarah withered to a distant hum. She watched the kids, but didn't hear what they were talking about as they pointed out the windows and giggled. It was as if she stood between two realities— the one with her grandchildren having fun and the other with Maggie as she walked into the store. "Maggie, keep talking."

"OK. I've got the door open. Nothing out of place in the storage room. A few papers are scattered around."

"The wind could have done that."

"I know. OK, I'm going to open the door to the store."

"If there's someone in there, run outside and call 911."

"I will. I promise." She hesitated, and then whispered, "Thanks for being here, Sarah."

"You are never alone, you know."

"I know. OK, here I go."

Sarah held her breath and heard an echo in her mind of Gerry's voice. How many times had he reminded her that there was nothing that she could make better by fretting about it? Better to face it head on, he'd said. Only silence came from the phone. She shifted it, hoping she hadn't lost the connection, but the call hadn't dropped. She wanted to call Maggie's name. Remind her to keep talking. Tell her to describe what she saw. But she didn't dare to speak. If there was an intruder in the store, a single word coming through the phone might betray Maggie.

Could Sarah's heartbeat be heard in the store? It thumped in her chest like rain on a metal roof.

Then Maggie said, "Sarah, don't bring the girls here." Distress deepened in her voice. "Please take them straight home. I've got to call the police."

A Note from the Editors

Guideposts, a nonprofit organization, touches millions of lives every day through products and services that inspire, encourage and uplift. Our magazines, books, prayer network and outreach programs help people connect their faith-filled values to their daily lives. To learn more, visit www.guideposts. com or www.guidepostsfoundation.org.